HUSTLE LOVE AND BETRAYAL

JAY MAINSTRIP

D1519621

AUTHOR JUSTIN HILL
A.K.A. "JUSTO"
A.K.A. "JAY MAINSTRIP

CONTENTS

NOTE FROM AUTHOR

This book was written while I was incarcerated at Oaks Correctional Facility. I was on L.O.P. and tired of watching t.v., so I was inspired to write a book. This book was written during very long days and nights, when I was stressed out over everything from missing store, women problems out there in the world and missing my daughter. My plan was to just write a book to pass time but the more I wrote, the more I enjoyed entertaining myself. I always loved writing so it wasn't hard. That's how I did my time. Then, after a couple of inmates read it and gave me honest opinions I figured that I might as well keep doing it. Why not become a Writer and get paid for it at the same time? Why not get paid for something that I like to do? I hope something good comes from this book and if it don't, I felt good knowing that I completed something as good as the book is. If this book goes far then I want to dedicate it to my daughter Morgan Hill and my grandma Carol Hill, the two most important women in my life. I love y'all all the way to the moon and back! To my haters and all the people who gave up on me when I came to prison.....FUCK YALL!!!

Chapter One
The Beginning

"FUCK YOU THEN BITCH!! JUST HAVE MY MOTHERFUCKIN' CHECK tomorrow or imma' blow this bitch up!" I yelled while walking out of the McDonalds I was just fired from. I was pissed I was just fired, after all the overtime I done put in at that job. I should be able to come and go as I please, I walked a couple steps away from the restaurant and threw the middle finger up to the manager. I swear he was a faggot anyway. He always would switch back and forth like he was a female. While I walked down Jefferson Avenue to the bus stops I had a lot of things on my mind. What would be my next move? What was I going to do now that I no longer had a job? I was tired of working 9-5 jobs that don't even pay me enough so that I could buy myself a car. My mind was in a million places but I became quickly distracted when the loud sound system of an al white S550 Mercedes Benz pulled up directly in front of me with a sound system that sounded like it had a marching band in the trunk. Everybody including me was staring at the luxury car that had a man and woman inside looking like they were enjoying their lifestyle.

The white rims were shining and the rays from the sun made them look like they were flooded with diamonds. "Jay, Jay is that you?" the familiar voice yelled out of the passenger seat to me.

When I took a better look I seen it was Tiffany sexy Sack-Chasing ass that was calling me. Tiffany was a yellow boned, red hair chick from my hood and one thing about her was that if you didn't have any money, she wasn't fucking with you. I nodded my head saying "Whasup" right back to her and was wondering why was she was all jolly and happy. I guess anybody riding in a Mercedes Benz on a hot summer beautiful day had a reason to be smiling and jolly. Tiffany looked over to the man driving like she was asking him something, "Hey, where are you going? To the hood?" she asked me. I nodded my head answering yes when she yelled back, "Well c'mon boy and hop in before the light turn green" She told me then rolling her window back up.

Any other time I would be stuck in my ways and refuse a ride from a nigga I didn't know but under these hot weather circum-stances I quickly ran into the streets and hopped into the back seat of the Mercedes Benz. We pulled off when the light turned green and when I looked back, I saw all the people staring from the bus stop wishing they were in our shoes. While riding I seen Tiffany lighting a blunt and taking a couple of puffs, From the strong smell I could tell that it was some exotic weed that I never smoked before. "Wassup Young Dog, what's your name?" The man driving asked me. Looking at him from the back seat I could tell that this nigga was heavy in the streets by the ice chunks in his bracelet and the diamonds in his watch. He was a DopeBoy and far from being anybody Worker. Just by looking at him I could tell that he was a Boss.

"My name is Jay ,Bro. I appreciate the ride..." I was saying before he cut me off. "Aw man it ain't nothin', real niggas do real things. My name is E-Bo by the way." He told me while puffing on the blunt that Tiffany just passed him. The way he spoke, the way he carried himself and his whole demeanor just proved to me just how Articulate he was. "So you just got off work huh? How is that working for you?" He asked while him and Tiffany chuckled and coughed at the same time.

Any other time I would've taken offense to being the epitome of a joke but being that I no longer worked there anymore I didn't let it bother me. "I just quit that whack ass job today, fuck them!" I said not caring that I was straight lying. The car quickly had gotten clouded with the weed smoke when E-Bo turned on the air conditioning and passed the blunt back to me. "That's whasup Youngin'. Now it's time for you to start getting some real money." He said turning down our block. After hitting the blunt a couple of times it didn't take long before the effects began to take a toll on me. The weed only opened my mind to focus on getting my money all the way up. Luckily I had a thousand dollars saved up and my last check would be at least three hundred dollars. I had to figure out a way to double it up.

We pulled up in front of Tiffany's house which was across the street from mines when I seen my niggas Darien and Rizzy standing outside busy admiring the Mercedes we pulled up in. I passed Tiffany the blunt and got ready to get out the car, "Yo Lil' Homie, you seem kinda cool and if you have any trouble finding yourself a job hit me up. I might be able to figure something out for you." E-Bo told me while handing me his business card. I was so high but wasn't high enough to miss out on a good opportunity. I stepped out the car and walked across the street to where I lived.

I walked up the driveway toward Darien and Rizzy and they were still glued to the Benz that I just hopped out of. E-Bo then pulled off throwing up the deuces. I threw up the deuces in return and looked at my niggas, "Yo niggas!!" I yelled snapping them back to reality. "Man who the fuck was that you just got out the car wit'?" Rizzy asked me. "How much you think we could get for that in the streets?" Darien asked. He was always on some hot shit. He didn't even know E-Bo but wanted to rob him.

- Darien, Rizzy, and Myself all had been Best friends since we were toddlers. Jeff better known as Rizzy was my Cousin and being that all our parents were good Friends as well it only made Us feel close as Brothers. Rizzy parents who were my Aunt Tracy and Uncle Jeff had no problem taking me into their care when my parents died in a car accident. We all lived on the Eastside of Detroit and grew up like inseparable. We done everything together from school, fucking the same girls, fighting niggas from different hoods, shid we even all lost our virginities to the same crackhead and ran off when it was time to pay her. These were my Niggas, my Brothers and most importantly my Family. "That's just one of Tiffany's old niggas. She hit the jackpot this time. They seen me at the bus stop and gave me a ride." I answered them as I headed inside the house. We all went inside to the living room when I flopped on the couch exhausted from my crazy day. "Just like a job to fire you after you do yo' whole shift." I thought to myself. If I knew I was going to get fired I would've cleared out a register or something. When I looked at both Darien and Rizzy I could tell that something was on their minds as well. The room was silent but I knew when something was bothering my Brothers so before they had a chance to vent to me I had to go first and tell them about my day.

"I just got fired from that Hoe-ass McDonalds today. I can't hold y'all Niggas up doe...after riding around in that Benz I'm thinking bout' saying fuck working a 9-5 and start Hustling. Fuck this trynna' live legit life!" I told them in a serious tone. They both sat up on the couch taking in what I was just saying when my cousin Rizzy said, "Why was I just telling this Nigga Darien the same shit before you pulled up that I was ready to quit that job at the airport!". Darien chuckled, "This shit is crazy, why did I just get suspended from my job today because they talkin bout' I'm under investigation for stealing some shoes!? They didn't catch me stealing shit cuz' I know wasn't nobody looking!". Rizzy and I burst out laughing because we were sitting there looking at the new shoes on his feet and he was talking about he didn't steal nothing.

"So we all fired, suspended and ready to quit on the same day? Yea this shit gotta' be some type of a sign for us to start Hustling." I said getting excited at the same time. "If it was meant for us to Hustle, what would we be selling?" Rizzy asked. "I don't know about y'all but I could sell that Dope to them fiends. I know all of em." Darien shouted out like he had already been planning to hustle. Rizzy nodded his head, "Im gon' sell weed. That Rego and that Exotic shit. What you gon' do Jay?" Rizzy asked me. It was a good question because I had no idea what I was going to sell. I was deep in my thoughts trying to figure out what would I do when the best thing I could come up with was to talk to E-Bo first. I told the guys that I was going to get back with them in a few days but what I did know was that it was official that we were leaving the legit life alone and going into the street business as a Team. I walked away from my brothers when I pulled out E-Bo's business card...

Chapter Two
The Meet Up

A COUPLE OF DAYS AFTER THE CREW AND I MADE IT OFFICIAL THAT we were going to start Hustling, they had already copped their Work and was out getting their hustle on. Rizzy had bought Hisself a half of pound and Darien bought Himself a ounce of Hard from somebody he knew. They were already posted at our hoods hot spots and getting their clients up. Me on the other hand wasn't doing anything yet, I called E-Bo earlier and he agreed to come and pick me up so we could have Ourselves a lunch meeting. I was eager to hit the streets and get my hustle on but truth be told I didn't know much about the street hustle. The most hustling I ever done in the streets were selling my little nickel bags but that was it. With the 1,300 I had saved up I knew that I would be able to fit somewhere.

Standing outside of my house waiting on E-Bo to arrive, the sight of seeing his white Benz bend the corner was just a piece of the lifestyle I dreamed of. He pulled in front of my house sitting behind the wheel on his cell phone looking like a true boss. He was on the phone and on both wrist were chunky ice pieces of jewelry. This nigga looked like he was a celebrity straight from Hollywood. When I hopped in the passenger seat just from the exotic weed aroma I began to cough. "Where is this Nigga getting his weed from? Afghanistan?" I thought to Myself.

"Whasup Lil' Jay, you good?" E-Bo asked as he handed me the blunt. I took the blunt and began smoking. "Whasup Big Dog, yea I'm straight. You?" I returned the question. He told me he was good and slowly pulled away from my house, as we cruised down the block we seen Tiffany running from inside her house and chasing the car like we forgot to pick her up. "Wait! Wait! E-Bo!" She yelled waving her hands like a crazy person for his attention. I passed the blunt back to him in disbelief in how Tiffany Sack-Chasing Ass was desperate and literally chasing him for attention.

"Look at this thirsty bitch chasing my car down like I owe her something. Listen homie and I want you to remember this forever. You could lose money chasing them Hoes but you could never lose Hoes chasing money, feel me? Now look at her for example...I'm on my money shit right now and dat' bitch is fiending for a couple dollars and some dick. Bitch, imma' call you!" E-Bo was saying as he cruised right passed ignoring her like she was a dog in the streets I laughed not only because I was high but because this was the same girl from my hood that everybody thought was one of the baddest bitches and here was straight dogging her and showing that she wasn't shit. E-Bo was a smooth Nigga and I admired that from the jump about him. We smoked another blunt during the drive to wherever we were going and we ended up at The Original House of Pancakes that was in a Suburban Area named Grosse Pointe. As we pulled into the parking lot I noticed that this must of been a high class restaurant judging by all of the foreign cars and business people that were around. There were only a handful of black people around but all the people that were around looked like they were all very wealthy. It was clear that I was out of my element, this place looked like a membership was needed just to enter the building.

Before we got out the car he reached over to his glove compartment pulling out two different kind of colognes and sprayed hisself with one of them and handed me the other one, "Here, spray yourself with this one, we can't go in smelling like the same shit, feel me?" he said to me as he reached back over to the glove compartment putting his glock nine millimeter inside it. I then sprayed myself twice and we both got out heading to the entrance. I felt so out of place when I noticed what everybody else was wearing compared to what I had on. Everybody was either dressed casually or in their business suits. E-Bo was dressed casual and the way how he dressed I could tell that he was a Hood Nigga at heart because he was in Gucci from head to toe but looked presentable to the atmosphere we were in. Me on the other hand looked like a average Hood-Rat wearing a white t-shirt, blue jean shorts, Air Force Ones and a Detroit fitted cap.

There was a long line that ran from the front door to the parking lot with people trying to get in. I couldn't believe how many people wanted to eat breakfast food this early, there had to be something else to this place. E-Bo told me to follow him and he walked right passed everybody standing in the line straight to the Hostess that stood at the podium. "How are you today Boss, Your table is set and ready for you." The pretty blue eye Hostess told him as she led us to the back. I was looking at all the white people that were already seated and waited to be seated and surprisingly they were not paying us any mind, almost like they were use to being around blacks such as Ourselves. This was surely the V.I.P Treatment we were getting and I wasn't complaining. What I was curious about was why the Hostess kept calling him "Boss"? Could he actually come to this place that much?

The restaurant was even more crowded inside than it was outside, by this time I had to know if the food was this good that it would make the white people wait outside just to be serviced. We sat at the table and I looked around the restaurant admiring just how fancy it was. I never been to a place of this magnitude. The ceilings had glass Chandeliers over every table, and each table had big vases of fine flowers sitting in the center of the table. This place was far from the Coney Islands I was use too.

E-Bo gave the Chef a head nod that he didn't hesitate to return back. The Waitress came to the table with a smile on her face that could make the saddest person happy, "Good afternoon Boss and how are you today? Will you be having your regular meal today?" she asked. On her name tag read Alicia and damn she was fine as hell. She was brown skin with short black hair. She had to been no taller than 5'6 and even through she was in her work uniform, it wasn't hard to tell that she had a nice ass. "Hey Sweetheart, I'm good today so far. Yes I will have my regular and give Lil' Homie a OHOP special." he told her. I tried to make some type of eye contact but for some reason I felt like that's exactly what she was trying to avoid. I liked my women Siddity, now the question was would she like dealing with a Nigga of my Caliber.

Alicia walked away to fill our orders leaving E-Bo and Myself enough time to finally get to business. "How old are you Jay?"E-Bo asked me. When I told him I was 18 years old he nodded his head.." And what is it that you want me to do with your life? Do you have a goal or a dream? What is it? He asked me. All of a sudden I felt like I was being questioned by my Aunt and Uncle who were constantly on me. Instead of becoming irritated by his questions I decided to tell him the truth, "I just wanna' get money and shine like you. I want to become my own Boss one day and want to be remembered as the greatest to had ever done all the things that I accomplished, feel me?" I answered him.

E-Bo sat there silent for a minute before answering me as if he was deep in his thoughts, "That's a good answer, that's a damn good answer! You remind me of myself when I was growing up and that's how I taken a like to you and barely even know you. Listen to me Jay and listen good, I'm thirty years old and I'm rich as hell but didn't get here overnight. It was alot of long nights and hustling, working crazy hours, alot of sacrifices and even taking a few losses but now I'm living a comfortable life because I earned it. Once upon a time I had to work and report to somebody as well. You have to crawl before you walk and if you don't understand that then you won't last long in this street shit. To get your money up you will need multiple hustles that you could turn your dirty money into clean money. I'm telling you all of this because I want you on my Team. I think that with you on my team it could be beneficial for the both of us. "E-Bo told me. "Here's you guys food, you two enjoy your meals and call me if you need anything else." Alicia the pretty waitress said as she placed our food in front of us before leaving.

- In front of me was a big breakfast that looked great but the fact he was willing to put me on his team was more exciting. "'Well I understand everything your saying but I have a question..What would you be wanting me to do exactly? I have 1,300 of my own money so I figured it would be good toward something, feel me?" I said to him. With the speech he had just given I would've swore that he wanted me selling Bricks or something. Patiently taking his time to answer my question he began eating a couple of his sausages before replying, "Ecstasy Pills." he answered. I was surprised by his answer but them being as hot as they were on the streets I could understand why thats what he would want me to sell. I knew alot of people from my hood that popped pills on a regular so finding some of my own clientele wouldn't be a problem for me.

"So...Do you accept my job proposal? I would be able to start you off with some of my good customers that is willing to spend some good money. I'm serious though Jay, you have to be willing to put in some long hours. It's time for you to grow up and start getting some real money so you could one provided for your family, feel me? With the E-Pills I guarantee that in the next 5-6 years you would be as successful as me. You would be making 2-3 thousand dollars every two days. Growing up in the hood I'm sure you already know the rules but just in case you don't, don't mention my name and I will have my very good lawyer come and fight your case for you, that's my word. "E-Bo told me with the most serious tone. How could I not accept the great job opportunity? Sounded like the best job with benefits to me.

- It didn't take long for me to answer his question, without hesitation I accepted the job offer and had a big smile on my face. We then shook hands officially sealing the deal and I told him that he would not regret it. My crew was finally about to start seeing some real money in our future like we always dreamed of. After eating our meals my curiosity was bugging me to ask, "Yo E-Bo, Why everybody keep calling you 'BOSS' ? Do you really come here that much that they call you that now?" I asked him. He chuckled and looked me in the eyes, "Nawl Young Dog, I own this place and several other businesses." E-Bo answered shutting me up. Right then I made an oath to myself that one day I would be as successful as him, if not more. . . . .

Chapter Three
Getting Money Now

(3 years later)

RIZZY PULLED UP ON OUR OLD BLOCK LAKEWOOD IN A CRANBERRY colored Dodge Magnum that was sitting on 24inch rims that was the same color as the car. Near his rear tires he had to 24inch plate on the car just in case anybody wondered what size rims he had they wouldn't have to ask. He was meeting up with me so I could buy a couple of pounds of Kush from him. Over the years I developed a bad habit for the best weed and I'm sure I picked it up from smoking so much with the Big Homie E-Bo. There was many things he taught me but one of them were that I should always treat myself and not cheat myself.

Rizzy parked directly behind my Dodge Charger that I just recently bought Myself. Now my car was Cocaine white with white 24inch rims also. Observing how E-BO always bought white cars and matching rims, he made me love it too. My windows were tinted preventing the hating ass niggas from looking directly inside at me. I was getting money now and been getting it for a minute so with money comes thirsty haters that wants to see me dead.

Rizzy hopped in the passenger seat of my car already passing me a blunt of the strong shit he was selling me, "Whassup Cuzo?"

he said to me reaching out his hand giving me a play then pulling out the pounds from up under his shirt. "1 thousand, two thousand, five thousand, six thousand and...ten thousand. There you go Fam. These bitches betta add up too Nigga, don't make me start bringing my scale wit' me. "I told him handing him the money with a grin on my face. He looked at me like I just offended him, "Nigga my shit always add up!" he replied. I put my pounds of weed in the back-seat and pulled out a box of Cigarellos so we could roll up. Darien or as we began calling him "D-Money" had just sent me a text message telling me and Rizzy to meet him at the Strip Club that we handled all our business at so he could holler at us. We knew the Owner of the Club but we were the ones who damn near owned it because we did what ever we wanted in there and the Owner wouldn't do shit about it.

We were what you called "Regular V.I.P"and everybody in the Building showed us made love. The Bouncers, D.J's and of course the Strippers treated us like Royalty whenever we were in the build-ing. One of the funny things about this Strip Club was that between the three of us we done fucked damn near every Stripper that ever walked in there. We would have full group Orgy's in the Owners office and wouldn't even let him in. Even the Bartenders loved us because we constantly bought bottles and tipped heave every time we were in the building.. 007 was the name of the Strip Club that we became legends and we were only twenty one years old making history and respected like the Bosses we were.

Rizzy and I pulled up at the 007 in my car when we seen that D-Money's burnt orange box Caprice was already here. His shit was laid out with an immaculate paint job, interior the color of peanut butter and unlike us he had 26inch Davens that had his shit sitting high up in the sky. "Look, we getting all this money and this Nigga still wanna' ride around driving his Old School. That hot ass Caprice is known everywhere he goes, he's lucky we ain't beefing wit' nobody right now or else he wouldn't be hard to find." Rizzy said as we headed into the Strip Club.

"Nigga we all got rims on Our shit, we all hot." I replied." But we both have two other cars that don't have rims on them and thats

not hot, his other cars all have rims on them and is hot as fuck!"
Rizzy complained. I was use to Rizzy steady complaining so I knew
how to just ignore him, what he complained about the most was D-
Money these days. "I'm so far gone, i'm on another planet..." the
sounds of the Detroit Rapper Juan's song screamed through the
speakers. It was 3pm and that song had the Strippers in there
shaking and clapping their asses.

Up on the stage was our brother D-Money with a stack of
money in one hand and a bottle of Rose- in the other while he
danced with the Strippers. I couldn't help but to smile as I watched
my Nigga enjoy Hisself but Rizzy just shook his head is disgust. It
was never to early for D-Money to be drunk because that was an
everyday thing. While on stage dancing with all the Strippers, there
was one Stripper named Honey who was the only one avoiding him
and focused on getting her money. Honey was strictly about her
cash and even though she was a Dancer she constantly reminded us
that a Stripper was only her job and nothing else. She was unlike the
rest of the Strippers because there was never a price that could get
her to change her mind. She was the only one at the club that none
of us ever hit and for some reason that made me more attracted to
her. Every time D-Money would try and cop a feel from Honey she
was quick to pop his hand and check him. She was a red-bone short
light skinned Cutie that had to weigh nothing more than 135lb and
had hair that flowed down to her pretty breast. Surprisingly she had
the fattest ass ever know for a woman her size. My whole Crew tried
shooting their shot at her and every time she was quick to
respectably turn us down. She wasn't impressed by the money or
cars which was proof that she had morals and respect for herself.

There were many times I would catch her solo and shoot my
shot in the most respectful way in attempts to show her that I was
different and every time she would hit me with the same answer,
"Boy please, you better stick wit' them Hoes you been messin' with."
laugh and walk away. It was clear that I was attracted to the
forbidden fruit and the fact that I couldn't have her made me want
her even more.

"Ms. Perfect she right, "Mrs. Perfect and I'm Mr. Right.." the

Gucci Mane song played through the sound system, "Oh shit, my Niggas here! Whassup my niggas!? Hold on Baby!" D-Money said as jumping off the stage when he seen us. Breathe smelling like Rose- and stumbling, D-Money put both his arms around our shoulders and we headed to the Owners Office where we talked and handled our business. We liked handling our business in the Owners office because it was sound proof and we could monitor the entire inside and outside of the club through the surveillance system.

I could tell that Rizzy was irritated at how D-Money was drunk but called us to this meeting. We all took a seat and before starting any meeting we always put three blunts in rotation.. One thing about D-Money was that even under the influence he still knew how to handle his business, "Alright Fellas, imma' get straight to it and tell y'all I got a fasho way for us to make anything between a hundred thousand dollars to three hundred thousand a piece…... Now that I have y'all attention, who's ready to get this money?!" he asked. Both Rizzy and I looked at each other then back to him wondering what was this mission he had up his sleeve. Hearing that much money caught both out attention and we were for sure interested in hearing it.

With D-Money putting this plan together I knew that whatever it was that we had to do that it wouldn't be easy, both Rizzy and Myself had to been thinking the same thing because in unison we both asked what would we have to do to get it. Seeing how interested we were, D-Money finished telling us the details." I have a Customer who owes Me his life damn near, He drives an Armor truck and Instead of paying me all cash he is willing to set up a Heist for me to rob his truck and that way he could pay me and have some more money for Hisself. He only wants fifty thousand dollars and the rest would be for us. Im telling y'all, this is the one right here. This is the Lick thats gon' make us and we gon' be straight!" he explained to us then inhaled the kush smoke.

"So let me get this shit straight, your willing to hit an Armor truck because some Fiend owe you Some money?!C'mon man, be smart!! That Crackhead is probably trying to set you up to get you off the streets so he ain't got to worry about you killing him." Rizzy said to him sounding like he was the least bit interested in the job. "Look, I know fasho he ain't trying to set me up because he wants the lick badly. And lets just say he is, I know where is mother live so we could go over there and threaten her with a gun to her hand and I bet the Nigga act right!" D-Money explained. Rizzy looked at me, "Bro do you hear this Nigga?! This Nigga is trying to get us Fed time!" Rizzy said to me. I sat back and hit the blunt a few more times thinking about the plan that D-Money had just put on the table. Seeing that I wasn't fast to respond, D-Money looked at me, "Bro if y'all scared to get this free money I could understand but with or without y'all I'm doing it. I would grab my Young Dogs and we riding. I bought this to y'all cuz' y'all my Fam so whasup? I need to know because this is going down in the next week. The Driver will be giving me his routes later on today. Whasup, y'all in or what?" D-Money asked.

I hit the blunt one more time and looked at Rizzy, "This will be a Lick of a Lifetime right here and it most definitely could be done as long as its done right. We will fasho need somebody at his Momma's house and we will need heavy artillery and not the regular pistols and choppas....Im in, Just let me holla at E-Bo and Im sure his connects could provide all our proper gear.

Both D-Money and I looked at Rizzy for his answer when D-Money asked him again what was he going to do. Rizzy exhaled, "Aight Man, Im in!" he answered with a grin on his face. We all were on board for the Armor truck Heist and we were going to see the type of money that was life changing.

After the meeting we all stepped out the office and made a quick stop at the bar when we all seen Honey dressed in her regular clothes. She already was sexy in her Stripper gear but seeing her with regular clothes on she was even more sexy forcing me to say something to her. "Whatup doe' Honey, let me holla at you for a second." I said to her. She had on some little tan shorts that was squeezing her fat little ass and she had on a blue halter top that had her titties glistening and looking good. Honey was surely something to look at. She wore some heels that had complimented her petite frame and just like the woman was suppose to on a regular.

"Whasup Jay, I have to go and pick up my Son from the Day care." She told me.

"Oh okay, this wont take long at all. Look right, I was hoping that I could take you out to lunch or dinner one of these days? I just wanna' kick it wit' you and get to know you more than when your working, thats all." I told her with a smile. She chuckled, "Boy you are persistent aren't you? I tell you no almost every time I see you and you still always ask me if you could take me out. Let me ask you something, if I let you take me out what do you consider is taking me out? Im not going to no hotel room or none of the spots you be taking all yo' lil' Groupies. Yea I heard about you!" Honey told me sounding like she heard alot about me. I laughed and promised her that I would not take her to any of them places but only to the finest. She took a long look into my eyes before answering, "Mmmm-hmmm, Im going to give you one chance and you better make it a good one." Honey told me. When she agreed to let me take her out I wanted to damn near jump up for joy, I couldn't believe she finally said yes.

"Fasho imma' make this one chance worth it." I answered reaching into my pocket and pulling out my cell phone, handing it to her. She smiled, 'Umm, just give me your number and when I call you, that's when we could set up a date." Honey said with a smile on her face.

Usually when a Woman would tell a man that she would call him that meant that there was a big chance that she wont but in this case I felt like she would call me. I gave her my cell number and soon as she put her phone away from storing it D-Money came from behind me," Yo Honey, you gon' call me too?" he asked her with a slur. "Ohh, umm sorry D but I'm not trying to take your number too and make all the other girls jealous. See y'all later Fella's." Honey said as she headed toward the exit.

After we all shared a few drinks we made our way outside to the parking lot so we could all go and prepare for the upcoming heist that we agreed to do. We all gave each other Plays before Rizzy and I hopped in my car and D-Money hopped in his. D-Money started up his loud motor and burned rubber the way out into traffic, "Do you think we could pull this off clean and with him being on point, nor drunk or high?" Rizzy asked me referring to our Brother. With all the money we been getting over the last few years we all picked up a few bad habits but D-Money's bad habits were the worst. I reminded Rizzy that D-Money does alot of things but one thing we never known him to mess up was his money. I took Rizzy back to his car and made the call to E-Bo telling him that we needed to meet up so we could talk…

Chapter Four
Its Time

THE WEEKS HAD PASSED AND LIKE HIGH SCHOOL STUDENTS PREPARING for their SAT's, we had done our homework on all the Lay-Outs, The Armor Drivers, the type of guns they carried and even the routes they would be taking. I was so focused that I haven't even smoked nor drank any liquor in the past week just trying to stay focused. It was 10:30am and in the next hour the truck would be leaving the bank from picking up the load of money. With us only having a Crew of three we had to make sure we moved fast and smart.

Rizzy, D-Money and Myself were at the Marriott Courtyard Hotel when it was time to call one of D-Money's Lil-Homies to make sure he was at the Armor Truck Drivers Mothers house with the pistol to her head. When D-Money made the call, the Lil-Homie put the phone to the Mothers face, "Don't kill my Son please!? Please don't kill me!" She begged. We were all set and all we had to do was make sure that the Armor truck Driver met us Six blocks away from the Bank that we told him to meet us at or we would kill his Mother. D-money made the call to the Armor Truck Driver telling him that we had his Mother and only when we made it away safe we would spare her life. He agreed to be at the spot we told him to be at and now it was all the way official.

We were all dressed in our black protective armor and carrying some of the finest artillery ever. We wore masks and even had walkie-talkies so we could communicate whenever we were separated. E-Bo really came through with all the gear and from the prices he charged us it better been the best. The time was finally here and we all headed out of the Hotel we gave each other Plays and hugs not knowing if this could be the last time that we seen each other again.

We all went our separate ways and I sat in the stolen car a block way from the Bank that the Armor Truck was loading up at. I was nervous as shit but there was no turning back. We all were in positions and the time had come for us to complete our mission. The Armor Truck was pulling off from the Bank when my Walkie-Talkie chirped. "Jizzle, The truck is on the move and your up first. Lets get it Baby!" Rizzy told me. I maneuvered through the Downtown traffic until I was directly behind the Armor Truck like I was suppose to. I followed the truck a few blocks when me Walkie-Talkie chirped through again, "Yep, one more block Bro" Rizzy said. As we approached the six block mark, the bubble guts in my stomach was going crazy. I never been this nervous in my entire life. I quickly threw my mask on and cocked back my AR-15 preparing to kill anything that gets in our way. The light turned red and soon as it turned green and we passed through the intersection was when it was supposed to go down. I had a feeling that I should check on D-Money to make sure he was in position and when he didn't respond I got worried. "Why wasn't he answering? Was he okay?" were all the thoughts that were going through my head.

The light turned green and the Armor Truck was now in motion when the bright yellow school bus came from the left side full speed ramming into the Armor Truck and knocking it on its side. The impact was so loud that it sounded like thunder. The debris and smoke had covered the entire accident.

"Let's go Jizzle!! Let's go get this money!! Rizzy yelled through the walkie-talkie. I jumped out the car with AR-15 aimed at the back door of the armor truck where he met me at. He reached in his backpack pulling out small dynamite and sticking it to the door when he yelled for me to step back. "BOOM" Was the sound of the loud explosion and the doors being blown off the hinges. When the smoke cleared, giving us a visible site of what was inside of the truck, both of our eyes were in total shock. Without hesitation Rizzy put a bullet in the Armor Guards head. We wasted no time before we set the dynamites on the Armor trucks hinges."Oh shit Bro" was all that I could say when I seen all the bricks and bricks of money. The driver started climbing through the window and before he could even know what was happening, Rizzy sent six bullets through his body. The people that were around began screaming and running away from the scene. Watching Rizzy being quick to kill whoever was when I knew if we wanted to make it out of this alive then I had to be ready to kill whoever. It was also clear that now the driver was dead that we didn't have to give him his cut. Rizzy began loading up the money into our duffle bags when he asked me to cover him. Covering him like I was asked, I turned around watching for anybody to run up and try to stop us. This shit was on the floor and it wasn't anyway i was going to let anybody stop us.

We completely forgot about the Armor guard that said in the passenger seat because he hopped out of the drivers window covered in blood. I turned around and sent five shots through his body and one of them through his head. Then the police sirens started wailing Meaning that our time was running out. Rizzy throughout bag after bag, "Time to go Bro!Time to go!" I shouted As the sirens sounded like they were getting closer. He jumped out of the truck holding three big bags of money and I picked up the other three big bags. We started running to the car when shots started being fired at us from behind. "Freeze!" The Detroit Police yelled. Leaving us no choice we had to duck and hide behind the car just to dodge the bullet. "Man, what the fuck?! Where the fuck is that nigga D- Money at?!" Rizzy asked while shots riddled the car we were hiding behind. Just when I was ready to give up hope on him, the sounds of the biggest rifle were being shot from afar, "GO! GO! Y'all clear! "D-Money yelled through the walkie-talkie. We both stood up and were surprised to see seven dead Police Officers bodies on the ground.

Rizzy and I jumped in the car and swerved through all the cars that were abandoned and in the way of our escape until we were clear. There was only a matter of time before all types of police made it to the scene so we had to get out of there while we could.- Fire trucks, unmarked and marked police cars, and ambulances sped past us as we were going the opposite way. I picked up my walkie-talkie and chirped through to D-Money asking if he was alright and got away safely. There was a long pause, "Fasho, I'll meet y'all at the first checkpoint." he answered.

We pulled up to the first checkpoint miles away from the Heist when we saw D-Money leaning against the side of our get away truck. He saw us approaching and his smile reached from ear to ear. We all were happy to make it away without anybody getting hurt but most importantly we were happy that we accomplished such a big mission. We all got out of the car and loaded the getaway truck With the six big bags of money. D-Money pulled out his phone and called the Lil' Nigga that had the Armor trucks mother at gunpoint and told him to kill her and get out of there. I walked over to the first getaway car with a can of gasoline and lit it on fire. No finger-prints, no evidence was the motto. We hopped in the truck and headed to the second checkpoint where another getaway car was then We would've been heading to the hotel where we would be counting our money up. We had multiple checkpoints just to make sure that we weren't followed or seen by anybody. After this Heist our lives will be changed forever, we will be three young rich niggas that could be able to do whatever we wanted to do and live good for a very long time....

Chapter Five
Two Weeks Later

I walked inside 007 Strip Club and as usual the music was loud and it was packed. Strippers were on the poles clapping ass and niggas were throwing money at them while I rushed into the Owners Office late for the meeting that the Fella's had called. I was sure that they just wanted to talk about what we should do with all the money that we collected from the armored truck Heist so this meeting was needed.

I opened up the office door and there was Rizzy and D-Money sitting on the couches already with blunts in rotation, "What's up nigga, you late." D-Money said as if he was happy that he could finally tell somebody else that. I just shook my head without an excuse, I gave both of them a play and sat down, "Look, the reason I called this meeting was because I think it's time that we start investing our money. I think that we should buy this club. Shid, we be in this bitch enough.W should just own this Muthafucka'.Yeah we gon have to do a lot of remodeling but I also know that when we become official 007 Owners that we would watch this place be bigger than we ever knew it to be." Rizzy suggested passing me a blunt. He was right, we were always there so why not be Owners of this Strip Club?

"I like that, that's a good idea but how much will we individually put in on this piece of shit place? 10-15 thousand?" I asked. Rizzy laughed, "Nigga we just made 500 thousand a piece with that last lick, I'm talking bout we put at least a hundred thousand a Piece into this place and y'all know it's gon' come back. We are winning, plus all our other hustles we should be able to make our Enterprise one to be talked about forever." Rizzy said to us. The room became silent but the thoughts inside our minds were louder than anything. "I'm wit' it but you know what else I'm wit'? I think we should all invest in each other's hustle and guarantee our Bags will be the biggest in not just Detroit but Michigan period." D-Money also suggested while catching his smoke clouds. Both guys had great ideas for the simple fact that my Pill hustle, D-Money's Cocaine and heroin Hustle and Rizzy's Weed hustles were all very successful.

I trusted these men with my life so turning down a Partnership wasn't even an option, it would make us even more richer than we already were. "I like both ideas and I'm in." I told them as I stood to my feet. Both Rizzy and D-Money stood up as well giving each other a play. This was rare for the two of them to be on the same page and it was a good look.

We were finally becoming a real Team and with all of us determined to do nothing but succeed there will be nothing to stop us. We were all working with at least or close to a million dollars a piece and we were going to see nothing but more money as long as we continued being the Hustlers that we had become."Hey!Hey!Hey! We are getting money now right? And what do niggas got when they are getting money? A group name, Feel me? What should we name Ourselves?" He asked. He was right again, we were already referred to as a group but we were called by our names when we should be called by a name that represented us all. "What about the Money Boyz?" Rizzy suggested. "M.O.B (Money over bitches?" D-Money suggested. I laughed, "Nawl man, it gotta be something that's exclusive and haven't been used by every Nigga sometime in their life-time.it has to fit Us!"I told them.

We all sat there continuing to guess more group names that really would fit our Crew, "What about The Mainstrip Niggas? MSN for short." I suggested. Everybody paused considering what I just said, "MSN huh? I like it. I really like it. Mainstrip Niggas, shid we from Jefferson the Mainstrip so why not? Im wit' it." Rizzy said. D-Money nodded his head repeating the name, "I like it too. As a matter of fact, I love it! Mainstrip Niggas it is then!" D-Money said, pulling out three bottles of Rose' from the minibar and handing them to us. We all took a bottle and raised them to the sky, "To the Mainstrip! To the Mainstrip Niggas!" I said and both of them repeated before we popped the bottles. This was the beginning of our movement that even the most famous and legendary groups from Detroit haven't even seen. If you weren't with us then you were against us, I was riding for my Brothers and would do anything to protect them.

We all stepped out of the Office with bottles in hand when we saw Harry the Owner standing behind the bar doing an inventory check. That's when I realized that we haven't even talked to Harry about whether or not he would sell us his Strip club. We needed the Deeds to the building before we could actually become Owners and begin remodeling. Rizzy and I gave D-Money the look which meant he already knew what to do and that was to make Harry sign the Deeds over. Rizzy and Myself were always real smooth and cool with him but D-Money was the one he was scared of and whatever D-Money told him to do Harry made sure he did it. D-Money was always known for getting people to agree with him and do whatever it was he wanted done.

We all sat at the Bar when Harry's big fat, stanking ass turned around reaching over the bar trying to give us a play, "Whasup Fella's, did y'all leave me any Rose' in there?" He asked playfully. "Don't worry about that, I need to holla at you real quick so come and take a walk with me. " D-Money said, throwing his arm around Harry's shoulder and walking him back toward the office.

"Let me know how they meeting went, I gotta go meet up wit' my Young Dogs and pick up some money. "Rizzy told me before standing up to give me a play and heading out the door. As Rizzy walked out, Honey walked in looking fine as hell as usual. It had been a couple weeks since I gave her my number and she still never called, "Oh shit, what's up Liar, oops I mean Honey?" I said to her.

She just chuckled knowing exactly my reasons in calling her that, "Hey Jay, I am not a Liar I just really been busy lately. I just found me a great job finally and now my life is about to do a drastic change. I just came here to let Harry know I quit and to pick up a few things from my locker." Honey told me. She was looking good, not just attractively but like a big weight had been lifted from her shoulders. She was proud of Herself for finally being able to shake the Stripper life she been living and to tell the truth I was happy for her too.

"Oh yea? That's what's up, I'm proud of you. Give me a hug Girl." I said as I stepped closer with open arms hugging her tightly. "Thank you, have you seen Harry around here? I want to see his face when I tell him I quit." Honey said with a smile on her face. "Umm Harry ain't your boss no more, Well wasn't your boss anymore. Me and the crew finally decided to buy this place so we are now the new Owners of the Strip Club. There's about to be a lot of changes around here too so I'm excited about that." I told her. "Wow, I am so proud! Congratulations!" she said as she jumped back into my arms giving me another hug. "We should celebrate" Honey suggested being just as excited as I was. Both our lives were doing a total 360 and we were proud of each other.

"You see, I already started celebrating. Let's go out somewhere, go eat and get some drinks."I said to her. She paused giving me a look, "Okay, let's go" she answered. I was shocked that she agreed to let me take her out, out of the million times I've tried, I couldn't believe she finally was with it. I had to take advantage of this opportunity now because it may never be available again.We both started walking toward the exit when I heard D-Money calling my name as him and Harry exited the Office. D-Money had that look in his face that I know all too well and meant that he was on that tip. "Harry here has some papers for you to sign before you leave. It's the Deeds to the club. He told me with his slick grin. D-Money had got Harry to agree to sign the club over but at what cost? Knowing my Brother he probably threatened Harry's entire family. I took the paperwork and signed them telling them I will get my copy later.

Honey and I walked outside to the club's parking lot when she saw my new car, "Damn, I see who's getting money. Buying new cars and clubs. I can only imagine what your crib looks like." She asked. "Do you wanna find out?" I asked jokingly. She gave me a funny look stopping at the passenger door, "Oh you got jokes huh?" I just shrugged my shoulders with a grin on my face telling her I was just playing. We both jumped into my new Cadillac XLR hard top-drop two seater. The car salesman that sold me the car told me that there were only three people in the state that were owners of this particular new styled car and he was pretty sure I was the youngest one out of them. Of course it was white like the color of all my cars and with one touch of a button it will transform into a drop top like it was an Autobot.

We went out to eat and had a few drinks at one of Detroit's most famous restaurants, Sweetwater Tavern. We ate and talked for hours like we've been friends for years. We were having such a good time that between the both of us we cleared a bottle of Rose' that left us drunk as hell and talking with slurs. I had been drinking and smoking all day so when I saw Honey's eyes bloodshot red I knew she was as high as I was.

"So why don't you have a woman Jay? I mean, you seem like a good catch but do you really want to be chasing Hoes all your life? You don't want yourself a woman to come home too? A woman that you could spend holidays with, go out on dates and all that good stuff?" Honey asked me. I thought long and hard about the question she just asked me before responding. "Umm, I never really had a woman before, I always just had...." and before I could finish my sentence, she finished it for me" Hoes! You only had Hoes, right!" She said, shaking her head already knowing the answer. We both just laughed knowing that it was pathetic that I only been dealing with Hoes instead of women my entire life. I took a sip from my glass, "So why don't you have a Man Ms. Honey? If I was your man I wouldn't of had you dancing in no Strip Club." I told her. My question must have been a really sensitive subject because she couldn't even answer it. The Waitress came back to our table placing the check in front of me. "You ready to get outta' here? "She asked me. I nodded my head yes and reached in my pocket peeling off two hundred dollar bills placing it on the table.

When we stepped back into my car I lit up another blunt but felt bad that my question ruined the good vibe that we had going on all night. As I began smoking Honey broke her silence telling me that she had a boyfriend which is her child's father who was in the street life. He was killed in a drug deal gone bad and the day he died was the day she went into labor. "When he died was the day my life changed drastically because he was the Provider. I had to find a way to make money fast and my only option was to dance. The difference between me and the other girls that work there is that I came in with a plan I was the only Dancer that will go to med school through the day and dance at night and still found time to be a mother to my son at the same time...I haven't had time for a man and haven't even thought about having one since my child's father was killed" Honey told me. Honey had just opened up her heart to me and for some reason after hearing her story I was even more attracted to her just by how strong she is.

As we cruised down the City streets and I continued smoking, she asked for the blunt.I didn't even know she smoked. She told me she didn't smoke on the regular but under the circumstances she wanted too. I passed her the blunt. "Now enough about me and my life, tell me your story." Honey demanded. I never was the type to open up and tell about how crazy and fucked up my life was but how could I refuse after she just told me about hers? What was I supposed to tell her, how I been broke up until the past three years when I began hustling for a big-time Hustler by the name of E-Bo? Or how I came up after me and my crew hit an armor truck?" Well I don't really got anything good to say about my life, I'm just out here hustling hard and getting my money up that's all. I answered by keeping my answer short and simple. "So what do you hustle?" Honey asked. I wanted to tell her what I told most women that asked what I did for a living which was construction but Honey was too smart to believe that lie. A young nigga driving a new Cadillac XLR, spending money without a limit and buying Strip Clubs, how could I lie?

"I do a little bit of this and a little bit of that but some of every-thing, feel me?" I answered she just nodded her head and said "Mmm-hmm", she knew I was trying to avoid her question and she left it alone for the time being. We pulled up to one of my favorite spots which was the casino that I often visited. The MGM Casino was a great spot where people gambled, they had drinks, you could eat good and if you're lucky enough you could win some money and get yourself a suite in the hotel for $550. Honey seen where we were at and grinned, "The Casino, you're a Gambler huh? "She asked as we parked in the hotels V.I.P. " Yea I do a little gambling, you?" I returned the question while reaching under my seat for my pistol and putting it on my waistband. When she saw my pistol she became a bit distracted and answered she's a Gambler too, "Don't worry about this my Baby, this is just my insurance and for our safety. I told her, referring to why I had my pistol on me.

We walked into the well lit casino both high and still feeling all the Rose' and liquor that we consumed. Soon as we got to moving through the casino people were speaking and acknowledging Our presence, "Yo Jay, what up doe'! Jay! Whats good Fam!?". I just would throw the deuces up at them and continue walking with one of the finest women by my side. Detroit fucked with me the long way and being that I was getting money and in the streets, it was only right that the Streets show me respect.We walked over to the bar, "Yo baby girl, could you get us a bottle of that Rose'?" I asked the female Bartender who was a short distance away. When she turned around a smile was already spread across her face but when she seen it was me it quickly turned into a frown. The bartender was a female named Simone that I met one drunken night I visited the casino and ended up fucking her the same night and a couple nights after that. I have not been in contact with Simone in weeks so I knew seeing me with another woman would make her a bit upset being that I never returned her many phone calls.

Simone was a cool female from what I knew but wasn't my type of female to continue to pursue. Her body was banging, her face was so-so but one thing that I could tell was that her thirst was real. She was attracted to all the jewelry I wore and the unlimited spending of money I was living by. I just wasn't interested in giving her any time for the simple fact I felt like we both were using the other. I used her for her pussy and she used me for a good time and a couple of hundred dollars I always would leave on the table before I would leave the hotel room.

"Well hello Jay, You don't know Anybody anymore?" Simone asked . Never being in a situation like this, it forced me to say the first thing that came to mind. "Umm, Whasup Simone? Simone this is my Woman Honey, Honey this is the best Bartender in the world. Simone." I introduced both women to each other. Simone spoke to Honey with the driest tone possible. When Honey peeped the whole attitude that Simone was giving out from the beginning is when she reached over and placed her hand on top of mine until they locked, "Nice to meet you Ms. Simone. So you're the one that gets my Baby all liquored up before he comes home to me huh? "Honey asked with a smile and played the role of my woman.

It was small but the physical contact that we were sharing felt good and I was enjoying her acting skills. "Umm yea, I guess so. I have to get back to work so I will be coming back with y'all bottle and y'all enjoy y'all night, Jay and Jay's Woman." Simone said before dismissing Herself. Flirtatiously Honey leaned over closer toward me and placed her lips onto mines, "We certainly will." She replied afterwards. When Honey places her soft lips on mine it is like being struck by lightning. It was electrifying and just off a small kiss caused a slight erection.

As Simone walked away in disgust Honey gave me a look, "Next time you bring me some place make sure is not a place where one of your sex victims work at please." Honey said with a grin on her face. I just laughed and admired how smooth Honey played the situation. Any other woman would've tripped out and called me all kinds of "Male Hoes and Sluts" but she was cool with Hers. After having Ourselves another bottle we were officially drunk and decided to hit the dice table to do a bit of gambling. About 30 minutes later Honey had to use the restroom and refused to use the public restroom telling me it was something she'd been totally against for years. "Just get us a room or something Jay because I have to go and we are both way too drunk to be driving home anyway." Honey told me. That was a demand that didn't need repeating and without arguing we went right over to the hotel side of the casino and got us a suite for $550 a night.

The suite was decked out and had a beautiful view of the Detroit River with a balcony to watch it from. Sitting on the table were bottles of champagne complements of the casino, there was a jacuzzi sitting in the middle of the floor, 60 inch flatscreen television posted on the wall and a mini bar that had more liquor than anybody could have possibly needed. How fast Honey ran to the bathroom when we first walked in I was sure she didn't get a chance to see any of the nice decor of the suite. I sat on the edge of the bed and started to roll up another blunt and stripped down to my basketball shorts, wife-beater and ankle socks making Myself comfortable. How faded we were feeling, I knew anything was possible tonight.

When Honey stepped out of the bathroom she finally noticed how nice the Suite was and how I made Myself comfortable. Now I had blunts rolled up and glasses of champagne already poured.I had everything set up perfectly for what I wanted the night to be, I've wanted Honey for so long and now I had the chance.

"Oh shit, look at you... All ready and comfortable like you about to get Some or something. Honey said flopping on the bed behind me with a smile on her face. My heart dropped at the thought of me really not getting no pussy tonight. I remained cool and just laughed her comment off when I began sparking up one of the blunts. Sitting there smoking, Honey made it her business to get closer to me and threw her legs and feet into my lap, "My feet are hurting, can you rub them for me? Please?" She asked me in an innocent tone. Staring down at her pretty white painted toes, I reached for her feet and began massaging them with a smooth caress.

After ten minutes of receiving hr massage, Honey sat Herself up and stepped out of the bed "Alright it done got a lil' hot in here. I'm taking my clothes off and getting comfortable like you." She told me as she stripped down to her sexy matching bra and panties. She wasn't hot and knew exactly what she was doing but I for sure wasn't complaining or calling her a liar. I've seen Honey's body naked a million times but it was different being on display only to me. Her body was amazing! Her titties sat up in her bra nice and right, her panties were so thin that I could see her cleanly shaven pussy. The tattoos that were wrapped around her body was doing something to me as well.

Honey slowly and seductively walked over closer to me when she began rubbing my head softly. Her hands went from my head down to my ear, down to my neck and then chest. It was clear that she was feeling me just as much as I was feeling her and our time had finally come. She leaned down and whispered in my ear, "Are you ready for me?" She asked. "I been ready, let's go." I replied being the smooth Nigga that I was. I stood up pulling my Wife-Beater over my head and had her lay flat on her back in the big king sized bed. I climbed on top of her and began passionately kissing her soft lips. I then kissed her from her lips down to her neck down to her breast when I removed her bra. I began sucking on her pretty nipples which caused her to moan and rub my head while she was being pleasured. Kissing her down from her nipples down to her waist line I just had to taste her. I was a freak beyond my time, I had to been one of the youngest Niggas that was already eating pussy. I was the biggest tease because after munching, sucking and licking on her Clit, I then would lick all around her pussy until she begged for more. This was Honey I had in the bed so I was for sure going to make this an experience she would remember. I was sucking on her Clit then would put a finger inside her pussy finger-fuckin her at the same time. Honey's moans got loud and she began to slide up to the top of the bed in attempts to get away. I then added a second finger that really made her try and run but now I had a lock on her that wouldn't allow her to go anywhere. "Oh shit!! I'm Cumming!" she yelled as her legs began shaking and she gripped the sheets on the bed tightly. Moments later my mouth was full of her juices and she was frozen still on the bed with a wet puddle underneath her. She had Cum all over my face and onto the bed.

Honey then stood up pushing me onto the bed laying flat on my back. She slid my shorts off and her eyes widened when she seen my already hard dick standing tall, "Damn Babe you are ready, huh?" She said in shock by the python standing in front of her. She then kneeled down to her knees and placed my dick on the tip of her tongue then into her warm mouth. She began slowly stroking it inside her mouth and against her tongue forcing me to grow bigger than already was. Honey's mouth was magic and I couldn't believe how talented she was. She started to speed up her pace while massaging my balls at the same time like she knew that I liked that. She was sucking and licking on my brick hard shaft with so much passion that I couldn't resist my moans and toes curling.

"Hold on, I got something for you." Honey said standing up and walking over to the table where our glasses of champagne were. She grabbed her glass and came right back to the same position when she began pouring the bubbly drink onto my dick. As she poured her champagne on to me she licked and sucked it all off of me until I was dry. Honey's Head was so good that I knew at this rate I wouldn't even make it to her pussy before I came but I couldn't allow Myself to bust so fast."Wait! Wait! Wait! You gotta' get up for a second. I can't take no more!" I told her taking a cop to her outstanding performance. I stood up lifting her from her knees and having her lay flat on her back in the bed. It was time for me to bless her with this A-1 Dick game that I been wanting to give her for the longest. I climbed on top of her and just getting ready to put the dick inside of her when she stopped me, "Listen, you better not hurt me with that thing either! I ain't like them otha' Hoes, my pussy can't take all of that so you better take your time and go slow okay? If you hurt me Imma' punch you!" She told me with a bawled up fist in my face. I laughed and promised her I will take my time and go slow. I then put just the tip of my dick inside her pussy and I couldn't believe how tight she was. I could barely put it in her so I knew she wouldn't be able to take the whole dick. This was going to take some time so what I knew I had to do is get her to relax a bit more then in no time her tight pussy would allow me in.

With just the tip in I slowly penetrated back and forth inside of her and at the same time I was giving her the most passionate tongue kisses ever. I kissed all over her neck and chest and like I predicted, she began to loosen up and allow more of me inside her. Her walls were so tight, her pussy was so wet that I just wanted more and more of her. I then started to speed up just a tad bit and the headboard was banging against the wall. It was clear that we both were enjoying the other because Honey moaned for more and more as she held a tight grip around my back.

This experience with Honey was amazing and I wanted to make sure that I didn't miss a piece of it. I lifted up sitting straight up so I could have a perfect view of her body while we were fucking and the fact that her body was was just as beautiful as she was made the sex even greater. I placed my hands on both her waist and began stuffing more of my brick hard dick inside and fucking the shit out of Her. Now that Her pussy was allowing all of me inside it was time for me to go hard on that pussy, I even got to talking shit as I was feeling Myself. "Who's Pussy is this!? You like dis' dick?! then say it! Tell me you like this Dick!!" I told her while I was giving her long strong strokes.

By now Honey done caught her second wind and she was just as amped up as me," This is yo' Pussy Babe! Do you love dis' Pussy?!" She asked taking the dick like a Pro."Yea I love dis' Pussy Girl!" I answered pulling out my Dick covered in her Cum. "Turn dat' ass around, it's time to switch it up!" I demanded. She sat up and before she got in the Doggy style position then she took my dick and shoved it into her mouth until she sucked it dry. I had to literally snatch my dick from her mouth to prevent me from cumming so fast.

She was in the doggy style position when I stuffed my long hard rock dick inside her pussy, it wasn't hard to find out what her favorite position was. She was in her comfort zone and she was ready. With both of her hands she gripped both sides of her ass and spreaded them as I pounded her from the back."Jay!! Jay!! Harder! Harder! Hit this pussy Nigga!!" echoed throughout the room. She was taking all of the Dick I threw at her. I reached on the side of her table where the bottle of Moet was sitting and while still fucking Her I started downing the bottle like it was water. Honey started throwing that nice ass of Hers back and soon after that I knew I was about to Cum. "Damn Baby, I'm bout to Cum" I told Her as I continued fucking from the back. "Oh, oh, oh Jay I'm Cumming!! I'm Cumming!!" She moaned and at the same time we both came together. We flopped on our backs tired from exhaustion and after a good ass day, we ended our night with great Sex or did we make Love????

Chapter Six
The Mainstrip

(3 MONTHS LATER)

I WALKED INTO OUR NEW STRIP CLUB THAT WE'VE BEEN OWNING FOR the last three months and it was finally done being remodeled. It looked better than it ever did and was for sure going to attract new Dancers and new money. We all invested a lot of money and time into this place so we all were very excited and eager for our Grand Opening. We had made a lot of changes like getting rid of the old Bouncers, old Dancers and even the Stragglers that use to hang around the club and not spending any money. We even added food to the menu, We had flat screen television mounted up on the walls so videos could be played or even sports games could be watched. There wasn't nothing like getting a lap dance and being able to watch the Pistons playing at the same time. Not to mention that we renamed the place from 007, to "The Mainstrip" which was where we were from and our Crew name.

I stepped into our Conference room that use to be the Owners Office and I just nodded my head impressed by how good the place turned out. We all had our own separate Offices and the Conference Room was where we discussed our business. "Whasup Nigga? I been calling you and you ain't been answering. Get yo' face outta

Honey's Pussy and answer your phone!" Rizzy said with a grin on his face. Even though I knew Rizzy was joking, I knew him and D-Money was still wondering how I pulled Honey and they couldn't. Honey and I were spending any available time that we had together and the crew loved talking shit to me and saying that I was tricking with her to get her.

"Yea me and Honey was at the mall and lost track of time. She finally had a day off, you know them Nurses be working crazy hours...Anyway, what up doe'? Everything here looks good and ready for the Grand Opening." I said as I looked around. "Yea, tonight bout' to be packed Bro, our Grand Opening is the most talked about Event going on this weekend. This bitch gon' be rockin'!" Rizzy said in an excited tone. D-Money came into the conference room looking like shit. His clothes were hanging all off of his body, he was still wearing the same stuff from yesterday and the smell of liquor ripped from his body like he was a Wino. Rizzy and I haven't seen him in two days so there was no telling all the stupid shit he been into. "Damn! Whasup Dog, where you been at and why you look like that?!" I asked, looking at him in disgust. Before he could even respond, Rizzy answered the question for him, "He's a Fuckin drunk, can't you tell!? Straight the fuck up!" Rizzy said like he wasn't surprised. "I just left the fuckin' Casino and lost 75,000 dollars at the tables! "D-Money answered. Rizzy and Myself looked at each other and back at him in disbelief in what he just said.

"75,000 dollars?! Why would you sit up there and even play that much? Why are you even carrying that much D? You know we are all working out of the same Bag and you went and gambled with it? Man you betta..." Rizzy was saying before I interrupted him. "D, Man...Are you going to be ready for the Grand Opening tonight? You pose to be right wit' us shining and looking good like a Owner pose to and you standing here all the way fucked up!" I told him disregarding the fact he just told us he lost 75,000 dollars. D-Money put his hands over his face trying to shake off the liquor," Yea, yea imma' be ready. I just gotta' get home and shake this shit off for a couple hours then I would be straight." He answered. "Good, we will worry about the loss at the casino later, for now we gotta get you home and ready for the night.In fact Imma' have one of the girls take you home cuz Me and Rizzy gotta' lot of shit to do." I told him.

I jumped on the surveillance cameras to see what Women were already here at the Club when I seen Kim heading over to our Bar. "Bingo!! Got one for him!" I said referring to D-Money. I stepped outside the office when I went to approach Kim and I knew that it would be a big chance she would refuse to do me this favor. D-Money wasn't as Liked as Rizzy and Myself. He was a Hot-Head Maniac and a lot of people didn't like to deal with him but i needed Kim to do this favor for Me so that D-Money would be on point by the night.

"Hey Kim!! Kim!! Whasup my Baby?! I said to her as she stood over at the Bar with one of the fattest asses I ever seen. She turned around grinning, "Whasup Boss Man?" Kim asked. Returning the smile and knowing that I had to be my charming Self, it was time for me to work some magic. " Whatchu bout to do Kim? I need a big favor?" I asked her. Checking me out from top to bottom she had a grin on her face, "And what is it that my Boss needs me to do?" Kim asked. Kim was Honey's Best-friend who had Worked at the Club and before there was a Honey and I Situation there was a Kim and I situation that never had its time to expand. It was when Honey and I became official was when all the flirting and Fucking had to stop. "So you know the Grand Opening is tonight and I need everything to be perfect! Saying all this to say, my Bro D-Money is upstairs stupid drunk and since Rizzy and I are Crazy busy I was hoping that you could do me this favor and make sho that he gets home straight and dressed for the Grand Opening. You think you could do that for me?" I asked with my hands together like I was begging. She shook her head while staring into my face, "You know I could never tell you no, yes I will take him home Jay." Kim agreed. I was so thankful that I gave Kim one of the tightest hugs ever. I thanked her a million times and told her that I owed her before walking away to get D-Money ready. On my way up to the Office I seen Rizzy staring down at us threw the picture window and shaking his head. I walked into the Office, "Kim's going to take him home?" Rizzy asked. I nodded my head answering yes, "That's a bad idea to send them together while that nigga drunk."Rizzy said to me. "Kim is good, she wouldn't try nothing on him or nothing." I replied. "Im not talking about her doing anything to him, I'm talking about him doing something to her." Rizzy said.....

Chapter Seven
Grand Opening

(HOURS LATER)

I PULLED UP INTO THE STRIP CLUBS V.I.P PARKING SPOT THAT WAS directly in front of the Club in my new white on white Lexus I only drove for special occasions like this. In front of the Strip Club was a line damn near down the street with people wanting to party at "The Mainstrip" and when I stepped out the car everybody began cheering and calling my name. I never been so proud to be apart of something in my life and to see that the City was fucking with us like this felt good. We had the entrance set up like a Red Carpet Premiere that led to a Photographer who would take pictures of only the people on the V.I.P. list.

I walked down the red carpet wearing Louis Vuitton from head to toe. On my feet were Louis Vuitton Loafers and all the jewelry I wore was flawless. On my face were my Cartier glasses with diamonds flooded all through them, in my ears were Cartier square-flat Diamond earrings, on one wrist was my Bust down Diamond Rolex watch and on the other wrist was my chunky Icey bracelet that ran me for a hot 60 thousand dollars. Last but not least I had on the chain that D-Money, Rizzy and I all went and had made custom at the Jeweler. It was the MSN letters surrounded by white diamonds. I stood in front of the Photographer posing taking pictures after pictures feeling good and ready to enjoy my night when I heard my Brother Rizzy calling my name.

"Yo!! There goes my Bro! Look at you, you shining Boy! What's good!?" Rizzy said as he checked me out and giving me a Play. He was fresh to death to wearing Gucci from head to toe, His jewelry game was just as icy and flawless as mine. Between the both of us we were looking like Celebrities. We gave each other plays and congratulated the other on the success we been having illegally and legally, the only person was missing was our third brother, D-Money.

Rizzy and I walked into Our Strip Club and it was even more crowded than it was outside. The Dancers were on the pole getting their money, the Bar was filled with people trying to buy drinks, the V.I.P. sections were packed and everywhere you looked there were some of Detroit's finest Women dancing and enjoying themselves." Bottles for the Owners." The pretty Waitress said as she delivered us bottles of Ace of Spade with the sparklers sticking from inside of them. We took our bottles and toasted them in the air, "We doing it Cuzo! Here's to making more in the future and to a Brotherhood that can't be broken!" I said clicking our bottles together.

While Rizzy and I made our way through the Strip Club I felt a hand from behind me cover my eyes imitating a deep voice, "Guess who?"the voice said. I turned around and it was Honey, "Oh, Whasup Baby!?" I said In shock in that she made it. She had told me this morning that she wouldn't be able to make it because she had to work, "Hey, I told my Boss that my Man was having a Grand Opening and I had to been there or we would be beefing so she let me off early and I decided to come and surprise you. So Surprise! Are you happy to see me?!" She asked. I stepped back taking a look at how good she looked and all I could do was smile and admire how fine she was, "Of course I'm happy to see you!! You look great!! Umm, and did I hear you say that you told your Boss that your 'MAN' was having a Grand Opening? That's what I heard right?" I asked smiling looking into her face. She began batting her eyes with a huge smile, "Yea, that's what I said, is that a problem? Did I lie or something?" She returned the question. With my hands on her small hips I smiled telling her that there was absolutely no problem with that and that in fact I loved that title she given me. She told me she thought I would and we kissed right there in the middle of the Club together. We were proud that we were finally in a official relationship with each other.

Rizzy being the sarcastic Nigga that he was, he started clapping, "Aww, ain't that cute! Looks like love in the air!" he said smiling and looking at Us. Honey and I stood there holding each other. I then handing her my bottle of Ace of Spade, She seen Her old friends that she use to dance with and told me that she was going to go and speak to them real quick and would meet me in the V.I.P. Section in a few minutes. I watched her walk away and was staring at her ass, "Wow Fam, public affection? Y'all really like each other huh?" Rizzy asked. I nodded my head bashfully," Yea Man, I cant hold you up. I'm really feeling that girl, forreal!" I answered. Rizzy stuck his hand out, "Thats Whasup then, if you like it then I love it." He said giving me a play. "Welcome to the Hottest Place to be in the city, The Mainstrip!! Shouts out to the Owners, them Mainstrip Niggas Jay, Rizzy and D-Money!!" the Dj announced over the speakers. The entire Club started clapping and cheering when we realized that D-Money still wasn't here.

"Where is that Nigga D-Money at? He pose to be here! Call Kim and see if she's still with him and tell her to bring him here asap!" Rizzy told me. I pulled out my phone and began calling Kim's phone but she wasn't answering. Rizzy pulled out his phone and started calling D-Money but he wasn't answering either. Maneuvering Hisself through the Clubs shoulder to shoulder traffic, our biggest Bouncer Big Tee came to us "Jay, Rizzy, y'all gotta' come wit' me quick! Right now!" He told us with a confused look on his face. We followed Big Tee all the way to the back of the Club and there stood D-Money dressed but covered in blood smoking a cigarette. "What the fuck happened to you?!" Rizzy asked. "Where the fuck is Kim?!" I asked. D-Money stood there with a look on his face that read that he fucked up and his silence had both Rizzy and Myself scared for whatever it was that he done.

Off top we were worried but as we took a look at Him we could tell that He hadn't been shot or hurt so now the question was what happened and what did he do. "I...I just wanted to kiss Her and...And, and she pulled my gun out and...And I hit Her. I hit Her and..She tried to rob me!" Rizzy was saying but could barely explain what happened. Rizzy wasn't even trying to hear nothing that D-Money was talking about and rushed him putting both his hands around his throat. "Where is she D?! Where the fuck is Kim?!" He yelled. I stepped between the two breaking them up, I felt exactly how Rizzy felt but we wasn't going to get any answers with him trying to kill him. When Rizzy let him go D-Money just started crying which was an indication that shit was bad. Neither Rizzy or Myself haven't seen D-Money cry since we were kids, Rizzy stepped away putting his hands over his own face expecting the worse but I couldn't accept it. I stepped to our Mans, "D, Where is she Bro? C'mon where is Kim? Did you hurt her? Where she at?" I asked in a more settle tone. The tears rolled down his face even quicker while he nodded his head answering yes. "I had too..She's dead. I'm sorry." He cried. I stepped back from him in disbelief that he killed that girl. It was only so long that I could keep my composure, I ran up on him and started beating his ass down to the ground with steady punches to the face. Rizzy and Big Tee could only stand there and let me express the anger I was feeling toward him. I was furious that he would do that to that innocent girl, I knew for sure she didn't try and rob him.

Exhausted from the beating I just put on D-Money, I flopped on the ground beside him putting my hands over my head. He sat next to me drunk and crying telling me that He was sorry but his apologies couldn't erase what he had done. Rizzy kneeled down in front of him, "Where is her body?" He asked. D-Money wipes the tears from his face and told Us that her body was in his trunk. I stood up shaking my head," I can't believe this shit..Y'all know what we have to do now right?" I asked Rizzy, Big Tee and D-Money. Rizzy nodded his head while still in front of D-Money, "Your my Bro but you are a fuckin' Dummy and I can't stand the sight of you right now. You are the one that's going to bring MSN down and I swear to God, before I let you do that I will kill you Myself!" Rizzy told him before standing to his feet.

"Yo so look y'all, Rizzy and Big Tee. I need y'all to take this Clown to a Hotel and get him cleaned up and when y'all done with that I need y'all to meet me on Jefferson in our old hood down at the water. I'm going to handle a few things here first then I would be on my way down there. Make sho' y'all get some garbage bags and disinfectant spray." I told them. Rizzy knew what we had to do because we been down this road many times before but the fact that we were doing it for somebody that we knew was the hurting part. Before heading out the back door Rizzy mugged D-Money while shaking his head in disgust, They hopped in D-Money's truck and right as they were pulling off, Honey stepped out the back door as well. "Hey Babe, everybody's looking for y'all...Ain't that D-Money's truck right there? Where is Kim, Rizzy and Big Tee going when they pose to be here celebrating with you y'all's Grand Opening?" She asked me.

"Umm, Kim wasn't in there and they had to go and take care of some important business and in the next thirty minutes I have to meet up with them." I told her as we headed back into the Strip Club. Honey could see in my face that what I was talking about had to been important for me to leave my own Grand Opening that I was so excited about. She turned toward me and stared into my face asking me was everything okay. Before I could answer, she reached up to my chin, "Is this blood? How did you get blood on you and who's blood is it?" Honey asked now concerned. I wiped my chin off with my hand and indeed it was blood that was on my face. It had to been from when I was fighting D-Money that the blood from his shirt got onto me. I was still in shock from the whole situation and I needed to pull Myself together, especially in front of Honey. When I didn't answer her question quick enough she became worried, "Jay is everything okay? What's going on? You and one of your best-friends fighting?whats up?" She asked me. Putting on a fake but selling smile," Yea I'm okay baby, why wouldn't I be?

Everything's good. I just have to handle some business with them real quick." I answered her. The fact that I knew Honey's Best Friends was in D-Money's trunk was sickening to me so I knew if she knew that her Best Friend was dead that she would be sick about it. That's why she could never find out about this.....

Chapter Eight
Detroit River

I LEFT THE STRIP CLUB IN OUR MANAGERS HANDS WHILE I WENT down to Rizzy and I old neighborhood to the Detroit River. Rizzy, D-Money and Myself been to this specific park on numerous occasions for reasons such as throwing pistols in the water that had bodies on them and whenever we had to throw a body over to prevent from being found. Living off the water, everybody and they mama had things that needed to be thrown away and never found so we all did so. I had a lot of memories from our past that made us had to visit the park but unfortunately none of them were good.

I walked towards Big Tee and Rizzy and they already knew the procedure as to why we were here. By the time I arrived they already had Kim's body wrapped up in garbage bags with some weights to make sure her body doesn't float to the top. "Is it all ready Big Tee?" I asked. When he nodded his head yes I gave him the head nod to toss her body over into the water. Big Tee picked her body up and tossed it into the river like a sack of laundry.

Rizzy stood over the rail staring into the Detroit River sparking Hisself a blunt in complete silence. I knew he was fed up with D-Money's actions but it wasn't the time nor place to talk about it. "Big Tee, I need you to go to D-Money's house and make sho' he didn't leave any evidence laying around, aight?" I asked him as I handed him a band of money for his services. Big Tee was a solid Nigga that we all trusted like he was a Brother and he been around for a long time. He stayed to Hisself so we didn't have to worry about him talking to anybody. "I got you Jay." He replied.

I walked back toward my car when Rizzy called my name, "You know we gotta' talk right?" He asked. I opened my car door," Yea man, I already know. Imma' come and get you int the morning." I told him before getting in my car and pulling off. What D-Money did had to been discussed and handled accordingly. He killed my woman's Best Friend since the age of six and now her Son had to grow up without a mother just because of his stupid decisions. I knew Rizzy was upset about Kim's murder but I felt even worse because I put him off on Her and asked her to do me a favor. It was all my fault Kim was dead and now I had to live with it......

Chapter Nine
Next Morning

I WOKE UP THE NEXT MORNING WITH HONEY BESIDE ME WHEN I noticed that I was covered in sweat like I had been working out or something. "Baby, you tossed and turned in your sleep all night. Are you okay? We're you having a bad dream or something?" Honey asked. I told her that I was fine and that I just needed some water. I looked at the time on my phone and it was already 9:30am, I had told Rizzy that I was going to pick him up so I had to get up and hit the shower before starting my day. While in the shower I heard Honey come in and she began brushing her teeth, "Hey babe, I know the party was packed last night but I didn't see Kim anywhere, did you?" She asked me. I stood still trying to figure out the answer I was supposed to tell her, "Nawl I ain't see her, she was pose to been working too so I don't know what happened to Her. Did you talk to her yesterday?" I asked picking her brain trying to figure out what it was that She knew. "Last time I talked to her she told me she was doing you a favor and taking D-Money's drunk ass home. I haven't heard from her since." Honey said before brushing her teeth. The bathroom became silent, "Hello?" She said waiting for an answer. "Well yea, she took him to the crib and then called me to tell me she would be a little late. I didn't know she was going to be a no-show though. If she wasn't yo Girl I probably would've fired Her" I answered trying to make a joke of it. She looked over to me with a grin, "You bet not fire my Girl or no Sex for you for the rest of the year, think I'm playin!" Honey playfully threatened. I hopped out the bed, "No sex?! You couldn't go two days without this dick!" I told her as I headed to the bathroom turning on the shower. Honey smacked her lips, " You right cuz I can go longer than that!" She replied back.

I stepped out the shower butt naked and still wet when Honey was standing in front of the sink brushing her teeth. We been messing around with each other that it was still crazy that she was now my Woman. She was just so Beautiful to Me and I was enjoying every moment with her at the same time. I stood behind her lifting one of my big t-shirts that she slept in right over her head and gripping her titties and fat ass that I was infatuated with.

It was an easy access for me to treat Myself so of course i took advantage. I then picked her up and sitting her on the bathroom sink where I began eating her Pussy for breakfast. She moaned and had both hands gripping my bald head, "Ooohh Baby, Oh my God! Oh shit!" She moaned in the sexiest tone. There was something about her moans that made me go harder than ever, she just sounded so sexy and that was arousing to me and brought out some of my greatest performances. After a few minutes and cumming all over my face, Honey pushed me back off her and dropped to her knees stuffing my already erected dick inside her mouth and began slobbing me down and sucking me up. How good her head game was, even though our bathroom was big, it just wasn't big enough for me to take what she was serving. She was known for always making me squirm from being unable to take her head.

I pulled her up to her feet, picked her up and carried her back into our bedroom placing her in our king sized bed. She assumes her favorite position which was the Doggy style position, " Fuck me Baby!" She demanded ready for the Dick. I stood there loving the sight of her fat ass and had no problem sticking my rock hard Dick inside Her. Not wasting any time I was giving her what she wanted and was fucking the shit out of Honey. I had both my hands on both of her shoulder stuffing the dick inside of her causing her to moan and scream my name until I came all inside of her and she came all over my dick. That was one thing I like about when we made love, we always came at the same time and together.......

After getting up and getting Myself dressed for the day we agreed to call each other later that day, "Hey Jay, now that we are in a Relationship together and damn near live with each other, what do you think about me moving in permanently?" She asked. I told her that I didn't have a problem with it because it was like she already lived her anyway, all of her stuff was already here. "One more thing...Can you promise to always be honest to me? No matter what?" She asked. I stood there staring into my Baby's eyes, "I promise." I told her as I leaned down to kiss her.My answer put a smile on her face, I then grabbed my pistol, keys and cell phones before leaving out of the condo.

Forty five minutes later I pulled up to Rizzy's Apartment Complex where he was already standing outside waiting on Me. He hopped in and we both gave each other a play before speaking to the other. I pulled off and now it was time to head to the hotel where D-Money was staying. "What are we gone do bout' that Nigga D-Money..I mean Darien? I can't call that Nigga D-Money no more cuz' he don't deserve that name, so Darien. What are we gon' do bout' Darien and all the stupid shit he's doing? He's risking all the things that we done worked so hard for!!" Rizzy said before sparking up a blunt. "I don't know Bro, what are we pose' to do? He's family, shid he's part of the reason we made it to where we are. Plus He's the one who got the Cali Plug that's bringing in a lot of money weekly." I replied back. Rizzy and I didn't know what we were going to do with D- Money, he was becoming more of a problem that was getting harder and harder to handle but at the same time he was profitable.

We walked into the Hilton where D- Money was staying and we had Big Tee posted outside the door making sure that he didn't leave," Good looking Big Tee, you could get up outta' here now. We got him." I told him. Big Tee gave us a head nod and left. Both Rizzy and I walked into D-Money's Suite where he was laid out across his bed staring out the window in his jogging fit with the hood

On. Rizzy sat on the couch and I sat at the desk by the window, knowing that this was about to be a difficult discussion we had to light up another blunt. I was so disappointed in my Dog and the route he was going. He was letting the money we were getting change him and he was taking on bad habits such as becoming a drunk and a coke head.

"D-Money Man, I need to know why you killed that girl and I need the truth." I told him. He sat up and took a deep breath, "Bro, she took me home right? And I was already drunk so my mind wasn't right but all I remember was she got my gun somehow and tried robbing Me. I couldn't believe it! My gun?! Rob me?! And then,," before D-Money could finish Rizzy had jumped up and leaped across the room hitting him with a Hay-Maker that sent D-Money to the floor. "Stop fuckin' lying! You think imma' sit up here and let you lie like that!?" Rizzy yelled at him. I jumped up standing between them and telling Rizzy to calm down. Rizzy pushed my hand back, "Nawl fuck that! I didn't even tell you cuz' I didn't want you to feel even more guilty but before we wrapped her body up, Kim was butt naked and raped and badly beaten. He raped and beat her ass and now this Nigga wanna' lie in our face?! Nawl fuck that!" Rizzy said in a furious tone.

The room fell silent and the pain in my heart had worsened at what Rizzy just told me, "D-Money, tell me he's lying on you. Tell me you didn't beat and rape that girl. Tell me!!" I yelled at him. D-Money stood to his feet, " I ain't gone lie, after I wrestled my gun back from her I beat her ass and I fucked her! She got what she had coming, she tried to rob me and I beat and fucked the Bitch!" He answered hyping Hisself up. "Do not call her no Bitch! Do not! You fuckin' killed that girl and we had to clean up your mess as usual!! She had a lil' boy that don't have his Mother anymore Darien, you didn't think about that shit! Even if she did try and rob you, after you got the gun back you didn't have to rape and kill her Stupid!" I told him. I was Pissed because he didn't understand how big this was going to get. "I'm sorry yall, I'm fuckin' sorry!!" D-Money said beginning to drop a Tear knowing that he fucked up. "Look D, your Fam and we love you but if you don't change with all of the drinking, smoking and snorting whatever, then....." I paused. D-Money's head lifted up wondering what I was going to say. "Or we will have to continue our money movement without you. Now as long as I'm alive you would never be broke nor need anything but we cannot risk all the things that we have going on because of your stupid decisions." D-Money's head just fell down to his chest knowing that he was going to have to get his shit together.

"Look my girl Honey was the last one that Kim talked to and this morning she asked me if I seen her after she dropped you off. I told her that Kim called me and told me that she would be late in to work, that is the story we gotta' stitck wit' aight?" I told both Rizzy and D-Money. Both of them looked shocked wondering just how much did she actually know, "You Wifed that Stripper Bitch Honey, Bro?" D-Money asked standing to his feet like he was mad. I stood up as well, "watch yo' fuckin' mouth Nigga!" I told him raising my voice. "Jay if that Bitch start talking..." and before he could finish his comment I hit him so hard that he fell back to the ground holding his mouth.

He looked at me crazy, "Honey's my Woman now and I won't allow you to disrespect her like that." I said shaking my hand and looking at my hurting knuckles. I gave Rizzy a head nod toward the door indicating it was time for us to go. Before leaving I turned looking at D-Money, "Take a couple weeks off to get Yourself together and we will handle all your business affairs until your back good. Leave all of them stupid ass drugs alone, forreal Bro." I told him before we left his suite.....

Chapter Ten
Meeting E-Bo

(2 WEEKS LATER)

AFTER ALL THAT'S BEEN GOING ON I STILL HAD TO KEEP MY OWN Hustle Operations up and running going. It was time to pull up on the Nigga E-Bo and re-up. I met up with him at the same restaurant in Grosse Pointe that he owned and where all our meetings were held. E-Bo and I had been dealing with each other for years and with him putting me in the game, I was honored to refer to him as a Big Bro. I visited his restaurant at least 2-3 times a week so I was something like a regular and knew and spoke to half of his staff whenever I came in.

I walked straight to the back where E-Bo favorite table was where I reached over the table to give him a play, "Whatup doe' Fam, you good?" I asked happy to see him. "Whasup Young Dawg, I'm good. It's good to see you. I see you shining and looking like money." He smiled referring to the jewelry I had on. I just grinned and told him I'm just trying to be like him. I sat down and checked out the menu, before the Waitress came I reached in my pocket pulling out an envelope that carries sixty five thousand in cash. E-Bo already knowing what it was for just smiled and put it in his pockets. "I been meaning to tell you, I appreciate you supplying My Crew wit' that Artillery a month or so ago. Some of that is just showing how much I appreciate you, feel me." I told him as I watched the Pretty Waitress approach us.

As she got closer I realized that she was the same Waitress that I met the first time I ever been here which was back when I was a broke young Nigga. "How are you doing today Boss, could I get you some more coffee and something for your company?" She asked. I couldn't help but to smile, "Wow, how are you doing? Do you remember me?" I asked her. She smiled but looked a bit confused, "Umm, you do look a little familiar. Have we met before?" She asked looking at E-Bo first then back to me. E-Bo sat there with a grin on his face, "Alicia, this is the same young Dude that came in here with me a few years ago and you were teasing him when he wearing his white t-shirt like he was on the block. This is Him, he's all grown up now." E-Bo told her. "Oh yea? Wow! My have you grown." She said looking me up and down admiring my growth and fashion." Yea I have, I'm a grown man now doing grown things. You should call me sometime, whenever your free." I told her handing her my MSN Business card. She looked even more confused," Wait, don't you want my number?" she asked. I shook my head, "Nawl, if you want to fucks wit' me you would call me, feel me?" I answered her. She took my card and smiled, I could tell that she wasn't use to men hollering at her like this, "Well I guess I would call you when I get the time." She replied. "What's your name again?" She asked. "My name is Jay Baby Girl, take a look at the card." I told her. Alicia took our orders and told us that she would be back shortly. E-Bo and I looked at each other and just laughed, "See what that real money do? These Hoes see the jewelry and money and they want in." E-Bo said reaching over the table to give me a play.

"So how is things going out here for you and your MSN Crew these days? Everything good, I hate I missed y'all's Grand Opening but I had a lot of business to handle." He asked. With E-Bo being like a big Brother to me, I always told him the truth because I knew that he would tell me an honest but real answer. He was somebody that I could vent to and not have to worry about what we talked about getting out or nothing like that. I told him the situation with D-Money and he wasn't even shocked. He told me that he understood that we were family and all but he also told me that at some point I had to realize that I can't do business with all my family. He was totally right, the type of lifestyle we lived was dangerous and it only took one fuck up to get us locked up for life and that I couldn't risk. I had the strongest loyalty toward D-Money so kicking him out of the business wasn't an option but after talking to him I realize that in order to stay successful that I had to pay a little bit more attention to him and keep him out of trouble if I wanted him to stay in the business.

I gave E-Bo a Play and thanked him for the talk and told him I would see him soon. As I walked toward the door he called my name, "Your loyalty toward your Crew is good but the consequences amongst friends is avoidable." E-Bo said. I just nodded my head and continued walking away. Before making it to the exit a waitress handed me a take-out bag and told me to have a good day. I got inside my car and opened the take-out bag and it was filled all the way to the top with Ecstasy pills. I pulled them out and it was six pounds of ecstasy pills. Six pounds of ecstasy pills would make me anywhere from 85-100 thousand dollars. I pulled away from E-Bo's restaurant thinking about all that we just talked about but right at the moment I needed to drop this work off to my Employees....

Chapter Eleven
Two Months Later

(10:24pm)

I walked into my Condo and it was a mess. Pizza boxes covered the tables, stacks of toys were all over the place and a television volume was turned up to its highest with the Pokémon playing on it. I knew when I agreed to let Honey and her six-year-old son move in that I had to do some adjusting and it wasn't a problem at all. I actually like coming home to her and her Son, it was fun and felt like I really had Myself a family. "Boom! Boom! Boom!" Honey's son Khari yelled pointing his toy gun at me. Khari was my little man's and I liked him from the moment I first met him. Honey and Khari only been living with me for the past two months and I was already attached to him. "You shooting me now Lil' K?" I asked as I picked him up flipping him in the air. Then out of the blue I felt something or someone poking something into my leg, I looked down and it was another little boy shooting his toy gun at me.

When I looked at him he looked so familiar, I put Little K down and grabbed the little boy up, "And who is this Lil' boy that's shooting me? I'm going to beat you up too!" I said playfully as I kneeled down to him. The little boy remained silent, "Dat's my friend Dez, Jay." Lil' K told me like I was suppose to already know. Soon as I heard his name I remembered I seen this little boy a few times before. This was Kim's little boy who was the same age as Lil' K. "Oh okay, Whasup Lil Dez?" I said standing back up. I told them to continue playing and I would be back shortly so I could play with them.

I found Honey in my Office on the Computer, " Hey Babe?" she spoke with a smile on her face. I walked over toward her leaning in to kiss her, "Whasup Love, I just seen Kim's Son in there looking just like her, that's crazy ain't it?" I asked her as I took a seat in the chair in front of my desk. "Yea that's crazy how much he looks just like his Mother. Umm I told his Grandmother that he could spend the weekend over here while she goes in to have surgery. You know she's real sick too but I hope that she gets better afterwards. I cant wait to hear from this Bitch Kim for leaving her Son over her Momma house knowing she's sick." Honey said sounding a bit worried. Being the good supportive boyfriend I was, I told her not to worry and she would be okay. "Besides, Lil' K need somebody to play with anyway." I told her. She looked at me and smiled, "That's why I love you Boy!" Honey said leaning in and planting a kiss to my lips. I loved kids so I had absolutely no problem with the boys running around and enjoying themselves. Plus, Honey and I been on such good terms and loving each other's company that I didn't care if she bought an entire daycare over here. I was so in love that she had total access to all my security codes, cars and my smallest safe.

One of my two phones vibrated in my pocket and when I pulled it out I noticed that it wasn't my money phone or a familiar number so I sent whoever to the voicemail. Even though I was in love with Honey, I still was a hood Nigga with hood Nigga tendencies that made me cheat. It could've been anybody calling between women or begging Niggas but being that I was in front of Honey I wasn't taking the chance. Honey seen me hit the side button on my phone, "Damn Baby, who is that your sending to the voicemail this late?" She asked being nosy. "I don't know, shid I didn't recognize the number so I didn't answer." I told her.

My money phone rang right after that, "What up Doe' ?
Yea..Yea..Aight I'm on my way..Umm, gimme 30 minutes." I said
putting the phone back in my pocket. Honey shook her head, "So
you gotta' go again huh?" Honey asked. "Umm, yea that was Rizzy
and he need me at the Club. I probably would be there til' late too
so I'll call you when I'm on my way home, aight?" I told her as I
leaned in to kiss her. She just said okay but I could tell she was tired
of the late nights being out, I told her that I loved her before leaving
the Office. I walked through the living room where the boys were
playing, "Aight Lil' K and Lil' Dez imma' be back a Lil' later
tonight. Y'all be good aight?" I told them as I headed toward the
door. "Jay! Jay! Jay! Can you buy us some juice and chips from the
store?" Lil' K asked me while jumping up and down in a hype.
"Don't buy them nothing Jay! Since they don't want to clean up
their mess in there they don't get them nothing.!" Honey yelled from
the Office. Both boys had an upset look on their face, "Aww Man!"
They both said in unison and stomping their feet. I thought it was
funny," Look, y'all clean this mess up and imma' bring y'all some
snacks when I get back alright?" I told them. Smiles spread across
their faces and they both agreed to clean up by the time I got back.

Forty-five minutes later I pulled up in the Mainstrip's parking lot
when my second phone rang. It was the same number I sent to
voicemail when I was in front of Honey. "Who dis'?" I answered.
"Umm, is this Jay? This is Alicia. Alicia that work at the breakfast
spot." She told me. When she told me who she was, instantly a smile
spread across my face. I gave her my number just a few days ago so
for her to be calling me so late was a little surprising. "Alicia, ohhh
Whasup? Yea this Jay, I was wondering who was calling from this
number." I responded. "Well whasup Mr. Grown Man, are you busy
right now?" Alicia asked me. "Umm, not that busy. I'm just walking
into my business right now to handle some business, what's good?
Should I make Myself free or something?" I asked her while smiling
over the phone. "Well, I'm at home chilling and drinking some wine
so if you wanna' join me then you should make yourself free. That's
if you wanna' spend some time wit' me that is." She replied. I
nodded my head looking at the time and how late it was, "Fasho

then, after I finish here imma' call you and get directions to your place then." I told her. She said okay and we both hung up the phone knowing what was soon to be going down. I could tell she was ready and it wasn't no question if I was ready because I have been ready since the first time I see her years ago....

I walked into our conference room and there was Rizzy and two guys in cheap suits, knowing what I knew about the streets and how things went, it wasn't a secret that they were either Feds or Detectives. Rizzy sat behind the desk as I approached him giving him a play, "Whasup Bro, what's going on here?" I asked referring to the two men. One of the men stuck his hand out to shake mines, "How are you Mr. Hill, I'm Detective Gordon and this here is my partner Detective Brown. We are from the Detroit Police Department, Homicide Division. We are here because we understand that a young lady named Kimberly Smith was employed here, so there is a missing person report out on her so we are here to ask if any of y'all seen her or heard from her lately? Her grandmother is worried sick about her and says she hasn't seen or heard from her in a couple of days." Detective Gordon asked. I looked at Rizzy first then back to the Detectives, "Well yea Kim was a Dancer here but we haven't seen her in days either. In fact, I called her grandmother asking if she heard from her because we began to worry about her too. She brought a lot of money in so for her to not come in to work was all new. You don't think nothing bad has happened do you?" I asked sitting on the couch folding my leg on top of my knee. The two detectives looked at each other first then back to me, "Well we hope that she okay, Could you do us a favor? If you hear from her or anything about her could you give us a call?" Detective Gordon handed me his card with his number on it. I accepted and told him I surely would. "So we understand you, Mr. Harvey and Mr. Johnson owns this Place huh? This is a nice joint here, y'all done fixed it all up and put some money into it. What is it y'all were doing before owning this Strip Joint?" Detective Brown asked. I could tell Detective Brown was Asshole of a cop and from jump I didn't like him. Both Rizzy and I looked at each other then back at the detectives," Well we definitely wasn't working a job that only thirty thousand dollars a year, we left that for the two of you." I told them with a short laugh. The look on both of their faces were pissed and I could tell all they wanted was a reason to try and book us. "Have a nice night Detectives, we will call if we hear anything new." Rizzy told them pointing to the door. Both detectives were mad but couldn't do nothing but leave.

We watched the detectives from the surveillance systems standing outside and they were pointing to our cameras, that was the last thing we needed was detectives snooping around our Club. What I wanted to know was how did he know who we were? D-Money was still laying low getting Hisself together and had no idea that things were getting rough out here in the streets. "As long as they don't come back then we should be good" I told Rizzy. He did what he did best and remained silent. I stepped out of the Office and made one last stop at the bar. Since I was planning on visiting Alicia I wanted to make sure I had enough liquor so that I could get nice and drunk. I grabbed a Fifth of the 1800 for it was known to be the drink that get the ladies fucked up an horny as hell. The Detectives, I'll worry about them later.....

Chapter Twelve
Alicia

(11:46pm)

IT WAS ALREADY CLOSE TO MIDNIGHT AND MY PLAN WAS TO BE AT home by at least 1am the latest. I had to get in and get out and the only way to do this would be to make this is clearly a Quickie Mission. When Alicia texted me the address to where she lived, I knew exactly where she lived. From the way she acted I thought she was goody two-shoes but she lived dead in the hood, in some Projects I was all too familiar with. The Projects she lived in was known for heavy robbing and murder so it wasn't a question if I was Strapped.

"I'm outside, come open up the door." I told her on the phone before hanging up and watching my surroundings. When Her front door opened I grabbed the 1800 out of the front seat and pulled out my 9mm from under my seat and put it on my waist. When I stepped out of the car I noticed that all eyes were on Me and I let it be known that I was strapped by the big bulging extended clip sticking out from under my shirt. I then walked into Alicia's place and she already had the lights dimmed down with a little bit of R. Kelly's TP2.com playing in the background. It wasn't a secret what I was here for and I was glad that she knew. When she closed the door behind me I turned to look at Her and was in complete awe in what she was wearing. She stood there wearing some of the sexiest lingerie, high heels and she had an ass so nice that I couldn't wait to fuck the shit out of her.

I pulled the 1800 out and sat it on the couch. I stuck the bottle out for her to bless the bottle how females did when she reached over and ejaculated the top. I slapped the ass of the bottle before opening and we sat there taking back to back shots. "Whew shit! That's my shit right there!!" Alicia said tapping her finger against her throat. I poured myself another shot when Alicia stood up and walked her sexy ass over and sat on my lap facing toward me. Automatically my dick started getting hard and I was more than ready to get the party started.

Alicia had her titties in my face and with her sitting on my lap had me anxious and eager. She began kissing my neck and un-buttoning my shirt so she could kiss me down my chest, "Pour me another shot." Alicia whispered in a sexy tone. I reached over grab-bing the bottle of 1800 and by Her request I poured her another shot. She threw it back so fast like only a professional would do. Right then I already knew the type of female she was and all at the same time I loved it. I then unsnapped her bra releasing her big pretty titties and without hesitation I began sucking and licking all over them.

After she gave her great head performance, I pulled her off her knees and threw her in the couch. I reached in my pocket and pulled out a gold Magnum wrapped condom and put it on. I had no idea where this girl been plus I was having sex with Honey unpro-tected so I couldn't risk bringing anything back to Her. I then slid her panties to the side and slid my hard dick right inside of her and started fucking the shit out of her. Alicia's pussy was so good that I was in another zone. I was feeling Myself and picked her up still in the Missionary position fucking her up against the wall. "Jay!! Jay!! Oh my God, Fuck me! Fuck me!" She yelled with her nails digging inside my back.

Alicia's Sex was so good that I fiend for more, I threw Her back on the couch demanding her to turn around and toot that ass up in the Doggy Style position. I stuffed my Dick into her tight Pussy and began pounding her from the back. I loved how she was throwing that ass back and forth forcing me to Cum all over her fat ass. Even though Alicia had some good ass Pussy, I knew it was time to get the fuck on. After Alicia went and got Herself cleaned up she came back into the living room, "Have a couple more shots with me and chill for a second." She suggested as she flopped beside me on the couch still naked. I was already exhausted from the hot Sex we just had and the liquor had surely taken a toll on my body which forced me to stay just a few more minutes until I gained the energy to leave. I told her that I could stay a bit longer and we sat there taking a few more shots and kicking it getting to know each other a little better. After my shots I began liking Alicia as a person rather than just how fine She was and how crazy Our Sex was. Our Sex was so crazy that Our next rounds we no longer cared any more and had to see what one another felt like without a condom. I knew it was risky being that We just started having Sex but this was a risk that I was willing to take. I shot all my nut inside Her that Girl without thinking about an outcome…

I woke up at 3:30am rubbing on who's Back I thought I was Honey's until I looked down only to see that I was still at Alicia's House. Here she was laying on my chest still naked and I fell asleep on some drunk shit. I couldn't believe I had got that drunk and fell asleep. I gently slid Alicia off of Me in attempts to make an escape and hopped up quickly getting dressed and picking up my Strap. I was trying to get up out of here without waking Her Up. Unfortunately Alicia woke up from all the movement I was doing, " You know you could stay the night if you want, I don't have a Man or nothing coming through." She told me. "I gotta' go! I gotta' get home to my Woman and Kid, Imma' call you doe." I told her as I rushed out of her place rushing to get home.

It was 4:39am when I pulled into the garage and I haven't came home this late since we first started dating. I know that I smelled like pussy so before getting out of the car I reached in my backseat grabbing an already opened bottle of water and poured it on my hands. With water on my hands I reached down into my pants and began scrubbing my Dick hard as possible. I had all type of hand sanitizers and smell good aromas in my car but I knew if I smelled like soap or anything else then that would make her suspicious of where I been. I then checked my phone for any incriminating evidence from any other female and erased it, Honey was far from stupid so I always had to be two steps ahead of her if I didn't want to be caught.

I tip-toed through the Condo hoping that everybody was sleep but between the squeaky floors and bag of snacks I had bought the boys it was kind of hard not to be detected. I made it to the living room where both boys were laid out sleep on the couch and the television was still on. I crept to the kitchen and softly placed my keys on the table when I heard Lil' Dez's voice, "Where is our chips and juice?" he asked, wiping the slob from his face. I just softly laughed, " I looked around the place and it was cleaned like I asked them to have it.

Hearing juice and chips was an automatic alert for Lil' K to wake up. "Yea, we been waiting on you. What took you so long?" Lil' K asked sitting up. I put my index finger up to my mouth signaling for them to be quiet and I crept over to the couch telling them to make room for me. I sat between them when I told Lil' K to go and make sure his mom was sleep first. He came back nodding his head telling me that she was sleep and jumped back on the couch beside me. Knowing that Honey was sleep, I could relax. I handed both boys a big dollar bag of chips and two big sprites so they could wash it down. I pulled out my favorite candy which was skittles and began munching on them still feeling all the liquor and weed I had smoked. I sat back trippin about the crazy sex Alicia and I had but tripping even more that I fucked her without a rubber on the second go round. I sat there and sparked up my blunt and a few minutes into it I knew I was high because I was kicking it with the boys like they been my Homies for years. "So what y'all gon' do when y'all grow up?" I asked them. Lil' K was the first one to answer, "I..I wanna' be a Construction Worker like you Jay so I could have sweet cars like you." He answered. I forgot his Mom told him I was in construction. Him telling me that actually touched my heart, I had someone that looked up to me and wanted to do what I did.

"What about you Lil' Dez, what you wanna' do when you grow up?" I asked. He was quiet for a minute and I could tell something was on his mind. I put my hand on his head and repeated the question. He looked up to me, "I wanna' be the Police so I could find my Mommy." he answered. My heart fell down to my stomach from his answer. He was only six years old but I knew that he knew that his Mother wouldn't just disappear on him. D-Money is my Brother but I hated how he killed that Girl for no reason. Now the Club was hot, a kid is without his Mother and only my Team knew that she was at the bottom of the Detroit River.

I grew up without my parents and even though I wasn't neither Lil' Dez or Lil' K's Fathers, right at that moment I promised Myself that I would be there for them for the rest of their lives. I was going to be a Role Model to them and show them how to become Men. After they ate their snacks they fell asleep watching cartoons and shortly after they fell asleep so did I. I had my arms around both of them ready to live with the promise that I just made Myself.....

Chapter Thirteen

WHEN I WOKE UP THERE WAS LIL' K AND LIL' DEZ STILL UP UNDER my arms with chips all over their face and knocked out with their mouths open. Standing directly in front of me was Honey with folded arms staring. I Wiped the cold from my eyes and sat up, "Y'all look so cute but I'm mad at you...What time did you get in last night?" She asked with her hands now on her hip like she dared me to lie. "Umm, late but not that late. Why? Whasup wit' all the questions?" I returned the question while softly placing the boys on the couch in attempts not to wake them. I headed to the bathroom with her following behind me, "Sooo, What time did you leave the Mainstrip?" Honey asked. I shrugged my shoulders standing over the bathroom sink trying to pull Myself together, "I don't remember Honey, Why?!" I asked, becoming irritated by her questions.

"I wanna' know where the hell my Man was last night, thats why?! I called the Club last night and they said that you left hours ago?That was at midnight!" She snapped back. I continued brushing my teeth and washing my face ignoring her question when out of nowhere Honey hit me dead in the mouth causing Me to stumble back from the hit. " Don't fuckin' lie to me Jay!" She yelled. Soon as I was about to grab her ass up, her eyes watered up and one thing I hated was to see her cry. She stomped out of the bathroom and into the bedroom closing the door behind her. I tried following behind her but she locked the door from the other side, I started banging and demanding for her to open the door but she wasn't budging. "Jay, what's wrong wit' my Momma?" Lil' K asked standing behind me. It was like DeJa'Vu, I remembered a time when I was little and asked my Dad the same question when my Mom locked him out. With no real logical answer, "Ummm, nothing. She's just a lil sleepy thats all. Hey, Im bout' to go out, you and Lil' Dez wanna' ride wit' me?" I asked. His smile spread across his face so fast and he told me that he was going to get Lil' Dez before taking off down the hallway.

I walked around the house and entered our bedroom through the back patio entrance that we always kept unlocked. Honey exhaled loudly upset that she didn't remember to lock that door too when she buried her head back into the pillow. I sat beside and placed my hand onto her back and began rubbing it, "Baby look, Me and Rizzy handled some business after we left the Club okay? All of my business I can't tell you about, that's why I need your trust Honey. Where is the trust?" I asked her. She turned around laying flat on her back, "I do trust, I just can't help but to think of all the Lil' Hoes that are in your face. I know about all your Groupies sooooo, I'm sorry I hit you." She told me. Not being able to stay mad at this Girl for nothing I cracked a smile, "Yea I almost pulled out my gun and shot yo' ass!" I replied. We both laughed as she playfully punched me in my side, "Boy shut up!" She replies. I leaned down and kissed her soft and luscious lips feeling good about our making up. As she laid in the bed I raised up my big t-shirt that she was sleeping in trying to get things started. I rubbed my fingers against her clitoris when she popped my hand quickly, "No Nigga, the kids are in the next room, Freak!" She whispered to me. "They not coming in here." I whispered back while steady feeling on her and watching for the door at the same time.

"Stop playing Jay, they could hear us..."Honey whined but wanting me just as bad as I wanted her. "Jay! Jay! Jay! We ready!" Lil' K yelled before running into our room and into our bed. "Damn!" I said low enough to only Honey and I could hear. She laughed getting out of the bed, "I told !" Honey said walking over towards Lil' Dez. Honey asked Lil' Dez what he had on and when I turned to look I even chuckled. Lil' Dez was covered in mud and Lil' K got dirt all in our bed. "What was y'all doing in them clothes, playing in the dirt?" I asked. "Mud" both boys answered in unison. Honey and I burst out laughing at the kids and their little boy ways."So where are you taking them anyway?" Honey asked. "Well I guess the first stop is the mall to get them some new clothes, you know they can't be riding wit' me and looking like just anything. Then we just gon' have Ourselves a Guys day out you know?" I answered her putting my hands on both of their heads with a smile. Honey gave me a funny look and told me to be careful with her boys and don't get them into any trouble.

After taking Myself a shower and getting Myself together for the day, I noticed Honey was getting up and dressed also. "Where are you going Baby?" I asked. "Im going to visit Kim's Grand-mother at Sinai Grace Hospital to make sure her surgery went okay. Today is Her surgery and I hope to catch Kim there so I could kill her for disappearing and leaving Her Son with her Grandmother. She knows that wasn't right." She said while fixing her hair in the mirror.

We all headed to her Chevy Impala, "Umm Jay, where y'all going?" She asked giving me a crazy look. "I told you that we were..." Then I noticed that I had the Boys with me and needed to drive a different, Bigger car. The only other car I could've chose was my White Lexus but I only drove that on special occasions. All my other cars were at my other properties. I did not want to take the kids in the Lexus because they were liable to fuck up something inside it, especially since my interior was all white. Honey had a big smile on her face asking me if I wanted to exchange cars for the day but I refused to be caught riding in an Impala, I had an image to maintain. "We want the fast car! We want the fast car! We want the fast car!" Lil' K and Lil' Dez cheered jumping up and down pointing to the Lexus. "Fuck it, We gon' take the Lexus." I told Honey. Both boys jumped up cheering and happy. Before we hopped in the Lexus I looked over to Honey walking over to her Impala, "Hey

Babe.....Take my other car, we getting rid of that Mothafucka' today." I said with a chuckle.

Honey and I kissed before hopping in separate cars and I turned up the music loud and rolled down the windows. Both boys started nodding their head when they heard the Jim Jones "Ballin" song come on. They both started reciting it and throwing their hands up in the air like they were shooting a jump shot. I watched them in the rearview mirror and couldn't help but to laugh. Today was going to be a hell of a day but fun at the same time, I never been in possession of no kids by Myself....

Chapter Fourteen

THE BOYS AND I SPENT HOURS IN THE MALL VISITING STORE AFTER store where I bought them everything they needed and wanted. It was crazy trying to keep up with two six year olds in a store. When one would disappear I would go looking for him and while in search, the other would disappear too. Trying to keep up wit these kids were crazy and driving me insane. Then at the same time both of my phones were blowing up, both legal and illegal jobs were in need of my help but it wasn't possible for the simple fact I made today family day. With all of the shopping we were doing we had to constantly travel back and forth to the car to drop bags off so we could continue shopping. Lil' Dez was so Bummy that I couldn't allow him to go on any longer like that. We went in one store where I had him put on his new clothes right then and there.

Exhausted from all of the crazy shopping we had done, the kids said they were hungry so I took them to the food court where we grabbed Ourselves a pizza. Sitting there watching them eat and enjoy the shopping spree we had, made me feel good. For the moment I felt like we were a real family. I also took them to the toy store where I let them pick out all the toys they wanted. I wanted them to be comfortable while living at my house.

One of my phones rang, "Hello, Hey Babe, what's wrong?

Whaaaat?? Wow! Umm, we are at the mall right now. Umm, Okay..Okay, well Imma' see you shortly cuz we on our way. Okay, don't worry Baby, we gon' be okay aight? I love you." I told her before hanging up the phone. I sat there in shock by what Honey had just told me. She told me that Lil' Dez's Great Grandmother, Kim's Grandmother didn't make it out of her surgery and Kim still hadn't shown up. What was crazy was that the Grandmother left all of Lil' Dez's birth certificate and important information with the hospital. It was like she expected the worst to happen before it did. Now Lil' Dez no longer had his Mother or Great-Grandmother in his life and it reminded me how I was forced to be raised by my Aunt and Uncle. We had no idea of any other family members that Lil' Dez may of had, we never even heard of who his Father could be. From what it looked like, it looked like Lil' Dez would be with us a bit longer.

I got the boys ready to go after our long day of shopping and it was time to get back home and see what was going to be our next steps. On the car ride home not even ten minutes after we got in the car both boys were sleep and totally worn out from all of the shopping and running through the mall. That reminded me that I haven't smoked all day and after hearing that news from Honey I couldn't find a better time. I pulled out a half smoked blunt from my ashtray and blew it all the way back to the Condo.

I carried both boys over my shoulder inside The house and into Lil K's bedroom placing them gently on the bed. I walked into the Master bedroom and there was Honey sitting on the edge of the bed sipping wine with her clothes still on but heels kicked off. As I approached her I could tell that she been crying, I reached down to our Mini-Bar and poured Myself a glass of Remy Martin, I knew that a deep conversation was soon to come.

I wrapped my arms around her bringing her closer to me assuring her that I was here and everything was going to be okay. "She been gone for almost two months now Jay, at first I thought she was just being irresponsible and ran off with some Man or something. That's clearly not the situation, I'm worried for my Best friend Kim now, something's wrong and I know it. She wouldn't have just up and left Her family knowing Her Grandmother's situation. I know it!" Kim said as the tears began rolling down her face. "Look Baby, whatever the case is we will figure out. Don't worry about nothing cuz' Im wit' you." I told her. Who was I to tell her to not worry when she had a Best-friend that wasn't coming back and had a Kid? "And her Grandmother must have knew that this surgery would be bad because besides leaving Lil' Dez's information, she left a note." Honey was saying as she pulled it out of her purse.....

"Dear Honey, I know if your reading this that my surgery didn't go well, therefore I'm on my way to see the mighty Lord that we serve. Since its the good Lords way, then it is an honor for me to obey. The purpose of this letter is to ask you to watch over my Grandson in case his Mother doesn't show up. He is a good boy and I will miss him dearly but you are the only Friend his Mother had that I approve of that is responsible enough to take care of him. I know that you already have a Son and it is kind of a lot to ask you to do but these are the things in life that we just have to deal with. I have no ideas where his Mother is and I know at times she could be irresponsible but this time I think its different and I'm worried about her. I pray and I pray that she is okay but I have a gut feeling that she isn't . Desmond has no other family and I hate to put this type of responsibility on you but my soul could rest in peace knowing that Desmond is in your hands. I left all of his important information in this box. Tell Desmond that His Grandmother loves him and I love you too. Be blessed and live by God's word." Sincerely loving Grandmother, Edna......

Hearing the letter that Lil' Dez's grandmother left, I was in complete shock. Honey already had a job and her own Son and now she was being asked to take on another son in her life. She was financially stable but having two kids was not in her plans anytime soon or wasn't easy. Honey and I only been together for a few months and to any other Bum Nigga it would've been all too much. I was different though, a real Man and was in love with Honey all the way to the moon and back. Her having two kids that wasn't biologically mines wasn't going to stop me from loving her.....

"Don't trip Love, we gon' be okay. I know we gon' be able to handle this, together." I told her meaning every word I said. She looked over at me, "We?? So you don't have a problem with me having two kids Jay? I mean, C'mon. Thats allot to ask anybody." Honey said to me with the tears constantly flowing down her gorgeous face. I smiled, "What? I love you and everything that comes with you. I wouldn't care if you came up in here with four kids, I wouldn't go anywhere! Now don't go and get no ideas or nothing now…" I replied making the both of us laugh. "Nawl but forreal, I'm already crazy bout' Lil' K and Lil' Dez is real cool so they fine with me. No I don't mind you now have two kids." I told her. Honey couldn't do nothing but smile and hug me tighter than ever. "Plus you should've seen all the girls they got me today at the mall!" I told her. We both laughed and since I wanted to be funny I caught a nice gut shot to the stomach. "I really do love you Boy!" She told me, releasing me from her hug. She stood up and popped me in the back of my head, "Now what Girls did they get you at the mall?" She asked playfully.

"Hey Ma, you been crying again? Your a Crybaby." Lil' K told his mom with Lil' Dez standing beside him at the door. We both laughed as Honey wiped her eyes, "Mommy's not crying, Im just happy thats all. Come here both of y'all, I need a hug." She told the boys. They both raced into her arms hugging her tight and asking why was she so happy. "Well, I'm happy that Lil' Dez will be staying with Us longer than we expected, How y'all feel about that?" Honey asked them. They both jumped up and down, "Yay!!! So he get to spend a lot of nights over?" Lil' K asked. Honey nodded her head, "Yep, he gets to stay over every night." She told them. Both boys jumped up and down for joy happy that what used to be just an overnight thing was now forever. They already called themselves Brothers so now they really felt like Brothers.

Standing there watching all of them hug and being happy made me feel good, I felt like a Father that had a family and responsibilities which I now did. Neither one of the boys were mine but from this day on I would treat them like they were........

Chapter Fifteen
Months Later

Everything in my life was going good and things were only getting better. The Mainstrip was doing great, the money from the streets was flowing constantly, Honey and the kids were adjusting just fine, in fact we even been house hunting in search for something bigger and last but not least, D-Money had finally shook his addictions and was back on the right track. Today he was coming back from California where he been laying low at from the whole Kim situation and the first thing he wanted to do is get right back to business and check out the Strip Club that he still partially owned. I was a bit skeptical about him jumping right back into the street life with all the liquor and women surrounding him but when Rizzy vouched for him I knew he had to been all good. Rizzy never vouched for D-Money so I knew he had to been fully recovered.

I made it to the Mainstrip around 11:45pm to check on things and make sure things were being ran smoothly and soon as I walked in I seen a group of Niggas wearing all black, a few of them wore chains that read "HUSTLE FAM" and those not wearing chains wore the t-shirts. This group of Niggas were clowning, loud, throwing money and the way they carried Themselves I could tell they were either on Powder or on E-Pills. I seen groups like this come in on a regular but this particular group I felt would be trouble. They were just doing too much but because they were throwing a lot of money at the Dancers and spending money at the bar I decided to leave them alone for the time being. I had to leave and head up to the Conference Office to check the Club books.

When I stepped in and seen D-Money and Rizzy already looking over the books, there was a big smile spread cross my face. I haven't seen D-Money in so long that I actually had been missing my Bro. "Whasup Bro?! Whats good?!" He replied. I stepped back checking him out and he looked good. I could tell that he been sober and leaving all of them drugs alone, he looked like he was back to the old D- Money. The last time I seen him he looked terrible and sloppy from all the drugs he had taken so to see him looking sober and good made me proud. He was back to the freshly well dressed Nigga we known him to be and wearing his MSN chain that we all went to have made together. D-Money was back to his old self. "Im good Man, No I mean I'm really good now. I needed them months away and now I'm ready to get back to the money, feel me?" D-Money said sticking his hand out to give me a play.

I nodded my head proud to have my Brother back, "Well we been waiting on you and the Businesses been waiting on you too. We been putting your money up so you got a bankroll coming. You been staying staying sober right?" I asked. He gave me a funny look "C'Mon Fam, I'm straight on all that drinking and smoking shit. I'm staying sober and focused on getting this money," D-Money told me. I actually believed him and without hesitation I trusted him to do his own thing…...

The night went on and we all were around the Club doing our own thing. Rizzy was checking with the Dancers making sure that they were straight, I was at the Bar making sure that all the liquor was stocked up and across the room was D-Money making sure that all the Guests were good and having a good time. On the other side of the room was the same Niggas that was repping their crew

"HUSTLE FAM" and they were good and drunk because they thought this was their Club or something. One of the Niggas wearing the chains jumped up on stage with the Dancers and Big Tee moved in quickly pulling him down. When Big Tee snatched him down the Hustle Fam Crew didn't like how he did it and they began surrounding him while cursing him out like they were going to attack him.

All the other Bouncers ran over to assist but through all of them I seen D-Money rushing over there too. "Yo!Yo!Yo! Calm down. All the big Man is doing is his job."D-Money began explaining in attempts to diffuse the situation. Seeing that shit was getting real I made my way over there and before I got there I seen a big bottle of Rose' raise high in the air and drop down over D-Money's head knocking him straight down to the ground. Next thing I knew Rizzy had ran over punching on anybody that was affiliated with the Hustle Fam.

Now there was a huge fight with the MSN, The Mainstrip Security and all the Hustle Fam Niggas and from the looks of it we were winning even with D-Money on the floor knocked out cold. I was stomping on the head of one of the Niggas I knocked out and when I looked over to my right I seen Rizzy doing the same thing. The whole Strip Club was a frenzy. Dancers and Guest all running for the exits while we continued our club brawl. One of the guys that Rizzy was fucking up was begging for him to stop but I was sure the thought of our Mans getting knocked out was his gas to keep him going and therefore we did. I looked over to my left and Big Tee was whooping three niggas ass at the same time. I wasn't surprised, he was 400 lbs and 7 feet tall, that's what he was supposed to be doing.

I looked around for D-Money and somebody had slid him across the floor where I seen one of the Hustle Fam Niggas taking off his MSN chain and money rolls out of his pocket. I immediately made my way through the clubs traffic in attempts to get to my Nigga, "Boom! Boom! Boom!" was the sound of a gun going off and echoing through the club. Everybody in the club ducked down and ran toward the exit but I was only focused on getting over to D-Money. By the time I made it over to him it was already too late. D-

Money's chain has already been taken and his pockets were turned inside out. I kneeled down to D-Money when I noticed his head was bloody from being hit with the bottle. I started shaking him but he struggled gaining consciousness, "What?? What happened??" D-Money kept asking. I just helped him get up and over to the Conference Office. The Club was a wreck and when I seen Rizzy walking toward me it was good to see that he was okay. He looked like he been in a war but he still had his MSN chain swinging and shining like I did. When he seen how fucked up D-Money was he was furious but he had to save it for another time, "Yo, gimme' y'all pistols so I could put them up before the Police get here!" He told us. He grabbed the pistols from both our sides and helped me get D-Money to the Conference Office.

Within the next ten minutes the club was totally empty all you could hear was the police sirens echoing from outside. We all sat in the office while we had one of the Waitresses nurse D-Money back in one piece. He just kept asking what happened and where were we at but Rizzy and I didn't have that kind of patience. Rizzy and the Waitress had to keep getting towels to clean up the blood on D-Money's head and seeing all that blood made my blood boil. The fact that this Hustle Fam crew thought they could come in our club and act an ass then they took my brothers chain? Shit wasn't going to end well for them for they must've not known who they just fucked with. Not only were we supplying majority of the city but we put in work Ourselves and was well known from the East to the Westside. We were The Mainstrip Niggas and the fact that they thought they could come and disrespect us and our club was unacceptable and they were going to have to answer for it…..

Keeping a close eye on our Surveillance Cameras, I just shook my head when I seen it was the same Detectives that came before to ask us about Kim. I told all of them to stay in the Office while I went to go and handle the Detectives in the Club. When I stepped out of the Office closing the door behind me both Detectives were all smiles as if they knew they would see us again.

"Well, Well, Well....If it isn't Mr. Hill. I see you done some redecorating, looks nice." Detective Gordon said being sarcastic. I nodded my head, "Yea just a lil' bit. How could I help you Pigs...Ooops, I mean Detectives tonight? As you can see, I have a lot of things on my plate." I told them while standing behind the bar fixing Myself a drink. "So there was reports that shots were fired, who do you think is responsible?" Detective Gordon asked while Detective Brown walked around the messed up Club. I gave him a look as if I was clueless, "I don't know what you're talking about Detective. Umm, ain't y'all Homicide Detectives anyway? What are y'all doing here anyway? Ain't nobody get shot or dead." I asked them. The fact that they were even here was baffling to me especially since no one was killed or shot and they are Homicide Detectives. They got her kind of fast too, so it seemed like they were close by.

"We were in the area when we heard the call and decided we would handle it. Yes we are Homicide Detectives but since we were the closest we could pick up the call. And while you're wondering why we are here, you need to worry about who was doing the shooting in here and tore y'all place up." Detective Gordon told me. "What my Partner has failed to ask you is do you want to tell us who wrecked your club tonight or not?" Detective Brown asked. I stared both of them in the face and told them I know nothing of a shooting and nothing to tell them. "We see that y'all have cameras all around here, can we check them out?" Detective Gordon asked. When I told them that they all were broke he got angry with my lies and I could tell I got under his skin, "Gordon lets get out of here. The next time Hustle Fam shoot this place up we won't be in the area." Detective Brown said as he headed toward the exit.

" Excuse Me Officer, Who said anything about the Hustle Fam doing this to our place?" I asked now interested as to how they knew without me telling them. It was clearly some bullshit in the game and I could see it in both Detectives faces. Detective Brown had a grin on his face, "Have Yourself a good night Mr. Hill and call us if you ever want to talk." He told me while leaving his card on the table again. "Oh yea, tell yo' Mans Darien a.k.a. D-Money that we are looking for him." Detective Gordon said following behind his Partner. I followed them to the exit, "Who said anything about the Hustle Fam Detectives?! What are y'all looking for Darien for?! Answer me!" I yelled at them as they ignored me and walking away.

Why was the Detectives looking for D-Money? It couldn't be for the Kim incident, How could they know that it was the Hustle Fam who tore my Club up? There was a lot of bullshit going on and I had a lot of questions. First things first, we had to handle the Hustle Fam immediately......

Chapter Sixteen

A COUPLE DAYS PASSED BY AND THE LOUD CARTOON SOUNDS BLASTED through my big screen television. Spongebob was the man in my house but I hated how he woke me up damn near every morning. I reached over to my phone that was on the charger and seen that I had ten missed calls from D-Money. He had been caught up to date of what happened the other night and that quickly he was back to the Hot-Head nigga he once was. He wanted to kill anybody affiliated with the Hustle Fam. Just when Rizzy and I thought D-Money was in a good place just like that he was taken out of it. In the business we were in we couldn't just go and shoot shit up because it was bad for business but Rizzy was suppose to reach out to the Hustle Fam Boss and get all of D-Money's belongings back to prevent any further violence.

My phone started vibrating and when I noticed it was Alicia I quickly silenced the ringtone and threw my phone on silent. I was at home with the family and it most definitely wasn't a good time. I quickly erased Alicia's calls from my call history just in case Honey went through my phone, I was sure Alicia didn't want anything but to know why I haven't called her in a while or haven't came to kick it with her. I had alot going on and was way too busy to be thinking about some pussy I could get anytime I wanted.

. . .

I got Myself together for the day when I walked in the living room and the boys had toys everywhere but their faces were glued to the television. "Whassup Boys?" I spoke and chuckled seeing how they reminded me of Rizzy, D-Money and Myself when we were their age. "Hey Jay!" They both spoke at the same time. I looked over in the kitchen and there was Honey behind the stove cooking breakfast. I stood there appreciating the moment and the sight of the cooking for the family, besides all the bullshit that comes with what I did for a living I was loving being the Hood Nigga I was.

"Baby you want some breakfast?" Honey asked me while standing there looking good cooking in her boy shorts and wife-beater. I walked up from behind hugging her from the back and kissing her on her neck, "I would love some breakfast Girl." I told her now kissing her on her cheek. She giggled telling me not to start something that we were not going to be able to finish. My phone in my basketball shorts began vibrating when I pulled it out exhaling loudly, "Yea, yea you know you gotta' answer it so answer it."Honey told me. It was Rizzy again, something had to been wrong for the simple fact he never called so much this early before. "Whatup doe' Boy?? At the Crib, where you at? Umm, aight Im on my way right now. Right now Nigga, Im on my way." I told him before hanging up the phone. I looked at Honey and she was all too familiar with the schedule that I lived by, " Imma' have to miss breakfast this time Love, this Nigga Rizzy is outside and I gotta go. I love you and I will hit you up a lil' later." I told her placing a kiss on her cheek and telling the boys bye. For Rizzy to be here at my place so early it had to been something important and for some reason I felt that today was going to be a long day.

I hopped in Rizzy's Escalade giving him a Play and nothing was better than the sweet smell of good kush already fired up to begin the day. When we pulled off I could tell that he was stressing over something because he already smoked half of the blunt to Hisself. I asked Rizzy what was up and what had him up and over my place so early, "Mannn, so I went to visit that nigga Marlo who is the head of them wack ass Hustle Fam Niggas last night right? Well off top before I could even say anything he was already apologizing for how his Crew acted in our club. Right then and there he pulled out D-Money's chain and a loaf of money and handed it to me. He told me that he added an extra five thousand dollars to it and told me that he got on His Crew ass for what they did. Dude was mad cool and I couldn't do shit but respect him just because he was so humble and wasn't on no bullshit. So after all of that, we gave each other a play and went separate ways. Now I called that Nigga D-Money to tell him the news and he was on tip. He was talking about he ain't gon' be happy til' he get his get-back and wasn't accepting no apologies. That Nigga is back to his don't give a fuck self and we gotta' make sho he don't do shit stupid, feel me?" Rizzy was telling me. I sat there smoking what was left of the blunt that he passed me and just shook my head in disappointment in D-Money. He was doing so good and back on the right path and just like that it all changed.

We pulled up at The Mainstrip and to our surprise D-Money's old school Chevy was already here. For D-Money to be this early out and about couldn't been good for nobody and I had a feeling we were going to find out shortly just what he was on. We then walked into the Mainstrip and went straight into the Conference room where we seen D-Money sitting at the desk with dark liquor in his cup with a look in his eye, Rizzy and I gave him a play and took a seat, "Wow, one lil' brawl and your back on the bottle huh?" I asked him. He gave me a look, "A lil' Brawl?! Is you crazy?! Them niggas cracked me in the head, took my chain and money and you talking about a lil' Brawl?! Yea you got me fucked up! They got me fucked up!." D-Money snapped back at me. Rizzy asked D-Money what had him up at work so early and a devilish grin spread across his face, "I gotta' plan to get them Hustle Fam Niggas back, full proof plan?" He answered. "Hold on, hold on, hold on...before you get to coming up with plans look what I got you." Rizzy said pulling out his chain and a loaf of money placing it in front of him. The look D-Money had on his face was like it wasn't his or something. "I don't want that shit! They paid for it so they can keep it! Give it back, as a matter of fact.....I'm putting it on a Nigga grave!" D-Money said sounding so firm with his decision. The Room grew silent when I asked him what kind of plan that he had in mind.

Happy to know that I was interested, "I been doing my home-work on this whole Hustle Fam Clown Crew and they are actually getting money, alot of money. I found out where their Stash house is at and Im telling y'all right now, them Niggas is holding. I'm sick we been slipping on these Fools for so long! Im talking Kush Bows, Cocaine and some E-Pills. I fucks wit' one of Mario's Hoodrats and she confirmed everything." D-Money told me while passing over a blunt. "How do you know this and how do you know that Bitch is telling you the truth and not trying to set you up?" I asked. "Are you really even considering this shit Jay when I just told you how humble the Nigga was about what went down?!" Rizzy asked me. For some reason Rizzy didn't hear all that I heard, what I heard was free money and work was on the floor and it could be all Ours.

"I know all this cuz' I really did my homework and been laying on them Niggas, where do yall think I been at since that shit happened? I knew what was going in and out of the house but the Bitch just confirmed it. The other night it was bout' 3am when Mario pulled up to the house and in the driveway backwards. Thats when he had his Crew unloading his truck. I even seen the Hoe Nigga that cracked my head wit' that bottle. I started to just shoot everybody ova that Mothafucka but I was thinking bout the long haul. This is something we gotta' do Jay, forreal. Them Niggas disre-spected not just our Club but MSN and what we stand for. Fuck an apology, lets hit Niggas where it hurts and get money at the same time you feel me?! If we don't do shit then Niggas Gon' think they got the green light to just come in and do whatever the fuck they want, feel me?! They gon think they can come in this Bitch and Clown and then pay they way out of it, hell Nawl! They got Us fucked up!" D-Money explained. The more he talked, the more I was convinced. He was right, we couldn't let Niggas come and fuck our club up and they think all they have to do is apologize to make it right. If we let that incident slide we would have many more on the way.

"I'm wit it, fuck it! This plan has to be well put together and I don't want them Niggas to know we did it off top. That's the only way I'm in Bro, they cant know off top! Deal?" I asked him under my own stipulations. I had a reason for my stipulations and it was for everybody safety. D-Money didn't hesitate to agree to my terms and it was on. "Let's get this money and make them niggas sick. It's MSN fo' life!" I answered standing up and giving D-Money a play. Once again we were waiting on Rizzy's final answer and we could tell he was deep in his thoughts while we stared at him. "Mannn, y'all Niggas is fuckin' crazy! I'm in too!" He answered. D-Money was hyped that he had us on board to get the same Niggas that robbed him," Bet! Now look , I already been doing my homework on the house and there is two big Ass Niggas that be working that Bitch but they soft as hell and all they do is eat carry out. All these Niggas do is order Pizzas and Chicken from the same place all the time. I mean these is some big Niggas and they answer the door wit' Choppas every time. The Delivery Boy is so use to seeing it that he don't even panic when he sees the guns." D-Money briefed Us.We haven't hit a Lick since the Armor Truck Heist so hitting a house had to be twice as much easier.

D-Money continued explaining all the ends and outs of the upcoming Lick we would be doing and I made the call to the Big Homie E-Bo so he could prepare us with all the proper Artillery once again. I've known E-Bo for years now and had mad respect for him but now that I was in this street life I hated telling Him or anybody else all of my business. I couldn't take the chance of someone ever being forced to Rat on me and I knew with my Crew I never would have to deal with that type of situation….

There was a lot of work I had to do at the club and I had to prepare for the upcoming Lick so I was racing against time to get things done when my phone vibrated again. It was a text message from Alicia telling me that I needed to come over ASAP so we could talk. I couldn't think of a reason as to why we would have to talk ASAP, couldn't nothing had been that important for us to discuss. Not up for any games I decided to just call her and see what was going on with her.

"Alicia, Whatup doe, I got your text saying that we needed to talk ASAP, what's going on??? Umm yea, I been busy lately...I apologize my Baby, don't be mad at me, I was going to call you today as a matter of fact...I been missing you too..You want me to come over??? Right now?? Uhh, aight I'll be there in bout' twenty minutes. Yep." I told her before hanging up the phone. I wondered could she want the dick that bad but at the same time it seemed like something was wrong. I just had the feeling that she wanted me to come over for something deep. Whatever the case was, I haven't fucked her in a while so I could use some of that good ass pussy again real quick.

Rizzy stayed at the Club while I used his truck to go and visit Alicia. I had to see what was so important that she insisted that I came by. After a twenty minute drive I pulled up in her Projects and the front door was already open. Of course I had my 9mm tucked in my waist band so if she was on some bullshit I would already be a step ahead. I then stepped into her place and closed the door behind me. Alicia sat on the couch with her hair in a ponytail and wearing some little boy shorts looking like the clean-cut Hoodrat chick I was attracted too. When I sat beside her I leaned over and planted a kiss on her cheek but I could tell she been crying. I instantly began to worry as to what was next and what she was about to tell me. Either she had an STD or she was pregnant, both would be life changing and if it was an STD her life would surely change because if it was something that couldn't be cured then I would have to kill her before the disease did.

"Whasup Baby, what's wrong?" I asked wrapping my arm around her. She sniffled, "Jay, I'm pregnant." She answered without hesitation. When she said that I felt my heart stop beating for atleast a minute, "What? Pregnant? Mann, by who?" I shot back at her. She looked at me crazy, "Really?! Nigga by you! I only been wit' you!!" She said getting loud. I didn't even mean to respond like that but hearing that she was pregnant fucked me up. I quickly apologized and tried calming her down. "Damn! Pregnant huh?" I whispered to Myself. Alicia could tell that I wasn't happy about the situation and truth be told I wasn't. I already had a Girl and kids now so they were all I was thinking about. "Jay if this inconveniences you then I could take care of this Baby Myself! I got my own money, my own place and I don't need a Man that don't want to be father anywhere around...." Alicia started ranting before I raised my hand needing some silence to get my thoughts together. This shit was crazy because I knew that she wasn't lying because I remembered shooting all inside of her that whole night. The way how Alicia was talking I could tell that abortion wasn't even an option. I had to think of something and think of it quick.

"Look, if it's really my child I will be here for the both of y'all. I'm not the type of Nigga to not take care of my responsibilities but I'm sho' I told you I have a Woman already. That's what I'm thinking about." I told her.

"No, you didn't tell me you had a girl but I'm not stupid, I figured you did how you got up in the middle of the night and wouldn't spend the night. Look, as long as you take care of what needs to be taking care of then I can't complain and have no reason to call your Girl and getting ghetto. My question is are you happy with Her? You haven't even given me the chance to make you happy," Alicia asked as she planted her hand on my face and started rubbing it.

Without hesitation I told her that I was happy with my Woman but I just tend to cheat every blue moon. I felt bad that I couldn't give her a chance, but my mind was already made up and couldn't be changed. I was in love with Honey and wasn't nothing going to change that.

After sitting there and discussing all of our next steps, I told

Alicia I had to shoot a few moves and would check up with her later. As I headed out the door, she stopped me and planted a big kiss on my lips that was electrifying as it was when we first met. She had that type of touch that reminded me why I even was risking losing Honey for her. Before I walked off, we told each other that we loved the other and I hopped in the truck and pulled off. I sparked up a blunt quickly inhaling the good Kush knowing that I needed it after hearing the news I just got. If Honey found out, she would be out done with me and surely would be taking the boys and leaving and that I couldn't have. The crazy thing about it was at the same time I was a little happy. I know what I was going to do to make this work, but I had to find a way, a smart way.

Chapter Seventeen
Sweet Revenge

(Friday)

I GOT UP A BIT EARLIER THAN USUAL WHEN I KISSED HONEY AND THE boys on the forehead before leaving the house. today wasn't promised neither was any other day being in the business that I was in. when I walked into the Mainstrip, Rizzy and D-Money were already there and preparing for the mission that was at hand. I dropped the bag of Heavy Artillery that I got from E-Bo and we all got suited and booted, "Yo, I'm 'bout to go and pull the cars up," D-Money said heading out the door. Rizzy and I began loading up the guns and since there wasn't a good time to ever to tell him, "Yo Cuzo, I got a Baby on the way Bro," I told him. He paused from preparing his AR-15, "Straight up? I already knew you and Honey was gon' have y'all one. how y'all be on each other, I knew it! Y'all know what it is yet? A boy or a girl?" Rizzy asked in an excited tone. I just shook my head, "It ain't by Honey doe, It's by Alicia. You know Alicia the one that work at E-Bo restaurant." I told him. Rizzy's face turned up, "Man, is you serious?! You got that bitch pregnant?! Honey gon' kill you! How do you even know that's yo baby? you gon' fuck around and that baby pop out looking like E-Bo." Rizzy said. I quickly became irritated by his response because I knew that it was my baby she was pregnant with. Then again, I would be lying if I said the thought didn't cross my mind. She been working with him forever and they often talked.

D-Money walked in the office, "The cars ready boys, lets go!" he yelled as he grabbed all his firearms and gear before heading to the truck. Rizzy and I then followed behind him, "Hey Jay, congrats Bro." Rizzy sad sticking his hand out to give me a play. We gave each other plays and a hug, "Aight lets do this shit the right way so I could get you home safely so Honey could be the one to kill you. I can't wait to see how that goes down." Rizzy said. We both laughed and got into separate vehicles. It wasn't a secret that when Honey found out that she would kill me.

Hustle Fam Mario's Stash House sat on a block that only three houses were on and he owned them all. We pulled up two blocks away so we couldn't be seen. D-Money and I were in the same truck and Rizzy was on the block directly behind the stash house on the next block. D-Money pulled out his binoculars looking down at the stash house, "Aight, I just called the pizza place they always order from so they should be here shortly. Soon as they pull up, we running up in that Bitch," he said. D-Money was already in his war mentality and I could tell he was ready to kill any moment. Times like this was when he showed how much of a killer genius he was.

We sat there waiting for approximately twenty minutes when the pizza delivery car finally pulled up. D-Money radioed to Rizzy for him to get in position because it was time and soon as the delivery boy walked up to the front door, I sped the truck down the street right in front of the Spot onto the grass. The front door was open and the confused look on the Pizza Boy and the Spot Workers face were priceless. Rizzy came from the side of the house and both D-Money and I hopped out the truck with guns aimed directly at the Workers demanding hem to get down on the ground.

As we all rushed the porch, we knocked the Pizza Boy into the bushes and demanded the Spot Workers to lay on the ground and not to move.that was dead-bolted. One of them decided to make a dumb move and try to dart to the back room but not before D-Money fired four shots into the Fat Man's back sending his big ass to the floor. D-Money and I moved in straight tactical style toward the back rooms where the dead Spot Worker tried to run too. Both standing on each side of the door we did a countdown to when we were going to burst inside the bedroom door but before we could do anything there were multiple shots being fired through the door at Us. Whatever it was he was shooting at Us was letting off loud shots but the sound of him clicking to shoot his gun but out of ammo was louder. D-Monet and I both turned to face the shooter behind the shot up door and we riddled his little body with the hottest shots. The Spot was now clear and we had minutes to get what we came to get and to get the hell out of here. D-Money stood guard at the front door just in case anybody else showed up while Rizzy and I scanned the house. we hit every room and came out with the most. This was surely a Stash House because there was bales of weed that had to been holding at least fifty pounds of cocaine and last but not least there was a closet literally filled to the top with E-pills. We hit a Lick with all the stuff inside this house, "Aight y'all its time to go, Niggas is pulling up and they deep as fuck! Let's go!" D-Money yelled as he sprayed shots at the cars and Niggas pulling up to the stash house. His AR-15 sounded like a helicopter was over our heads. Rizzy and I ran up to the front door and when we looked outside we seen that it was impossible for us to make it out that way. "We gotta go through the back! C'Mon let's go y'all!" Rizzy yelled ducking down from the incoming bullets that came from outside. "Y'all gon' head while I handle these Hoe Niggas! Go!" D-Money yelled. I refused to leave him but his loud demands and threatening me that he would shoot me Hisself made me leave.

Rizzy and I snuck out the back door of the Stash House undetected while carrying all of the heavy packages of work. We traveled through the backyard, jumped a few gates and onto the next block where Rizzy get-away car was parked. Even on the next block the sounds of the guns being fired sounded like fireworks. We loaded up the truck and both hopped in the running truck waiting on our Brother. I couldn't believe we just left him in the middle of a gun war. Suddenly we heard the gun shots come to a pause and the sound of men yelling loudly, I couldn't help but to expect the worse outcome. The block that we were parked on began to bring the neighbors out, they all were wondering what was going on, so was Rizzy and Myself.

"Bro, what we gon' do? If he was good, he would already be on his way," Rizzy said anxious to get out of there. I was confused not knowing what to do, was I supposed to stay or leave? "BOOM! BOOM! BOOM!" was the sounds of loud shots being let off and D-Money running towards us carrying another bag. I looked over to Rizzy and we both had big smiles on our faces when we seen that he was okay. We was yelling for him to hurry up and get in and soon as he did we stabbed off. Not even two houses down gun shots were fired into the truck during the getaway. I hit corner after corner until we were safely out of harm's way when we all began cheering and yelling. We got away with another successful Lick that was going to only upgrade the high-profile lifestyle life we were living. Now one thing that was for sure was that after what happened at the club the other night, we would for sure be suspects to the Hustle Fam. A lot of things were going to get even more crazier in the streets of Detroit. They done fucked up and made us the number one supplier of the city.

Chapter Eighteen
Three Months Later

THE HEAT IN THE STREETS HAD FINALLY DIED DOWN AFTER MARIO'S Hustle Fam Stash House was hit and Word on the streets was that they took a loss for 600 hundred pounds of weed, forty thousand E-Pills, and twenty bricks of cocaine. Rumors change up so much by the time it reaches the streets, it actually was only 500 pounds of weed, twenty thousand E-pills and 15 bricks of cocaine. Of course, the Hustle Fam had us on their list of suspects, they even came and hollered at us asking if we knew anything about it. We told them we heard about it but knew nothing of it. I promised that if I heard anything or came across any of it I would for sure let him know. Nobody but the MSN knew about the lick and it wasn't hard to keep it a secret. We sold all that shit to our peoples out of town and didn't leave a trace of our name on it. That lick was talked about heavily around Detroit for a while, it turned out that while Rizzy and I was waiting on D-Money to come to the truck, he done killed 12 of Mario's henchmen. The news called it a mafia deal gone bad and asked if anybody knew anything to contact the police.

Meanwhile things were going great with MSN. Honey and the kids were happy living in the new big mansion I got us far from Detroit,

Alicia was just as happy as I was about our little boy that was soon to be on the way, shid, I had to move her out the hood to and she wasn't too far away from the city in a nice suburban neighborhood. With all the money we were bringing in we were living the hustlers dream that we've been dreaming since were kids. Rizzy bought Himself a new big ass house with the latest model Mercedes Benz truck. Now D-Money used to be the type to go out and buy new jewelry and cars but now he picked up another hobby and became fascinated with the biggest assault rifles and best pistols ever created. He was getting ready for a war that nobody knew about but him. We were already rich young niggas but now after hitting that lick and cleaning up on free money, our net worth was in the millions, thanks to the Hustle Fam.....

It was a Monday afternoon when I was at home chilling with the boys while Honey went to run some errands. It was rare that I could chill out so I told her I would watch the boys while she was gone. I received a call from J.T and Gutta telling me they had my money so I told them I would be there in the next hour. The boys needed haircuts so while I was out picking up money, I figured why not take them to go and get clean cuts. I called Big Tee who lived not too far away from me to get here so he could drive us to the City. Big Tee was promoted from club Bouncer to my personal Bodyguard/driver and anywhere I went so did he. Now that MSN ran the streets, we developed Haters who didn't want to see us shine so I hired the biggest toughest guy I knew to watch my back and bust his gun when needed.

We all stepped outside, "Nawl not the Lexus today Big Tee, we taking the Range Rover since we got the boys today," I told him. Big Tee went over to my six-car garage and pulled the Range Rover out and the kids and I jumped in. I gave Big Tee the orders to take us to my Mans and personal barber J-Moss house so we could get cut up, I didn't go to regular barber shops because I didn't like all the traffic that came in and out. I was a getting money Nigga now, so I was super paranoid.

We spent an hour and a half getting all our haircuts and now we all were looking crispy with the fresh cuts. After picking up my money from J.T and Gutta the boys told me they were hungry, so we pulled up in a Wendy's where we heard the police sirens screaming from the unmarked car behind us. "Damn, Bitch ass Police is behind us. Gimme yo gun," Big Tee said to me looking into his rearview. I then slid him over my pistol for him to stash with his, "It's cool, it's cool. We ain't do nothing so they don't want nothing," I said as I Watched through my side mirror. "Jay is that the Police" Lil' K asked. "Yep Homie, just sit back and be smooth while I deal wit' this then we gone' get yo food," I answered.

Staring through the side mirror I seen the police step out the car and shook my head when I noticed it wasn't just any regular police. It was the detectives that visited the club months ago, I could only imagine what it was they wanted now. Big Tee and I rolled down our tinted window, "Mr. Hill, this is a nice truck you got here. Imma' have to get me a Strip club so I could afford one of these, this is nice," Detective Gordon said from Big Tee's side. I grinned, "Yes the Strip Club is pretty beneficial. I tell you what, whenever you tired of that tired-ass Cop check just come and holla' at me and I could pay you way more for being a Bouncer or something. I'm sure I could find something for you," I told him. He laughed but I could tell that I got under his skin by my statement. "I see they have y'all making traffic stops so what is it I could do for you good Detectives on this nice day?" I asked them, "Well my Partner and I just left the hospital after getting the good news that one of those Hustle Fam Members finally came out of his comma and was ready to talk. Could you believe that, he was shot in the throat and still survived. It's just unfortunate the moment we tried talking to him he had a seizure, so he was unable to talk again. My Partner and I are just dying to know who it is that he would say was responsible for killing all of his Homies. You know the word on the street is that it was MSN responsible for it in retaliation for the shit that happened at the Mainstrip. Now what do you think he would want to tell us when he come too?" Detective Brown asked as he stood over my window.

I couldn't believe what I was hearing, I also couldn't believe anybody survived the bullets that D-Money was firing but I had to keep my cool and not panic in front of them. "Well whatever the survivor says I'm sho' it won't have nothing to do with MSN and if it just so happens, he do, we got good lawyers on the payroll." I answered the Asshole Detective. "you fuckin' better because if you don't, I will personally make sure y'all get buried under the jail with no money to put in your accounts and bunking with one of the biggest faggots!" Detective Brown threatened. The back window was rolled down on Lil' Dez's side, "Uncle Mike? Hey Uncle Mike!" Lil' Dez yelled in excitement. I started looking around for Uncle Mike he spoke of then when I saw how lit up the Detectives face got, I knew exactly who Lil' Dez was talking to. "Lil' Dez?! What's up Nephew, how have you been Buddy?" Detective Brown spoke with a whole attitude changed. Lil' Dez told him he was okay, and the entire atmosphere had changed. Things were starting to finally add up to me now in why these Detectives were on MSN ass so bad. If he was related to Lil' Dez then that means they were related to R.I.P Kim.

Detective Brown gave me a look and asked me what his nephew was doing with Me. "Kim and my Girl are Best friends so after Grandma Edna passed, we took him in. that's my lil' Man's right here," I said as I turned around looking at him with a smile. Detective Brown opened my door and asked me to step out of the car. When I stepped out, we walked a few feet away from the car when he took a deep breath and exhaled, "So your Girl is Honey huh?

She is a pure Sweetheart. Look, I have to tell you that I really appreciate you taking my Nephew in, that's real good. I just work crazy hours and the lifestyle I live, I can't provide for a kid, shid its barely providing for me. we been on you and your Crew so hard because Kim was my little sister. So, off the books and I need you to be honest with me. this is between just me and you, do you know what happened to my lil' Sister?" Detective Brown asked me. I looked at him directly in the face giving him straight eye contact, "Brown, I swear I don't know what happened to Kim. She was like family, I ain't even heard shit from the streets man. I just don't know what happened to Her," I answered. Detective Brown looked me dead in my face, "Jay, you have my Nephew and I need you to take good care of him. Take care of him and I could take care of you, do you get me?" he asked. I nodded my head and answered yes. Detective Brown stuck his hand out and just like that, I shook hands with an officer of the law.

Detective Brown had a newfound respect for Me and at that point I took our handshake as a pass meaning the harassment was over. We both walked back over to the car where everybody was looking at us in confusion, even Detective Gordon. Detective Brown stepped to the back window waiving and telling Lil' Dez he would see him later and to be good. Then he told his partner to come on back to their car when they pulled off giving me a head nod. Big Tee and I pulled into the drive-thru in silence for a few minutes when all I could say was, "What a small ass fuckin' world."

Chapter Nineteen

TODAY I WAS SPENDING HALF OF THE DAY WITH THE BOYS THEN I dropped them off to Honey so I could visit the club to talk to the Crew. We were supposed to discuss future plans since we had so much money and Work now. It was time to step it up as Businessmen and become bigger than any Group of Niggas ever come out of the Detroit streets. We already had the streets on lock so now it was time to clean our dirty money up before it was too late.

I walked into a half empty Club and the only people that was in sight was Rita the bartender, a few dancers and a few Guests. "Yo Rita, where is everybody at? Where are the Dancers? Where is Rizzy and D-Money?" I asked. With a turned-up face she gave me a head nod pointing in the direction towards the Private Boom-Boom Room. The private Boom-Boom Room was for the highest paying Guest to take a female and trick top dollars off for any pleasure she allowed him to perform, as long as we got our cut we want complaining. Before MSN became Owners of this Club, we were known for tricking heavy with and fucking all of the Strippers in the V.I.P room.

. . .

I stepped in the boom-boom room and it was Déjà vu all over again, I done seen this so many times. Rizzy and D-Money were in this Bitch acting bad and both of them were holding bands of money in their hands. A total of Six Dancers were inside and over to the left two of them were pleasing each other with the freakiest tongue kisses while both fingering each other's Pussies to get the other wet. Straight ahead was one of the Dancers laying flat on her back getting her pussy licked and sucked on by another Dancer. They were in this Boom-Boom Room straight clowning, one of them were pouring 1800 Tequila from a gallon bottle all over another Dancer's body just so she could lick it all off and get drunk at the same time. To the right were two more Dancers that Rizzy and D-Money were blowing through and going to work on them. D-Money was butt ass naked hitting one of the Dancers from the back, the Dancer that was getting hit from the back was licking and spitting on the other Dancer's Pussy while that Dancer was getting her mouth fucked by D-Money. There was a full Orgy going on and even though I came to talk business I was still a Man at the end of the day that could in no way refuse joining the festivities. "Don't just stand there Nigga, you better get in where you fit in," D-Money said before drinking from his own bottle of Greygoose in a smooth and calm tone.

Not needing to be told twice, I walked over to where the two Dancers that was In the middle that was eating and getting their pussy licked and dropped my pants. After seeing all of this sexy ass fucking going on, I had no problem getting hard. "Damn Boss man Jay, I didn't know you were packing like this," One of the Dancers told me referring to my huge long Dick. She stopped eating on the Pussy and came straight over to the Dick and began sucking on it. She began gagging and choking on the Dick that she thought she could handle and with my hands palming the back of her head she knew that she had to take her time, or she would've puked all over me. now the Dancer who was no longer getting her Pussy ate sat up and joined in on the sucking of my Dick. With one sucking on my brick hard shaft and the other sucking on my balls I couldn't have picked a better time than to be here.

The Boom-Boom Room was popping and after they sucked my

Dick dry, I laid on the couch on my back with Dick standing tall. One of the Dancers came from the other side of the room and jumped right on the dick quickly regretting that she didn't take her time. She turned around so she could ride it from the back, and it could be easier for her. The sight of her pretty and fat ass was certainly something to see, she then started riding the dick smoothly and taking it all.In making me feel good and comfortable. I sat back loving her smooth riding style when I noticed that she was one of the new girls that I never hit before. Now that her Pussy was taking all of the Dick, she sped up her pace and was riding hard and fast making me feel like she was going to snatch my entire dick off. Every time she rode it fast frontwards it hurt but felt good at the same time. D-Money turned around and seen how much I had it popping and decided to leave the two females he was with to join the dancers that were beside me.

D-Money than came over and stood in front of the Dancer who was riding me from the back and stuffed his dick in her mouth, palming her by the head. A few minutes after she rode the dick hard it was time for me to switch things up and my turn to fuck the shit out of one of these Dancers.

Over in the corner was a bad ass little pretty Red-Bone petite Dancer who was only getting her pussy ate and I wanted her. I had never seen her before either, so I knew I was going to enjoy this new Pussy she had. I lifted her up from the head she was receiving from another Dancer and turned her around stuffing dick inside her from the back. I began pounding on her soaking wet pussy and how tight her shit was I knew I wouldn't last long. She moaned and yelled for more Dick while at the same time throwing that plump ass back at me. This little Dancer Bitch was a soldier because she wasn't running or giving up but actually giving me a run for my money. She was fucking the hell out of me and was talking shit at the same time. "Fuck me Boss! Fuck this Pussy like you pay this Pussy!" She yelled. Her demands turned me the fuck on and made me go harder. Her sexy moans and screams gained everybody attention in the room, some even stopped just to watch. Knowing that we had an audience now, I reached up to her hair and wrapped it around my hand into my closed fist. I began yanking back on her hair making her neck cock back, moans got louder and she begged for more and more good dick. Her pussy was so good that I couldn't go any longer, I could only take so much of the good Pussy she had. "Damn Baby, I'm 'bout to Cum!" I moaned. D-Money, Rizzy and the rest of the Dancers were entertained and cheered for me to continue, "Nigga you bet not quit! Nigga you bet not!" They yelled. "Oooooh, I'm Cumming too Boss Daddy!" She looked back at me and moaned.

"Keep going! Keep going!" The Dancers chanted and cheered for the new Girl. For a minute I felt like I was on a basketball team being cheered on by the fans and cheerleaders. They wanted me to score the game winner and I only had a few seconds left before the buzzer beater. I continued pounding on her Pussy, she kept throwing it back, I continued pounding on the Pussy, she kept throwing it back, "Go! Go! Go!" They all cheered. "I'm 'bout to Bust!" I yelled. "I'm Cumming too!" She yelled back. I looked down admiring the nice ass she had and every time I went in back and forth, my dick was covered in her creamy Cum which sealed the deal. "I'm Cumming!" She screamed again. The Dancer quickly jumped up and turned around taking my Dick ejaculating every drop of my nut inside of her mouth and swallowed every bit of it.

It was so nasty but so sexy at the same time, she made my Brothers start clapping from her performance and her fellow Dance friends cheered her on by tapping on her back telling her she did her thing with the dick.

We all grabbed our things and like after any type of game, we all gave each other plays, we slapped the Dancers on the ass and told them good shit. As we headed out of the Boom-Boom Room I was so impressed by the Girls Work who I just fucked I had to stop her and ask her what her name was. "My name is Ciara," she answered with a smile. All the Dancers hit the showers and MSN went into the conference room.

Rizzy went and flopped on the couch, D-Money went to the mini-bar to pour us some drinks and I flopped in the chair behind the office desk. Everybody was still trying to catch their breath from the big Orgy we just experienced, and I was totally exhausted. It's been a long time since I played part in the sexual activities such as these. D-Money came back handing everybody a glass of hard liquor then it was time to talk business.

Just when we were about to begin, there was a knock on the door. "Come in!" I yelled. One of the Dancers that was just with us in our Orgy stepped in, "Sorry to interrupt guys but D-Money, that tape you asked for is..." she was saying before he quickly cut her off. "Okay, okay, okay just give it to Rita and I'll grab it from Her. Thank you." D-Money said dismissing her from the office. D-Money's whole-body language was different and after knowing him damn near all my life I knew something was up. When the Dancer left the office, I looked at D-Money, "What was that about," I asked him. D-Money just waved me off, "Oh ain't nothing important, now what were you about to say?" D-Money asked while drinking from his glass.

"Umm look, I was talking to my Realtor and asking him about properties around the city and some in the suburban areas so we could start a lil' Mainstrip franchise of Titty bars. With Rizzy having a big out of Town Lane and D-Money fucking with his Cali plug, then with all the shit I got going on in the Chi and NY, I think it's time for us to clean up as much money as we could and what's a better way than to start us a Strip Club Franchise. What do y'all think, y'all ready to put a Mainstrip all around Michigan or what?"

I asked them with a grin on my face. Rizzy and D-Money looked at each other then back at me and without hesitation they both answered, "Hell yea!" I knew that they were going to jump at the opportunity as well they should, it was a good business transition that we needed to do, "Well there it is then, imma' talk to my Realtor again and get the locations of the places available and get y'all the paperwork. One time for the Mainstrip," I said raising my glass in the air for a toast. Both of them did the same thing and toasted to the Mainstrip.

Another knock at the door followed our Group toast when I yelled for them to come in, "Hey Baby! Hey y'all, what y'all doing?" Honey asked as she entered the conference office. She walked over to me leaning in giving me a kiss, I was Totally surprised by her pop-up visit and was damn near speechless. My heart was racing at the thought of the idea of her getting here twenty minutes ago. What were the odds that she pops up right after we just were in the Boom-Boom Room acting a nut? Both of the guys spoke to her but was just as surprised as I was. I hit the button on the computer that enabled the surveillance system that I should have seen her enter the building on. I sat there praying that I didn't smell like one of them freaky ass Dancers. "Hey Baby, what's up? What you doing here?" I asked. She told me that her mother asked her to pick something up for her so while she was heading back over there to drop it off and pick up the boys, she decided to come visit me. "Why y'all look so tired and it looked like y'all are celebrating something, did I inter-rupt?" Honey asked. "It's just been a long night. Um, we are toasting to the Mainstrip franchise that we are about to begin soon. We will be looking at locations so that we could start expanding," I told her.

She looked around at all of us when a smile crossed her face, "Well let's celebrate then! Congratulations Guys! Bottles on Me!" Honey cheered us on before turning around heading towards the door. We all gave each other a look like we couldn't believe she was here but happy she didn't come while we were in the Boom-Boom

Room. We all followed Honey to the bar where she asked Rita to give all of us a bottle of Rosé on Her. "Honey is that you?" a voice yelled from across the club. We all turned around and the bubble guts instantly attacked my stomach when I seen who was speaking to my Girl. "Ciara? Girl what are you doing here," Honey asked with her hands on her hips. Ciara made her way over to us with a towel in her hand from drying herself off after a shower, Rizzy and D-Money both had the same confused look on their face that I had. I'm sure we all were wondering how did they know each other and this Ciara girl was new to the Club. "I just started working here a couple of weeks ago, what are you doing here," Ciara returned the question. Honey proudly looked back at me and then back to her, "Oh, I'm just here visiting my Man Jay,one of the three Owners. How old are you now lil Cuz' the last time I seen you was at your high school graduation?" Honey asked. Ciara in a sassy way struck a little pose and smiled, "Girl I'm 19 years old now, I'm grown!" she answered. Honey looked back at me, "Baby did you know that this was my lil' Cousin right here?" She asked me. I shook my head no and told her that she knows I'm too busy to pay attention to the girls that's hired at the club. I looked at Rizzy and D-Money who both had looks on their faces like all they needed was some popcorn and they were good. "Here's y'all bottles, Honey girl." Rita said bringing the bottles over. I was the first to grab my bottle because I badly needed a drink. "So y'all are actual cousins or just call each other that?" D-Money asked. "Actual cousins." They both answered at the same time. Both Rizzy and D-Money reached over the bar grabbing their bottles and taking their drinks to the head as well.

"Well Ms. Grown Lady, we are celebrating my Man and his Brother's New business investments, wanna join us?" Honey nice ass invited her Cousin. Looking at me first then back to her cousin Honey, "Nawl not today big Cuz', I just got out the shower and have to get ready for my shift tonight. It was good seeing you though, maybe we could go shopping some time or something," Ciara told her. "Yeah Girl, call me." Honey replied as we watched Ciara walk away. Honey turned around, "Wow that's crazy, my lil' Cousin is all grown up now. Which one of y'all hired Her?" Honey asked Rizzy and D-Money. D-Money slowly raised his hand telling her that he had no idea, or he wouldn't have done it. Honey gave him a look, "I tell y'all what, I don't want none of y'all touching her or having her in that damn Boom-Boom Room. I know she's a lil' Freak but that's my Family so don't touch her. Especially you!" Honey told all of Us. Both Rizzy and D-Money agreed to Honey's terms and said they won't touch her. I was just glad that Ciara played her role and didn't say or do anything stupid. I couldn't believe I just fucked the shit out of my Girl's little Cousin. For Ciara to be so young I was a little surprised just how smooth she actually was. It was like maybe she knew that Honey was my girl.

Chapter Twenty
Stressing

(Few nights later)

IT WAS A REGULAR SATURDAY NIGHT WHICH WAS ONE OF THE Mainstrip's busiest nights and the club was doing numbers as usual. I went straight into my office so I could take care of a lot of Paperwork regarding the new properties that MSN was trying to Purchase. While sitting at my desk I sipped on my favorite drink Remy Martin VSOP when I received a text message from Alicia. She told me that she decided to name our unborn son Jay Hill Jr. I couldn't help but to smile knowing that in only a few months I would be having my very first Son. As fast as my smile appeared it quickly disappeared when I realized there was no way I could raise a Son and Honey not know. Honey was my heart but I just couldn't take being the one to hurt Her. It would break her heart to know that I had a Son by somebody else. I had to also pat Myself on the back at how well I was hiding it from her. I put Alicia in a crib far from everything and anytime I wasn't at home with Honey and the boys I was with Alicia. I sat there in my thoughts wondering how I would continue to keep the secret of another child when my thoughts were interrupted by a knock at my door. I looked at the camera outside my door and saw that it was Honey's Cousin Ciara, clueless to what it is that she wanted I buzzed her in.

Ciara walked in my office shutting the door behind Her and turning to face me. As she stood there in her dance gear, I couldn't even lie to Myself, she may have been the sexiest Dancer we had working at the Mainstrip. She had nice pretty titties, a small waist, nice plump ass and the tattoos she had made her red-boned skin look even more sexy. Seeing her standing in front of me I couldn't help but to reminisce about the sex session we recently had, it even made my dick grow at the thoughts. "What's up Jay, or should I keep calling you Boss?" She asked with a smile on her face. "Jay is fine, so you're my girls Lil' Cousin huh? I'm guessing that you already knew I was her Man, am I right?" I asked trying to stay focused on her face and not her amazing features.

Ciara had a devilish grin spread across her face, "I can't even lie, yeah I already knew but that doesn't mean that we have to stop doing us. I'm a Big Girl that can keep a secret," she told me as she slowly made her way over to my desk. I wasn't even shocked by her answer but at the same time she was right, what was done couldn't be changed. As bad as I wanted to accept her offer to continue our fucking, I just couldn't now knowing what I knew. Even though I was fucking her and many other women I just couldn't continue fucking the Cousin of my girl. I was a Dog because I was cheating period but knowingly fucking her Cousin was dead wrong. I smiled, "As good as the Pussy was, I'm going to have to respectfully decline your offer for us to continue. I enjoyed Myself surely but you're my Girl's Cousin and I can't do it," I told her. By the look on Ciara's face it was like what I just said went through one ear and out the other. She still had a sneaky grin on her face and began walking her sexy ass around my desk until she was directly standing over me.

. . .

It was clear that this Chick Ciara was trouble but the temptation she put on me wouldn't allow me to refuse her. As bad as I wanted to tell her to step back away from me, I just couldn't. Ciara dropped down to her knees and began unzipping my pants. She pulled the pistol from my side and placed it on the desk, then she reached inside my boxers pulling out my mid erected dick. She seductively licked around the tip of it. "You really wanna' give all of this up Jay?" Ciara whispered looking me into my eyes at the same time. I struggled trying to get my shit together but She started massaging my balls with one hand and was sucking on my Shaft with the other hand. For Ciara to be so young she had mad skills on how to arouse the man she dealt with.

I sat back putting my hands behind my head, "Suck this Dick then Girl," I coached. Ciara started pulling all her tricks out of her bag and went to work on the Dick. She spit, slurped and sucked on the dick like she was a professional and I surely appreciated how well of an effort she performed. She even moaned while sucking on it like it aroused her and that was a big turn on. Her Head was amazing but now she turned me the fuck on and I had to handle her accordingly. I snatched Her up to Her feet and turned her around over my desk like a Savage. I stuffed my brick hard Dick into her from the back and began pounding her soaking wet gushy Pussy. Her Pussy was so wet that I felt her juices running down my dick while I was fucking Her. "Fuck me Boss Daddy!" Ciara yelled. I quickly reached over to put my hand over her mouth so she couldn't be heard while I continued ramming this hard dick inside of her. Just like the last time she began throwing that ass back and now we were fucking to the same rhythm . I looked down loving the view of the wave motion in her ass while I fucked her.

Ciara's pussy was so good that I couldn't control Myself from Cumming so fast, "I'm 'bout to Bust!" I moaned. "Me too Daddy! Me too!" She said back to me. I was so much of a Dog that I could really care less if she got her nut off but I couldn't allow my good dick name to go bad so I continued fucking her lights out. A few seconds later I was no longer able to prevent Myself from Cumming when I yelled that I was about to bust. Without thinking I bust all inside of her juicy Pussy and she came shortly after that.

I pulled my pants up and put my pistol back on my hip, "It's almost time for my performance. I'll get with you later or something," she said as she headed out the office door. I flopped back in my chair putting my hands over my face wondering why it was so hard for me to turn her Pussy down. Was I in love with her Pussy already? With all of the things I was already going through I most definitely didn't need anything else on my plate. I couldn't believe I just couldn't shake Honey's little Cousin.....

Chapter Twenty-One
Business Trip

MSN HAD JUST FINISHED SIGNING OFF ON ONE OF THE PROPERTIES that would be our second location of the Mainstrip, and we were excited. All of the Contractors and Decorators predicted that we should be open for business in the next 6-8 months. In celebration for our new Mainstrip location we all decided to go out and sit at a nice restaurant to discuss further business ventures. It was surely a blessing how well all of our businesses were doing both legal and illegally, we were so busy that we had to hire all Ourselves more help so that we rarely had to even touch the work. The only thing we were trying to touch was the money that we were picking up and the money we were dropping off to the Plugs.

The Waitress bought everybody's order to the table and we began eating, "So tonight I have to shoot out to Ohio for a drop-off and pick-up to keep things running smooth, so who is going to drop that half a mill off to D-Money's Cali Plug since he gotta pick up the package that's already on its way." Rizzy asked. Both D-Money and I looked at each other when I pointed at him. Everybody started laughing how I threw him under the bus. "I can't do it this time, y'all know I'm the only one them niggas gon' let pick up the incoming package. Jay you gotta do it," D-Money said. "Man, that's yo' Boo ain't it?" I asked, being funny. D-Money hated when we accused him of having a woman. Ever since we were little, he made a vow not to ever have a girl and all the way up until now he lived by it. We just all knew that Carmen was the girl he liked, and he often talked about her like she was his.

Rizzy and I teased him like we were kids for liking a Girl and even though he hated it, he sat there blushing knowing it was true. "I told y'all she's not my Girl! I do like her and we went out a few times, but she told me not to rush anything. Really, she's spinning me, but I'm gone to get her one day," D-Money told us. "Nawl but all jokes aside, Jay you gotta go this time. It doesn't take long at all, just go out there and drop that cash off to Her, maybe go out and see what the Cali life's about and come right back. it shouldn't take long at all." D-Money said making it sound easy. "There it is then, Jay gon go and handle the Cali business and we gon take care of the rest," Rizzy said. As bad as I didn't feel like flying out to California this was for MSN, so I had to do it.

On my way home to pack up I knew that Honey wasn't going to like that I had to leave on short notice. I also had to call Alicia and tell her that I was going to be gone for a few days. She had a doctor's appointment coming soon too but one thing about Alicia was she never really tripped. She knew what this hustle life was about and the fact that I kept her in some of the finest jewelry she was quick to understand. Alicia just told me to be safe and to call her when I made it there. I already knew with Honey it would be completely different.

I walked into the house and as usual the boys were glued to the television when I walked past them palming their heads making them bump into each other. They both just laughed, I asked them where Honey was at and they told me that she was in the basement washing clothes. I went to the hallway closet and pulled out two of my Louis Vuitton travel suitcases so I could begin packing.

Ten minutes into packing Honey walked into the bedroom with a basket full of clothes, "Hey Bay, oh… where you think you're going?" She asked me already turning her face up. Honey wasn't like Alicia by far, even though she knew how this hustle life was, she still wasn't for some of the stuff that she knew came along with it. "Umm, I have to go out of town for a couple of days and handle this business. It shouldn't take long though," I explained to her while continuing to pack clothes into my suitcase. She looked at the time and saw that it was late in the day, "So you're telling Me that at 8pm you have to take a trip? Where are we going then," she asked in a plural sense. I chuckled, "I have to go to Cali to handle this business and then soon as I'm done, I'm coming right back. you can't come with me with for this type of business I'm doing Baby but next time I promise I'll bring you with me." I told her. She gave me a crazy look, "California?! So, you're going to fuckin' Cali and you don't wanna take me after I been telling you that I wanted to go to Cali? What type of shit is that? why can't Darien or Jeff go? She asked. I told her that they couldn't go because they were all handling other business and the questions started coming back to back to back to back. she even went as far as telling me that I didn't love her because I wouldn't take her with me and everything. Over time I learned that whenever she got like this that I should just ignore her and remain silent. I continued packing and before heading out of the bedroom I tried kissing her on the cheek, but she quickly dodged me not wanting me to kiss her.

I walked to the front door with my luggage and there wasn't any way I would leave without talking to the boys. I called both boys over and they walked up to me with their pajamas on asking me where I was going and if they could come with me. I told them not this time but promised them that before school started back that I would take them to Disney World. I kneeled down on one knee, "Now if y'all want Me to take y'all to Disney World y'all have to do me a favor. I need y'all to be good and watch over ya' Mama. Make sure she's not bad and if she is y'all call me. I also want y'all to be good while I'm gone and I might bring y'all something back," I told them. Lil' K stepped closer to me, "Okay but since we gotta wait till school is almost back to go to Disney World, can you at least buy us something from where you're going," he asked. I laughed at his negotiating ways. I reached in my pockets and peeled off two hundred-dollar bills handing one to each of them, "How is this, is this good enough for you cuz I don't think imma be able to go shopping because Imma be busy," I told them. They both smiled and jumped for joy running back to Honey asking her to take them to the mall tomorrow.

Honey had a fake smile on her face like she was happy for the boys and told them She would take them if they are good. The boys ran back to the video game when I stood up and walked over towards Honey with an attitude. I reached back in my pocket handing her a band of money that was ten thousand inside it, "Is this enough to last you until I get back," I asked trying to buy her smile. she took and looked at the band of money like it wasn't enough, I shook my head and reached down in my pocket pulling out another band of ten thousand and handed it to her and a fake smile came across her face. I just chuckled as I leaned in placing a kiss on her cheek before heading out the front door. I turned back around, "I love y'all, call when I get to a hotel," I told them. They all told me they loved me back and I was out the door, To California I go....

Chapter Twenty-Two
Carmen

(4 hours later)

I WALKED OUTSIDE OF THE OAKLAND AIRPORT WHERE D-MONEY told me that his Plug Carmen who was a red-head Puerto Rican Woman would be waiting on me. I knew of Carmen but I never really actually met Her. Rizzy been out here a few times before when D-Money couldn't make it but I never been out to California. D-Money had given me her number before I left Michigan so we could communicate and I texted her telling her that my flight was scheduled to land at 12:30Am. She agreed to be here to pick me up but I didn't see anybody fitting the description.

As I stood there looking stupid, I was calling D-Money to curse him out for having me on a bullshit mission.Then I seen two all black Range Rovers pull up in front of me and behind them was an all red Ashton Martin that was followed by two more Range Rovers. I put my phone back in my pocket when one of the windows in the Range Rover rolled down asking me if I was Jay. When I told him yes he hopped out of the truck big as hell and wearing all black with a bodyguard type look to him. He took my bags putting them in his truck and told me to go hop in the Ashton Martin. I walked over to the car and inside was one of the sexiest women I ever seen. She looked so much like a runway model that I couldn't believe that she was the famous Carmen that was supplying us the best Product on the East coast. "MSN Jay from Detroit?" she asked. I nodded my head answering yes, "Well get in baby and let's get outta here!" she told me, swinging her long red hair behind her.

I hopped in the Ashton Martin and she put her pedal to the metal switching four lanes onto the freeway while being followed by her security in Range Rovers. "So what's up Jay from Detroit, nice to finally meet you," she said watching the road and looking over to smile in my face. The way how D-Money described her was an understatement, she was more beautiful than he told us. She sat in the driver's seat wearing a long white sundress that had her cleavage trying to burst out and reveal just how pretty her titties were. I looked down to her feet and they were freshly manicured and done like her hands were. I knew and loved a woman that would go and get her manicures and pedicures. "What up doe Ms. Carmen, its nice to finally meet you as well. I heard a lot of great things about you and I speak for the entire MSN when I tell you that we appreciate your business." I told her to try to remain professional. She looked over at me, "Wow, what a professional and handsome young Man you are. I appreciate MSN's business too but do you want to know something? It's not about the money that You and your Team spends. That's just money, I have a lot of money…It's the Character of my Customers that makes me even trust in doing business with you, understand?" Carmen said to me with that sexy ass accent. I knew I was here on business but I still couldn't believe how beautiful Carmen was.

Carmen looked over and caught me looking at her when she smiled asking what was it I was thinking about, "Huh, oh nothing, I'm just tripping at how all the times D-Money been out here, Rizzy been out here and none of them told me you were this Attractive! I mean, no disrespect intended but you are stunning!" I complimented Her. She laughed and blushed at the same time. "Well thank you, thank you. You're very handsome yourself, why are they just now sending you, you should've been coming to visit me!" Carmen returned a complimented back. "Usually I would take my out of town Guest to the best hotels available but in this particular case I'm taking you to my Mansion and that way instead of coming to pick you up in the morning we could discuss business over breakfast. I have an amazing Kitchen Staff, just wait and I will show you. Is that fine with you Mr. Jay?" Carmen asked me. I nodded my head, "Totally fine with me. breakfast huh? I haven't had breakfast in years," I replied. She just chuckled and turned up the music as we flew down the highway disregarding the speed limit.

After an hour and a half drive we finally pulled up in the front of a gated Mansion on top of a Hill. This Mansion was so big that I started to believe that she was really a real Queen. She even had a security booth that sat outside of the gates that checked over every car before entering. When we made it past the security booth and gates I asked her why was her security going around the cars with the dogs and this was her place, she told me they were checking to make sure no detachable type bombs or Fed wires got attached to the cars that enter the property. We headed down her very long street that led us to her front door where I seen security patrolling the perimeter with dogs and the same protective gear the SWAT teams wear. At that moment I knew Carmen was bigger than anybody we were dealt with, she was damn near Royalty.

When we finally pulled up in her drive-way I swore a party must have been going on by all the different foreign cars parked outside. Bentley Coupes, Maybachs, Rolls Royces, Ferrari and a Lamborghini. I was amazed by all of the different foreign cars, "Damn, it looks like your having a party here by all of these foreigns," I told her. She laughed, "Party? No Honey, these are all mine," Carmen responded. I chuckled, "God damn, I ain't doing shit in the D then!" I said. She looked at me, "Keep fuckin' with Me and you will have this shit too. Its all who you know is how you get rich." she said before stepping out of the car.

We both walked up the stairway into her Mansion when I seen even all of her security inside were heavily equipped and wore earpieces in their ear like they were Secret Service or something. Inside the Mansion looked like a fairy tale movie and even had the big chandelier hanging from what had to been a sixty foot ceiling. There were Maids and Butlers walking all around the place, "Rudy!?" Carmen yelled somebody's name. A short Mexican cute little Butler approached us with a smile on her face, "How can I help you Madam," she asked. Carmen looked back at Me with a smile on her face, "This is Jay from Detroit and he's going to be our House Guest for the next couple of days, see to it that he gets the nicest Guest room with the view of the inside swimming pool. Help him with anything he may need or want," Carmen turned back looking at her butler. "And you, Jay. You make sure you don't stay up too late, we have a busy day ahead of us tomorrow and I want your fine Self to be ready for business. I also want to show you around my City so get you some rest." Carmen told me. She then gave me this look only females that wanted the Dick would give me but maybe I was misreading her. Carmen was indeed a Bad Bitch and a Boss at the same time but how D-Money talked about her I figured she was off limits.

I gave Carmen a head nod with a short grin when I thanked her for her hospitality, "Good night Jay, I'm just going to take me a quick night swim before I go to bed." She told me before she walked away leaving me with Rudy the Butler. Rudy and I began heading to wherever she was taking Me and I couldn't help but to be amazed at how nice Carmen's Mansion was. This type of Mansion meant you made it and were officially a success at whatever you were doing. We finally made it to the Guest Room that had to take at least ten minutes to get to when Rudy led me in, "Good night Mr. Jay. If you need anything just push the button beside your bed and I will be here for your assistance," Rudy told me. I told her thank you and closed the door behind her. This Guest Room was big as a hotel Suite in Detroit and even had a bathrobe and towels just like a hotel.

I couldn't believe it. I remember when D-Money was telling Rizzy and I Carmen's story and it was the average everyday Hood story. She was the bad bitch she was today and met a Puerto Rican Nigga named Chico who just so happened to be part Of a Cartel and was the Plug supplying everybody in L.A. They were deeply in love until one day Chico was killed and left everything he had to his love Carmen. Carmen not only accepted everything he left her but she took over his Cartel business and kept his business very successful. Of course there were rumors that She had him killed so she could run things but no one actually knew the truth.She never looked back to the broke life since.

I flopped on the king sized bed picking up the huge remote that sat on the desk beside it. Like a little kid it was killing me to know just what every button on it did. I hit one specific button and the shades that I thought covered the window opened up and it was a view from the inside swimming pool. Just when I thought I seen it all I was amazed again. The swimming pool was one like I never seen before in my life, its baby blue water looked pure and clean. Seeing this beautiful sight of nice water reminded me that I didn't call Honey when I got off the plane. I knew she was probably going crazy. There was a three hour time difference between Detroit and California so it was 3am where she was. I still pulled out my phone and decided to call her to prevent any future arguments. She answered on the second ring, "Hello, whats up Baby." I spoke to her wondering if she was still mad at me. "Hey, so you made it safe huh?" she asked me with the sleepy voice. "Yes I'm here safe. Are you still mad at me?" I asked. "No, I was just tripping earlier, I'm sorry for that. I should be more understanding but.." Honey was saying but when I seen Carmen enter the indoor swimming pool area I was automatically tuned out on what it was she was saying.

"I just been stressing out lately, between worrying about You and keeping up with these boys, I be having a lot on my plate. Plus I be hearing how all them hoes be out there trying to fuck with you so that's why I be on you like that." Honey was explaining. I was hearing only half of what she was saying because I couldn't get my focus off of Carmen sexy ass. Carmen waved at me with a smile while I held the phone to my ear, of course I waved back. How could I not? Carmen was one of the most sexiest Women I ever seen, if D-Money didn't have feelings for this woman I swear I would've shot my shot at her but for my Mans, I restrained Myself. "Yes, I know Baby but I just need you to trust me and I know that I don't want nobody but you and whenever you need help with something just let me know. Imma always be here…" I was saying but couldn't even finish what I was saying because I was distracted by Carmen dropping her robe and standing there totally naked.

My mouth dropped at the beautiful sight of her naked body. Carmen stood there with a flawless body, her ass was sticking out, thighs thick as hell, nice big titties with the big areola and she was covered In diamonds. Instantly my Dick started to get hard just from looking at her. "Baby? Baby what were you saying?" Honey snapped me out of the zone I was in. Carmen looked directly at me and had a grin on her face, she knew I was liking what I was seeing and she knew exactly what she was doing. She then dived in the pool and began swimming, "And… and… I love you Honey, for real," I was saying and struggled putting my wording together.

Honey could tell I was distracted by something, "I love you too. Umm, what hotel are you at?" she asked me. I was quick to tell her I was at the Marriott Courtyard, I couldn't tell her I was staying at the sexy ass Plugs Mansion. I did a fake yarn, "Umm, Baby imma lil' tired from the flight so imma just call you tomorrow okay?". She said okay and we both told each other that we loved one another before hanging up the phone. I put my phone down and sat back relaxing, watching Carmen swim in the pool all night.

Chapter Twenty-Three
Business or Pleasure?

(Next morning)

THE SOFT KNOCK ON THE DOOR HAD WAKING ME WHEN I HEARD
Rudy telling Me that it was breakfast time with Carmen. I looked at
the time and it was already 11am. I got Myself up and the first thing
I was thinking about was how good Carmen looked swimming in
her pool naked last night. I headed to the Guest bathroom getting
myself all washed up and dressed for the day I had ahead of me. I
got dressed only how a Detroit Nigga would, I threw on Polo from
head to toe, my Cartier frames that was flooded in diamonds, with
my Cartier earrings and Rolex watch. Even though I was in California I still had to put on for my city. I walked through the mansion
and admired her taste in designing. She had paintings up by artist
that I couldn't even pronounce, her floor was a clear marble type
that was so clear that I could damn near see my reflection through
it. Carmen had her own Spa, inside gym that was connected to a
tennis court and a work out room. This mansion was fit for a boss
such as Carmen, it was also fit for a boss such as Myself.

I finally found the Dining room where Carmen was already

sitting at the head of the table that was covered in so much food it looked like a catering service prepared for a big party. On each side of the tables were ten chairs each, this looked like the same table from Godfather when all the five families met up at. "Good morning Handsome, glad you decided to join me. Did you have a good sleep?" Carmen asked me signaling for me to have a seat beside her. "Whats up Carmen, yes I had a great sleep, thank you. Wow this looks great, is this only for Us? All of this food?" I asked. She grinned, "Yes, this is for only Us. Rudy, will you fix Jay here a nice sized plate?" Carmen answered me and ordered her Butler Rudy. When Rudy fixed me a plate and placed it in front of me I no longer questioned why Carmen was so thick, she was eating the finest food every time she ate.

Carmen and I were eating when from time to time we both would catch each other staring at the other. "So Carmen, when exactly would you be wanting to handle the business part of this trip?" I asked her as I wiped my mouth with a napkin. She grinned, "A Man about his Business, I like that. Tell me are you in a rush to handle business or are you in a rush to handle business and get back home to Something or Someone?" Carmen asked. "Well I wouldn't say that I am exactly in a rush to leave this place, this is a very nice place that I wouldn't mind spending my time at, especially with you. Ya know? That's all, I just like to handle business first and anything after that is whatever we make it." I answered being the smooth Nigga that I was. Carmen nodded her head, "I totally understand, Rudy! Give Jay the numbers for me." She told her Butler. Rudy bought a serving plate in front of me with a card on it, "You could send the money to that account and the new package will be on Its way to Detroit." Carmen told me. I pulled out my phone and needed to transfer the money to the account number she had giving me. "$500,000 all done." I said sliding her card back over to her. Carmen called Rudy back over to the table and this time she came over with a laptop on top of the serving plate. "Bontago mi-su Cantago sierna pumacos." Carmen spoke Puerto Rican to Rudy. Rudy grabbed the laptop and began typing numbers. I already knew that she was having Rudy confirm the money was in her account.

"Si, si senorita." Rudy told Carmen. I didn't know any other languages, but I did know that Rudy told her the numbers were accurate. Carmen smiled, "Now we could go and enjoy Ourselves. I own a nightclub off on Rodeo Drive, would you like to accompany Me?" Carmen asked. I smiled back at her, "Carmen I would love to go anywhere you Asked me to go as long as I'm with you." I answered flirtatiously looking her in her eyes. We both sat there looking into each other's face, there wasn't no secret that there was an attraction between the two of Us. I could tell that she was attracted to me and I was also attracted to her as well. This was going to be a visit to California for the both of us to remember.

We finished our breakfast when Carmen decided to take me on a little tour around LA and she insisted we did a little shopping as well. Being that I never been to California before I was all for a tour and a shopping spree. We tore the Hollywood Boulevard up and had Ourselves a blast on Rodeo Drive visiting on the high-end Stores. California was fucking over Somerset Mall for sure. We hit everywhere From the Cartier store, to the Gucci, Louis Vuitton and the best jewelry stores L.A. had to offer. Carmen's money was so long that no matter how hard I tried, she would not allow me to spend my own money anywhere. When we visited the Cartier store my tab alone came up to 65,000 so I could imagine how much Hers came up too. We were doing so much shopping that we had to take multiple trips back-and-forth to her car and her security detail car just to drop off bags. I was getting things that I knew Detroit Niggas never seen before and since Carmen wouldn't allow me to spend any of my money, I made sure I got nothing but the best. Shopping was nothing for Carmen because even though she was rich, she still never had to spend her own money being that she was who she was. Every store we went inside insisted that she get whatever she wanted so everything that I was getting didn't cost her a thing. I even picked up some jewelry for Honey and Alicia.

. . .

With all of the heavy shopping we had done, both of Us had worked up an appetite and we're hungry. She insisted she took me to one of her favorite places and have lunch so that's where we went. It was a high-class restaurant that she told me Robert DeNiro owns and a lot of celebrities always visited. When we walked in there was a nice mellow vibe with the smooth, calming music playing, "Carmen how are you sweetie it's so good to see you again." The Waiter who was no question gay spoke while approaching us. When Carmen saw him she looked at him like they'd been friends for years as they kissed each other on both cheeks how they do in Paris. "Oh I'm doing great Reginald, just spending money as usual. You know how that goes. Umm, I need my same private table I always get, this time for two." Carmen told the Gay waiter. Reginald smacked his lips taking a good look at me from head to toe, "Ohh okay, darling. Table for two coming right up. He's cute." Reginald told Carmen in a whisper before leading us to the table.

    The gay waiter took us to the back of the restaurant that was secluded from everyone else, Carmen liked to stay behind the scenes like I did. "Okay Darling and Handsome friend, can I get y'all anything to drink to begin with?" Reginald asked. Carmen looked at me while answering him, "Umm, just bring us a couple of shots of Patron to start off with. Thank you Honey." Carmen told him. Smacking his lips like only a gay person would, "I'll be back in a jiffy." He said before walking away switching his hips from side to side.

    One of my phones vibrated and it was D-Money calling, I told her I had to answer it and asked for her to excuse me. "D-Money, what's up Bro? Oh yeah, everything's good. Yeah, I'm with Carmen right now. Aight, ummm, hold on real quick." I told him and handed Carmen the phone. Before she took the phone she whispered, "Is this Darien?" I nodded my head answering yes. She took the phone and rolled her eyes as if she didn't want to talk to him or something. Seeing that reaction made me wonder just how much they were involved with each other. If they were ever close before she wouldn't act like she didn't want to talk to him.

    "Hi Darien. I'm good you?" She responded to him in the most

driest irritated tone. "I just been busy Darien, that's all. That's why I haven't been returning your calls. Oh, no I don't even have time for one of those. You know what, here's your Friend. Call me when you're done with the Package." Carmen told him and handed me back my phone. Reginald returned back to the table with our drinks, "Can I take you Cute Couples order now?" He asked. We both gave him our orders when I put the phone back to my ear, "Umm, yeah, we're out eating right now. Umm, I guess I'll be back in the next couple of days. Yep, I'll hit you up." I told him before hanging up.

Carmen immediately began taking shots of the Patron with a stressed look across her face, "So what was your Boo D-Money talking about?" I asked, being funny. Her face turned up and she smacked her lips, "That Boy is not my Boo!" She snapped back. "He's not? What do you mean he's not your Boo?" I asked her. "And what would ever make you think that? Is that what he told you?" Carmen asked. I shrugged my shoulders answering yes, "Well he didn't say that exactly, he told me that y'all been out before and he was working on You and that he basically thinks that y'all are Working on something." I answered. She raised her eyebrows like she couldn't believe what I had just told her.

Needing to take another shot before responding, "First off we are not working on anything, yes we've been out before but it was only one time and will only be that one time. Darien is cool and all but I'm just not attracted to him like that. Now maybe I mislead Him by my flirting but that's a part of my job as a Hustling woman. I keep business running good and try to keep the men who spend a lot of money happy, that's it. Plus I did my homework on Darien and He just does too much and I dont have time for it!" Carmen told me followed by another shot. "So... there is no you and D-Money, like that? Hmm." I asked. Carmen chuckled, "No, there is no Darien and I." She confirmed once again. A smile spread across my face like I hit the jackpot, "So now that we know there is no You and D-Money, what about you and any other man?" I asked. Carmen knew where I was going with my questioning when a smile spread across her face also. "Nope, I am single and ready to mingle." She answered.

Reginald finally arrived with our orders and we began to eat and wash our food down with steady shots of Patron. Carmen told him to just bring us a bottle of the Patron so we wouldn't have to keep having him go and get us more shots. With the liquor we were consuming, we were feeling good and taking this time to learn about one another. We sat there laughing and talking about everything that came to our minds. I told her about Honey and the boys, my Son on the way and the Mainstrip Franchise the MSN Crew and Myself were expanding. After hearing all that I was into and so young at the same time, Carmen told me that she was impressed with the man that I was and told me that she thought I was real For handling business the way that I did. I came to find out that Carmen was only three years older than me and she even dropped a bit of knowledge on me telling me how I should handle Honey and Alicia. Carmen was so much of a Boss that I took everything she told me and planned to consider her advice. We continued talking and drinking for hours I could tell that we were certainly feeling each other and to tell the truth, I didn't want this Business trip to ever end…

Chapter Twenty-Four
Bosses Only

(HOURS LATER)

SINCE CARMEN AND I HAD PLANS TO VISIT HER CLUB THAT SHE
owned later tonight, it was only right that we went back to her
Mansion to properly prepare for our Date night out on the town.
Tonight was different from any other night that I went out with a
Woman. Usually I would be Dope Boy fresh just from head to toe
and wearing a lot of jewelry. Tonight I wanted to make a great
impression on Carmen so when she told me to dress real nice like a
Handsome grown man would, I decided to do just that. I wore my
Tom Ford three-piece navy blue suit with my navy blue Ferragamo
penny loafers on my feet. I never got this dressed up for anything,
especially a woman but for this occasion I decided to show out. I
wore light jewelry by wearing only my brand new presidential Rolex
watch that Carmen bought me earlier on today and my brand new
Cartier glasses that had transitional lenses. I was dressed so well I
felt like I should've been accepting some type of award. If my
people in Detroit saw this part of me they would trip out completely.

It was something about being in Carmen's presence that made me just want to step everything about me all the way up.

I stood near the front door waiting on Carmen to come down the stairs and when she did I was speechless. She wore a strapless cranberry skintight dress that stopped a few inches above her knees and complemented every amazing feature her body offered. She wore her red hair pinned up in a bun that revealed the flawless jewels she wore on her neck and ears. Beautiful was an understatement referring to Carmen and how she looked tonight. Hands-down she was more gorgeous than any woman we would see anywhere tonight. It was crazy that this very woman I was looking at was one of California's biggest Drug Suppliers and was actually taking me out with her as a plus one.

Carmen slowly walked down the stairs looking like a certified Model and the smile on her face lit up the entire room. She looked me up and down with a fallen jaw, "Wow! You really, really, really do look handsome I must say. You sure do clean up well Papi." Carmen complimented me. I gave her the same look up and down, "Thank you, but you.. Oh my God! You are surely the most beautiful Woman that I ever had the honor to accompany on a date. "You look amazing, Carmen." I told her as I continued to admire how great she looked. Carmen thanked me and began blushing by the compliments I just gave her. For some reason I got the feeling that it's been a long time since a man told her just how beautiful she was.

We both stepped outside with her Security detail following behind and her Phantom park directly in front of the Mansion. Carmen stopped, "Jay are you packing?" She asked. When I answered yes she just chuckled, "I don't know exactly how things are in Detroit but when you are with me you do not have to carry your pistol. That's what I pay all of these guys for, to protect me and whoever is with Me. Trust that you are safe as long as I am with you." Carmen told me. "Now would you please hand over your pistol to him please and I promise you it would not be far away?" Carmen asked me. I then reached inside of my suit and pulled my pistol from its holster and handed it to her security guard, "Wow, do you know that I never handed over my pistol to trust anybody else before?" I asked her. She smiled, "Well you picked the right person to trust, I got you Papi." Carmen told me before cuffing her arm up under mine as we headed to the backseat of her Phantom to be chauffeured. Dressing up in expensive suits, Not carrying my pistol, bad Bitch on my arm and being chauffeured was all new to me. What was I becoming? Who had I turned into? I wasn't the same Detroit Nigga I was used to being. Funny thing about it, I was liking the new me better...

When we pulled up in front of Carmen's club that was named Chico, I remembered D-Money told me She named it after her deceased boyfriend that left her the business. I thought it was cool that she named it after the Man she loved and never being a hater, I knew that if he was still alive he would be proud of the woman she became. Besides the name, I also noticed that the parking lot was filled with nothing but foreign cars. They all had bodyguards standing beside them. The valet opened the door for Us and greeted Carmen as Boss lady. I took a look around the parking lot and didn't hear any music playing or didn't see any line with people trying to get in. "Must be a slow night since there is no line outside here." I said. Carmen chuckled, "No, I'm pretty sure there is a nice turnout on the inside. This is a Members only club." She told me.

We stepped inside of her club when I saw a live jazz band that was playing smooth and mellow music, I looked around and was very surprised to see just how many people were inside. As we walked through everybody was acknowledging and speaking to Carmen. From what I was seeing, she was loved by everybody inside of the club. Everybody inside was well dressed just as we were which probably meant there was a dress code to enter. This club was nothing like the Mainstrip, I was used to shoulder to shoulder club traffic and the music blasting through the speakers. I didn't even see bottles of liquor being bought or sitting on people's tables. This club was on a totally different level that I soon want to be on.

We continued passing tables and booths that held Mexicans, Puerto Ricans, Asians, Koreans and a couple of white people, I could tell how well they carried themselves and that they all were as rich if not more than Carmen. I was probably the least paid Nigga in the entire place compared to who I was surrounded by but I was for sure I was the Realist. We finally made it to our private Booth and I guess Carmen could tell by the look on my face that I was interested to know the people that were all around us. "I bet you're wondering what kind of club I am running huh?" She asked me. She was right, I was. There wasn't anybody on the dance floor dancing or anybody sitting at the bar ordering more drinks and cursing out the bartender for neglecting them. "Umm, just a lil' bit." I answered with a slight chuckle. A Waitress brought over a bottle of wine to our booth, "Your favorite Boss Lady. Enjoy your night!" the Waitress told her as she poured both of us a glass. Carmen thanked her before she walked away, "Well to answer your question, this club isn't just for anybody. This is a club we're all the wealthy come to unwind and connect with others that are Bosses like Us. Take a look at that table over there. That short Asian man that's sitting with them women, he controls all the heavy fire arms that are transported over from overseas. He is the reason the U.S has all of the fire power needed to start a war." Carmen told me while sipping her wine and raising her mid level giving a toasting gesture towards him. I looked at the short Asian man and laughed, for a man to be so little I thought it was funny that he was the reason the U.S has guns.

Carmen continued pointing out many races of people that were powerful from the gun Boss, Pimps of the world and every type of Drug Boss there was. The more she pointed these people out the more I felt that I needed to be brushing shoulders with these people if I want it to be successful in the street game. After having Ourselves a few drinks and enjoying each other's company, we both were really buzzing and couldn't get enough of the other. "Damn Carmen, that wine you got there is strong because I am feeling it. I never got fucked up off of wine." I told her. She smiled, "Yes, wine is a fine drink. I am telling you Jay, being around me I could introduce you to so much more new things in life other than a bottle of wine that cost $3000." Carmen told me. I lifted my glass and couldn't believe that she just told me that this wine we were drinking cost $3000. I looked around the club then back to her, "Hey, so tell me why there isn't anybody dancing on the dance floor? What's the point of having a band if no one wants to dance?" I asked her. Carmen looked around and sort of shrugged her shoulders, "Wow, I never even noticed that doesn't any one dance in here. I don't know, I guess the people in here just are too cool to dance, to siddity." Carmen responded.

Interrupting the moment, my phone had rang and when I looked at it I didn't hesitate to ignore his call. I was a million miles away from Detroit and there wasn't anything to discuss being that I wasn't around. Plus I wasn't feeling Him anyway from all the times he had ignored my calls when I needed him. I stood to my feet and in front of her sticking my hand out, "Let's change things up tonight, let's dance." I said to her with a smile on my face. Carmen looked around not sure if she should do it, "But...But there isn't anyone else dancing out..." She was saying before I cut her off. "There yet, that is until we get out there, come on, I want to dance with you." I told her as I stared her in the eyes. Seeing just how serious I was she stood up with a smile on her face placing her hand into mine, "You're right, let's do it!" She said as she let me escort her to the dance floor. We walked past all of the Bosses of the U.S straight to the dance floor. I could tell that she was nervous of what people might think but after whispering into her ear telling her how beautiful she was and how proud I was to be with her she became comfortable.

The jazz band continued playing the smooth and mellow tones as I wrapped my hands around her waist and she wrapped her arms around my neck. We were the only two on the dance floor dancing and as we softly paced against the dance floor I could see that all eyes were on Us. For someone who never danced a day in my life, I thought I was doing a fine job. We stayed on the dance floor song after song after song and to both of our surprise, more people came over and decided to dance with their Dates as well. Carmen looked me in the eyes, "You could've never told me that you knew how to dance before me witnessing it right now." She said with a smile on her face. "Yeah I know a little something, something. So are you enjoying yourself with me tonight?" I asked her. She looked at me crazy, "Are you crazy, I'm having the most fun with you than I had in a very long time. We are going to have to get you to be the one to come out here more often." Carmen stated. Knowing that she was enjoying my company as much as I was enjoying being her company made me feel good. I then pulled her closer to me, "Well we just might have to make me the one to come out here, that way we could handle our business and handle each other afterwards." I replied. Our faces were only a few inches apart from each other and I was badly wanting to kiss the woman in front of me. She smells so good, I swore I heard her lips calling my name and at that time I could no longer resist. "Sounds like a plan then." Carmen replied back.

The jazz band turned up the tone of their music which intensified the mood that Carmen and I were in. I leaned in disregarding all of the issues I had back in the city and kissed her soft lips passionately. Our lips locked and the kisses that we were sharing were incredible. I felt a feeling in my body that I never felt before and it was remarkable. The jazz band slowed the music all the way down indicating that it was the end of the song, our lips separated and now we were staring the other in the eyes speechless. I was almost certain that she felt the exact way I felt, "Hey, You ready to get out of here?" I asked still in a daze from the kiss we just shared. She nodded her head answering yes and insisted that we did leave. As we walked past all of the tables that the big Bosses were sitting in and she thanked everyone for stopping by and told them they could call her at any time. Together Carmen and I left her club with my arm around her shoulders claiming my prize. We then hopped in the Phantom and headed back to the mansion.

Chapter Twenty-Five
Have 2 Respect It

DURING THE CAR RIDE HOME OUR BUZZ WAS STARTING TO SETTLE IN and make us a bit drowsy so she laid her head on my shoulder. "Jay?" Carmen called my name. "What's up Baby?" I answered. She paused before saying what it was that she wanted to say, "You wouldn't hurt me would you?" She asked. I sat her head up so she could look me in the eyes, "No... I would never hurt you but just to make sure we are on the same page, I have a whole family back at home and as long as you could accept and respect that then we would have no problem." I answered her. For a second her face turned up as if she was a bit upset but I needed her to understand that for no reason would I leave my Woman. I think that was the time when she knew that she had to respect my honesty and how real I was being, how could she not respect it? The car ride became quiet and now we were both sitting on separate sides of the back-seat. When we pulled back up to the mansion I could tell that she was confused as to how she should feel and all I could do was give her some space.

We both stepped inside the Mansion when she walked away without saying good night or giving me a hug or kiss. She went straight up the stairs and I headed to the Guest Room where I was staying. When I walked into the room I flopped on the bed flat on my back with my hands covering my face. We had Ourselves an amazing night together all the way up until the car ride home. I began to get undressed and put my basketball shorts back on while I grabbed my three phones to see what's been going on. I had nine missed calls and the majority of them were between Honey and D-Money, a few from Alicia and I even had one from Ciara. It was already late here so I knew it was really late in the D so I decided to just wait and call everybody back in the morning. I couldn't believe how the night ended with Carmen not speaking to me. Being in the business we were in I felt that she should understand the most. As I laid there in the bed staring at the ceiling I heard two knocks at the door, I didn't know what Rudy wanted but tonight wasn't the night and I wasn't even trying to kick it.

I snatched the bedroom door open ready to curse Rudy's ass out and to my surprise was Carmen standing there wearing a short pink and sheer nightgown with matching heels on, "Can I come in?" She asked. I open the door wider, "I don't see why, this is your Place." I answered her. Carmen stepped inside and walked over toward the bed. The walk that Carmen had on her was exclusive and even though I was a bit mad at her for being mad at me, I still wanted Her bad. She turned around facing me and sat on the bed, "I thought about what we were talking about and the way I reacted was selfish and a bit immature. It's just... You only been here for a couple of days and I can't believe just how attracted to you I am. You had a family before you came here so I didn't know why I was only thinking about Myself and for that, I apologize to you." Carmen told me. I exhaled and sat beside her listening to everything she had to say. "I haven't had feelings for anybody in a very long time and I haven't had anybody to seem like they care for me in a very long time so I'm just overwhelmed with all types of emotions that I don't quite know what to do with them. All I know right now at this moment is that I want to build with you, I want to know you and I want you to know everything about me. I want us to be a part of each others life." Carmen told me staring into my eyes.

I reached over putting my hand on top of Hers, "I want to build and be a part of your life as well. I don't think that it's a secret that I developed feelings for you and just these couple days I've been out here. How about we just start by taking things one day at a time and seeing what happens after that? Is that cool with you?" I asked her. Carmen smiled and nodded her head answering yes, I then leaned over closer to her and softly kissed her gentle lips pulling her down into the bed until she was flat on her back. There was something about the way that we kissed that was so arousing that I got an erection every time.

When Carmen felt the half erected dick poking her she then pushed me to lay flat on my back as she stood to her feet. She then slid her nightgown off slowly and threw it on the floor. She was even more sexy up close in person. Carmen reached behind her to unsnap her bra releasing her big pretty breast before climbing in the bed on top of me. I slid both hands from her slim waist up to her breast that I palmed in my hands. Her big areoles were calling for Me to suck on them and that I surely did. I sat up a bit when I begin sucking on her breast and licking all over her hard and long nipples. She pushed me back flat to my back and leaned all the way down kissing me for my lips all the way down to my chest, then all the way down to my waist.

I could tell that Carmen was used to being the dominant one in the bedroom and it was different for me so I allowed her to have her shine for the moment. She started pulling my shorts all the way down and over my ankles throwing them on the floor. Immediately my already hard dick was standing tall like a street pole, "Damn Papi, this might be too big!" Carmen chuckle looking nervous and staring it down. I just chuckled and told her that I promised to take my time and not hurt her. Hearing that I will take it easy on her was what she needed to hear to relax and feel comfortable and I was glad to put her at ease. She probably wasn't never getting a dick this big with them little Puerto Rican Niggas she was used to.

Carmen then took the big dick that stood in front of her and slowly placed it on her tongue licking all around and over it. She took her other hand and began ejaculating off my Shaft while the tip was still on top of her tongue. This was a sex session that wasn't going to be rushed and I was all for it, In a matter of seconds my dick was covered with her saliva and now she began sucking on the Dick from the tip to the mid range of the shaft. Seeing how much I was enjoying her mouth, she began sucking with no hands and was now slurping and controlling the dick by only her mouth. Feeling like I was going to cum way too fast I had to struggled trying to change positions, "Ohhhh, this how you wanna play it huh?!" I said starring at her like she just fucked up.

Thinking that she was about to get the dick first, I decided to switch the game up and when I laid right beside Her. I slid her thong to the side and began licking on her Clitoris how I knew she would love. Her pussy was shaved bald which allowed me to stay down there a bit longer than usual and my goal was to make her cum numerous times. I was licking, sucking and spitting on that Clitoris while my hands were underneath her gripping tightly onto her ass cheeks squeezing them. "Papi! Papi! Papi! More!" She screamed. I continued pleasuring her soaking wet Pussy when I slid one finger inside her Pussy and began fingering her. when she felt the finger the screams heightened to an even higher tone which was a clear indicator that she was enjoying it. Her screaming and moans were highly pitched but I wasn't stopping until she reached her climax. "I'm coming Papi! Make me come daddy! Oh, make me come!" She screamed with both of her hands on top of my head forcing me inside her even more. I then slid a second finger inside her pussy and with two fingers fucking her inside and my mouth and tongue pleasuring her clitoris, it was only a matter of time before she achieved her orgasm. When I looked up at her both her eyes were closed and mouth wide-open, her legs began to shake harder and harder and at that moment my face was covered with all of her pussy juices. I set up afterwards looking at her, "Oh no, we're not done yet!" I told her while licking my lips of her juices.

"Oh Papi! That was just what I needed you are good!" A big smile spread it across her face while she tossed and turned all over the bed feeling good. I stayed up and made my way in between her legs, "Come on Daddy, give me some of that monster Dick!" "Carmen demand it. I pulled her closer towards me by the waist and put just the tip of the dick inside of her. She instantly jumped like she was shot, the feeling of a dick this big was surreal to her. She told me she haven't had sex in years so I knew that Her pussy will be extremely tight.

Being considerate to her Pussy not used to a Dick like this one, I slowly put it inside of her wet and tight pussy and begin thrusting at a slow pace. "Oh that's right Daddy, just like that." She whispered. After only a few minutes I felt that her pussy was allowing more and more of me inside of her, now she was wanting and demanding for more. Her pussy was so good that she had me even moaning, "You love this pussy don't you Papi! Tell me you love this Pussy!" Carmen demanded with her hands wrapped around me and pulling me inside of her with every thrust. Her Pussy was so good that I couldn't even respond. While going at it we had the entire bed knocking against the walls. Again, I had to prevent Myself from Cumming too fast So I slowed down needing to catch my second wind. I pulled out when she smiled, "Yes Papi, take your time. Get your energy, I know it's good and I know you love it." Carmen said as she reached up wiping the sweat from my head feeling cocky about Herself. She knew I was stalling to prevent Myself from Cumming so fast. I took a look at her and her hair was all over the place but she still looked beautiful. Rubbed my hands all over her body appreciating how good her body looked.

Carmen sat Herself up telling me to lay down on my back, "Now it's my turn Papi." She told me. She climbed on top of Me and she placed my Dick inside Her. The feel of her nice fat ass sitting on my lap made my Dick grow harder. Carmen started taking charge Herself and began riding the Dick hard and like a professional. We both caught our second wind and she was now fucking Me at a faster and pleasing pace. Her big pretty breasts were bouncing up and down as she was riding when she grabbed them and licked on her own nipples. I was so turned on with everything about Carmen. Her Pussy was so wet every time she raised up and came down on the Dick I felt her Pussy juices flowing down onto my lap.

I was now at the point where I couldn't stop the fucking even if I wanted to, it was feeling so good that I felt Myself was soon ready to burst. "Oh shit, you bought to make me Bust Baby." I moaned with a turned up face. Looking down at me she smiled, "Cum inside me Daddy, I want you inside of Me!" She leaned down whispering in my ear. At that moment and without hesitation I released all inside of Carmens Pussy. She slowly raised up from the Dick and laid on my chest when we both exhaled. I think that moment we both realize that this wasn't just any regular type of Sex we had, we just were fucking like we belonged to each other.

Chapter Twenty-Six
Catch Up

(ONE MONTH LATER)

DUE TO THE FAST AND CONTINUOUS BUSINESS BETWEEN MSN AND Carmen, my visit to California was extended a lot longer than what we expected. With our business finally on track and up-to-date for at least the next couple of months, it was time for me to head back to Detroit. While in California Carmen and I spent every moment together and enjoyed every second of it. We had been all over California and she showed me everything from L.A, Oakland, Beverly Hills and San Diego. We visited the finest restaurants, hit a couple of Lakers games and even a couple of concerts. We were having so much fun that from the outside looking in you would have swore we were a couple that was in a happy relationship. Of course with Me being gone for so long that Honey wasn't feeling it at all but She wasn't the type to argue over the phone. Honey would play it cool all the way up until I returned and then it would be on.

. . .

Last night after making Love to Carmen I had to break the news to her that since our Business had come to an end and that It was to get back to Detroit. She was a bit disappointed but at the same time knew We knew this day would come and she understood. I assured Her that I will be returning in the next month or two for more Business but also to spend time with Her. We had developed a relationship that we both valued but I had to get home and take care of all of the many other business ventures I was responsible for. Her and her Security Detail dropped me off at the airport where we kissed each other goodbye and promised to call each other sooner than later.

It was a long flight back to Detroit where I had to walk to my car and I flopped in the driver seat. It has been a minute since I was behind a driver seat, in California we were either driven around by Carmen Security or she was driving us around. As I made the drive home one of the first people I decided to call it was Rizzy. I had talked to him a few times while I was away but there was only so much we could talk about while on the phone. "What's up Rizzy, what's good? Yeah I just touched down and on my way home to get cursed out by Honey, why? What's up? Right now? All right Man, I guess I'm bout to meet you there then." I hung up the phone shaking my head. I wasn't even home for 30 minutes and I was already coming home to some bullshit. Rizzy told me that I needed to meet him in the city ASAP at one of his properties that he owned. I could only imagine what type of shit been going on for the last month that I've been gone.

I hopped in his Escalade truck giving Rizzy Play, "What's up Dawg, now what was so important that I had to meet you before I went home?" I asked Him. Rizzy passed me the blunt that he was already smoking on, it's D-Money Man, that Nigga been tripping Bro. Now you remember the Lick we did on them Hustle Fam niggas? Well one of the niggas from the Stash House survived, the good thing was that he didn't tell the police that we did it to him but he did tell his Boss Mario. So now Mario knows we did it. He put

$100,000 tag on all of our Heads a piece. D –Money heard about the tag and been clowning. Him and all of his new Lil' Homies been going through everywhere Hustle Fam known to be and been shooting they shit up trying to kill them Niggas. One of the Hustle Fam Niggas well known Spots was shot up and Mario caught a bullet to the leg, so now Mario is on tip and ready for our Heads. It's official that we are an all out war with the Hustle Fam." Rizzy explained to me.

Taking in all that Rizzy just told me I exhaled the Kush smoke, "Wow... Things have been crazy since I left huh? $100,000 tag on all of our Heads? That's all!? We could double that lil" shit. We got money too!" I said with a slight chuckle. I was mad but it was what it was, all I could do is get us prepared for this war that was in process. "Where is D –Money at?" I asked. Rizzy told me that he didn't know but was sure he was somewhere shooting up some shit.

I stuck my hand out to give Rizzy a play before getting out of his truck, "Hold on, that's not it." Rizzy told me. I looked back at him and asked what else he had to tell me. "Detective Gordon and Brown are looking for D-Money too, they talking about they got information from a valuable source that he killed Kim. They've been coming to Mainstrip every other day and when they don't come in I see them posted down the block just waiting and hoping to catch him. Shit is crazy bro. I didn't even tell you that since the beef with Us and Hustle Fam, the Mainstrip in the city had been shot up a couple of times." He told me steady hitting me with bad news. I just shook my head reaching for his blunt again needing another hit.

I asked him how the new location for Mainstrip and Our other business Ventures were going when he told me that all the other businesses were doing well. The new Mainstrip location was almost ready and he put all of my money in the safe at the MSN condo. I nodded my head okay appreciating the bit of good news that he told me. I handed him his blunt back and reached over to give him another play before getting out of his truck when he stopped me again asking how was Cali. When I told him that it was cool and like any other trip he gave me a look like he knew I was lying or something. "You was out there for an entire month with a Bad-Ass Bitch and you're telling me that it was just okay? Nawl, I ain't buying that shit Nigga. Tell me the real." Rizzy told me with a grin on his face. I continue to play off like it wasn't a big deal, I told him that Carmen was one of the coolest women that I ever met before I tried getting out of his truck again. "Jay! You fucked that Bitch didn't you?!" He asked. My silence was as good enough an answer as me literally telling him, "Awww Nigga! You hit that Bad ass Bitch Carmen? How the fuck you do that? Damn you're lucky ass Nigga man." We both were laughing when he reached over giving me another Play. Then he paused again, "Oh shit, D-Money gon' kill you for fucking with his Bitch! Damn that Nigga heart it's gonna be broken when he finds out." Rizzy told me. It was right then when I first realized that he will be upset. I never kept a secret from Him because I told my Brothers everything. "Yeah I haven't even thought that far ahead but he gon' be straight. I got to tell Him. Alright Dawg, let me get up out of here and get home." I said before giving him another play. I headed back to my car when he pulled up beside me with his window rolled down, "Be smooth Bro and stay on point. I know that you didn't have to be all the way on point out here but now you're back in the D. Get on your Shit!" He told me before pulling off. I gave him a head nod and got in my car driving off....

On my way home one of my three phones rang and when I looked down and seen it was D–Money. We haven't talked in two weeks so for him to call me today was a bit weird. I didn't even tell anybody that I was coming back home today so I wondered how he knew. It wasn't like I was trying to dodge him anyways so I answered his call. "What up doe D-Money, what's good? Yeah, I actually just got back a few hours ago and was making my way home. Yeah it was straight, I did so much out there that we shouldn't have to go out there for a while now. Umm yeah, where at? All right, I'm near that spot anyways, I'll be there in a few minutes." I said before hanging up.

D-Money wanted me to meet him in the Home Depot parking lot off 7 Mile and Myers.

I pulled up a few minutes earlier than when D– money asked me to be but he was already here and In a low-key Ford Taurus. I parked directly beside him wondering out of all places, why did he want to meet him here. I jumped in his passenger seat sticking my hand out to give him a Play, "What's up Bro?" I spoke to him when I noticed the 9MM Ruger sitting on his lap. He gave me a Play while at the same time all and his mirrors watching his surroundings, "What up doe Fam, I know that Nigga Rizzy probably couldn't wait to tell you about the shit that's been going on, that's why I'm in my mirrors like this and ready for whatever. I had to do what I had to do so, you know how that shit goes. Fuck them Hustle Fam niggas! What I wanted to talk to you about was that Kim shit that the Hook is looking for me for. Did you tell anybody about it? Who else knew besides Me, You, Rizzy and Big Tee?" D–Money asked Me. I looked at him like he was crazy, "Why would I tell anybody about a fucking Murder?! I ain't told a fucking soul! Who did you tell cause Rizzy say he ain't told nobody and we know big Tee ain't told nobody." I reply back to his crazy question. D-Money sat back with a confused look on his face, "Hmm, so I wonder who the fuck they got info from if none of us told nobody? I know I ain't told nobody Shit!" I answered.

"Maybe they were just trying to pull a confession out of me then. They just so happen to be hitting it directly on the nose. You didn't tell yo Girl Honey did you?" D-money asked me. I gave him an even crazier look, "Yea, right. I told my girl that you killed her Best Friend and I helped throw her in the Detroit River." I said being sarcastic. I could see it in D-Money's face that he was tripping out, I also noticed that he had the jitters like he was back on that cocaine again. "My fault Bro, I'm just going through it right now. Homicide is looking for me, Hoe niggas looking for me, shid I just got a lot going on. My fault." D-money apologized. "Whatever the case is you know I got you and I'm riding. With the police and all the Hoe Niggas, I'm your family and I got your back." I told him sticking my hand out to give him a Play. He nodded his head after hearing that, "Fasho, that's good to know... Anyways, how was Cali? How is my Girl Carmen doing out there? Was she asking about me?" D-Money asked with a grin on his face. I wanted to avoid that question but it was obviously unavoidable.

"Cali was good, it was good and I kind of want to talk to you about that..." I was telling him. He turned towards me so he could give all his attention, "In Cali right, Carmen and I kind of hooked up. At first I was telling her that I couldn't fuck with her like that because of you but then she swore up and down that it wasn't nothing like that at all. So when she told me that, one thing led to another and... Yeah, we did our Thang." I told him. D-Money looked away and was completely silent. He was so silent that I had to ask him what was he thinking about. "Oh, that's all you wanted to talk to me about? Nigga I ain't tripping over no Bitch! Are you serious? Fuck that Bitch for real for real Bro" D-Money reply. I've known D-Money since we were kids and just by his facial expression I could tell he was hurt. My Brother was on fire, "Alright Jay, I got a lot of shit to do and handle so I'll hit you up a little later." D-Money told me indicating that it was time for me to go. "We straight right? We still Brothers and you ain't mad at me are you?" I asked. He gave me a look like I was crazy, "Of course, Blood Brothers." D-Money answer. We gave each other a play and I hopped out of his car. Before I jumped in my car D-money was already stabbing off leaving me standing there. I could tell he was pissed but was I supposed to feel bad when Carmen told me she wasn't even the least bit attracted to him? Whatever the case was, I just hope he got over it soon..

Chapter Twenty-Seven
Coming Home

I STEPPED THROUGH THE FRONT DOOR OF MY HOUSE WITH SO MANY bags that when I dropped them to the floor it sounded like light thunder. Immediately both boys came running from the living room when they seen it was me, "Jay! Jay! What's up Jay!?" They yelled. I kneeled down picking both of them up in the air, "What's up Boys! Y'all miss me?" I asked but judging by the tight hugs they were giving me I already knew the answer. When I put them down and took a look at them I noticed that they both grew an extra inch or two in the past month. "Hey Y'all, where is Honey at?" I asked. They pointed upstairs while staring at all The bags I brought inside, "Jay, so what did you get us?" Lil K asked anxiously. I grabbed all the bags that was full of toys and handed it to them, while they ripped up the bags I went up the stairs to see my Baby.

I walked into the bedroom where Honey was in the bed under the covers asleep. Looking at her in the bed asleep reminded me just how beautiful she was. I sat her bags down beside the bed when I quietly sat beside her rubbing on her stomach, "Watch out, Stranger." She told me with her eyes still closed and popping my hand. I chuckled, I knew that she wasn't happy with me for staying out there longer than I said I was. "Stranger? So since I am a

Stranger I guess you don't want this?" I asked pulling a jewelry box from my pocket. One of her eyes open so she could take a peek, when she saw it was a jewelry box she sat up, "What's that?" She asked. I pulled it back from her reaching hands, "Nawl, nawl, don't wake up now. You heard when I walked through the front door and now you want to get up. Naw, this ain't for you." I said playfully.

A smile spread across Honey's face when she playfully hit me in the shoulder wanting to know what was in the box, "Shut up, you should've called me more and I wouldn't be acting like this. Give me this damn box!" She told me as she finally snatched it out of my hand. Just when I was about to explain Myself her mouth dropped why open into the floor, "Oh my God Jay, this is Beautiful!" She said pulling out her diamond necklace. I pulled out two more jewelry boxes that had her diamond earrings and diamond bracelets inside. When she seen it she was speechless but thankful as she jumped in my arms hugging and kissing me. She jumped out of the bed to put on all of her new jewelry and indeed it looks good on her. She turned around and wrapped her arms around my neck, "You knew you better came in here with some gifts or it would've been World War III around here!" She said smiling into my face. I chuckled, "I already knew it. I don't see why it would've been all that, I'll talked to you every day." I said leaning down and kissing her. "But you didn't call me enough, you know I want to talk to you at least three times a day. We were only talking twice a day and sometimes it was once a day." Honey said. I exhaled picking her up and carrying her back over onto the bed, "Would you shut up Girl and just tell me how much you miss me?" I said to her as we laid in bed. Honey climbed on top of me, "I miss you big Head, don't leave for that long no more please? Could you promise me?" Honey asked. Laying there with Honey on top of me felt just so right, I actually missed her more than I thought. She was my true Baby and the Woman who had my heart. "I promise you I won't leave for that long again, okay?" I answered. She smiled and leaned closer placing her soft and luscious lips on mine. I loved kissing Honey, the way I felt about Her made me feel bad for all of the cheating and lusting I was doing with Carmen. I then got up and went to lock our bedroom door so the boys couldn't interrupt, it was time that I made up for all the time I've been away from her...

Chapter Twenty-Eight
Set Up

(NEXT MORNING)

I WOKE UP THE NEXT MORNING ONLY TO FIND LIL' K AND LIL' DEZ asleep in the bed with Honey and I. I smiled at the sight of having Myself a family that I cared for and they cared for me. I crept out of the bed not wanting to wake anybody and I went straight into the bathroom to get Myself together for the day. After showering and getting dressed I make my way downstairs to head out the door when Honey caught me, "Baby, can you stay at home today? I don't know why but I had a bad dream that something happened to you and my gut is telling me to ask you if you could please stay at home." Honey asked me as she walked down the stairs towards me. With all that's been going on since I've been gone, I had a lot to handle. I didn't have time for superstitions, "Baby, I have a lots of work to handle today, so much has gone wrong since I've been gone and now it's my job to fix it. Those are only bad dreams that I have all the time. Plus I have my pistol and Big Tee is waiting outside for me and you know He got Me. Relax, everything will be okay, okay?"

I told her as I walked back to her to kiss her before walking out the house...

I stepped outside and Big Tee was already standing out there beside the Range Rover ready for work. I gave him a Play, "Big Boy! What's up with you Man, you've been good?" I asked being happy to see him. He was happy to see me too, "Aww Man, I've been good. I know you heard how crazy everything's been though?" He asked me. I nodded my head, "Yea I already know, that's why we punching in early so we could get things back good. You ready to hit the streets?" I asked him. He stuck his hand back out to give me another play and have a smile on his face, "Fasho, let's do it Boss." Big Tee said as we both hopped in the truck and pulled off headed for the city. As we headed to the city Alicia and I were texting back and forth with me telling Her that I will be over there in a few hours. I had to hit the Mainstrip up first to make sure business was still good and after that we had to visit the new Mainstrip location and then I would have time to visit Her.

Big Tee pulled into a gas station when he said that he will be right back and that he was going to pay for the gas. I wasn't even paying no attention to Him or where we were because I was now texting Carmen and Alicia all at the same time. When I lifted my head and seeing the type of raggedy ass gas station we were at I got to wondering what made Big Tee stop at this gas station. He knew that I didn't want no cheap ass gas in none of my vehicles so I didn't under-stand our point in being here. I then looked over at the gas meter and it read that the truck was already on a full tank. "What the fuck is going on?! Did he say he was getting some gas?!" I asked Myself. Now I was worried and super paranoid of my surroundings, I reached under my seat because I always kept a pistol on both the driver and passenger side but there wasn't a pistol under there. I reached over on the driver side and there wasn't any pistol on that site either.

"What the fuck?!" I said starting to panic. Big Tee stepped out of the gas station and instead of coming towards the truck he went to an all black Caprice that sat on the side of the gas station that looked like it was waiting on him. All of a sudden two old-school Chevy Caprice surrounded my Range Rover with four Niggas hopping out each vehicle aiming their pistols directly at me.

Instantly my life flash before me. From Honey asking me to stay at home, Rizzy telling me to be careful, Carmen telling me that I couldn't couldn't go wrong fucking with her and Alicia pregnant with my Son. The shots from their guns ripped through the windshield and doors as I ducked for cover the only way I could. I felt the hot shells ripping through my body causing me the greatest pain I ever felt. After feeling so many shots I knew this was the end for me and at that moment I took my last breath whispering to the Lord, "Forgive me for my sins Lord, here I come..."

Chapter Twenty-Nine
Two Weeks Later

I OPENED MY EYES AND THE BRIGHT HOSPITAL LIGHTS AND SUNSHINE that they allowed inside the room made it hard for me to see. "Oh my God, he's woke y'all!! He's woke! His eyes open, Baby!? Baby, can you hear me?!" I heard Honey voice yelling in my ear. On one side of me was my brothers Rizzy and D-Money and standing over me was Honey with a face full of tears. The more my vision began to clear I begin to look around the room when I seen all the flowers and cards that read get well soon. I tried talking but I could only whisper, "What... What happened?" I asked. Honey tried telling Me but she couldn't stop this tears From falling down her face. Rizzy handed her some tissue, "Jay Baby, you were shot six times, it was pretty serious. You were out for two weeks." Honey told me while wiping the tears from her eyes. Not in the crying mood I gave Rizzy a eye to get Honey out of the room so that we could talk just the Guys. Smart enough to know that we needed to discuss business, Honey left the room but not before saying that she would return in the next twenty minutes.

I reached my hands and put them over my face, all the stress was overwhelming. Here I was in the hospital bed after being in a coma for two weeks and shot six times and I still couldn't shake being stressed out. "Jay, I need you to tell me what exactly happened."

Rizzy asked me. I pause for a minute before answering, "Big Tee, he was the one who set me up. He pulled up at a gas station, he went inside with the key, none of my guns that I stashed under the seats were there and the next thing I knew I was being shot up." I told him unable to hold back my tears. Just thinking about it had me pissed and wanting revenge. "Mario must've got to Big Tee and got him to turn, I also think that he is the one the police is talking about that's ratting on D-Money. I'm going to kill that Nigga!" Rizzy said balling his fist up. As mad as we both were we couldn't handle the situation like this. We had to remain smart and take care of whoever he worked for in a strategic and professional way.

"Calm down, calm down Cuzzo... I don't want nothing done just yet. I want y'all to catch him, hold him and we're gonna make him tell us who he who hired him. As bad as we want to, we can't automatically assume it was Mario's crew. So that's what I want done first, find him and hold him at the Warehouse." I told them. Honey and the boys stepped back into the room when Rizzy told Me TheY had me and was going to go and work on it right then. They gave me a Play and told Me they would be back in a couple of days before walking out the door.

Honey walk towards the bed and placed her hand on top of mine when I asked her where was her Mother. She told me that she had to leave because too much was going on, "Babe, Let me start by telling you that I am so happy that you survived. I don't know what I would do without you around Boy!" She told me leaning down to kiss me. "I don't know what I would do without you or the Boys either. I love y'all and y'all are my family." I replied. Honey stared at me with her big pretty eyes, "Jay, did D-money kill my Best Friend?" She asked with her Eyes beginning to water. If I told her the truth she would be not only hurt but could never forgive Me just because he's my Brother and I knew about it. There was even a possibility that she would leave me and none of them decisions I could allow to happen. I did what any other man in my situation with Do, " No...

No he did not kill Kim." I answered with a straight face looking her in the eyes.

A smile had spread across her face in relief when she leaned down and kissed me. Honey exhaled, "Well Babe, I have to go and put the boys together an overnight bag so they could stay over my Mothers house tonight, I have to go and get out of these clothes and take a shower then I will be back up here." Honey told me. "Honey you don't have to go through all of that just to get back up here. Go home and get you some rest, I'll be okay. Just be back tomorrow okay?" I said to her. She gave me a look, "Are you sure you'll be fine?" Honey asked me. I smiled, "Baby go home and get some rest, I'll be good." I told her. Honey kissed me and told me she loved me, "Boys. What are you gonna tell Jay?" Honey turns asking the boys. Both boys walked over towards me, "We love you Jay." They said in unison and they reached over hugging me. Them telling me that they loved me touched my heart. Knowing that Niggas tried to take me away from my loved ones made me even more angry and for that, Niggas was going to pay the price to the fullest...

Chapter Thirty
Recovery

I HAVE BEEN SHOT IN BOTH LEGS, ONE TO THE CHEST, ONE TO THE shoulder, and two in my hip that made the doctor say that it will be 2 to 3 weeks before I was released from their care.

There was still a lot of test they said needed to be taken and physical therapy was mandatory before I was released. Being in the hospital not able to take care of Myself or business was taking a toll on me. I had to walk around everywhere on a walker like I was a straight handicap until I learn how to walk again, I felt useless. I had already been in the hospital for the past month and all my phones were ringing nonstop. The rumors that I was hearing about me were even more crazy. I was rumored to be dead, some said paralyzed, I even heard that the streets thought I been shot so many times that I have brain damage causing me to be a vegetable.

The nurse had just bought me back to the bedroom assisting me back into my bed, wearing the hospital robe I would often feel breezes through the thin fabric But this time was because my entire ass was out. "Oh Papi, I miss that Black Chocolate Ass!" I heard the familiar voice from behind me. There was only one woman who called me Papi and had that accent but I was in disbelief that this was the person that I thought it was. I turned around and to my surprise it was Carmen standing there in the flesh. My heart dropped in shock that she came all the way to the East Coast to visit me. The biggest smile spread across my face when I seen her. Carmen and I had become very close during my visit to California so I was happy to see my Puerto Rican Baby.

"Get up Papi, I'm in the D now, you got to show me the D you've been trying to get me to visit. Just don't take me to the spot where they shot you at." Carmen said making both of us laugh. The nurse told me to call her if I needed her and left the room, "How are you Daddy, are you okay?" She asked walking closer to my bed placing her hand on top of mine and leaning down to hug and kiss me. I missed Carmen smile, her touch and just being in her presence, she was one of the realist females I've ever met so for her to come all the way out here it really meant a lot to me. "I'm good, you know me. I'm a soldier in battle but a general that makes the Calls. Feel me?" I told her with The slick talk I was always known for. She just smiled staring down at me, "Always the slick Talker. I've missed you." Carmen told me. "I've missed you too. It's good to see you, I never thought I could get you to come and visit the D and lookee here, you're here." I said with a smile on my face holding her hand. "Yeah, well when I heard that my Boo was shot up I had to pack up and come and visit you to make sure everything is good. So, is everything good?" Carmen asked. I already knew she was referring to the niggas responsible for shooting me. I exhaled, "Well it will be... My Bodyguard/Driver was the one who set me up so now we got a find him and see who hired him. Then we go from there. Everything will be good soon." I answered.

I looked behind Carmen when I seen her top bodyguard Diego who never left her side, then I looked outside the room when I seen what looked like two more bodyguards standing out there. When Carmen noticed I was looking around she placed her other hand on top of mine also, "Well you are right, everything will be good soon and it's going to start with your new Bodyguards I'm leaving with you. You will be escorted everywhere you go for now on by six of my bodyguards and I'm not taking no for an answer. These guys are certified and weapon approved bodyguards that are some of the best in the country. You remember Diego from your visit, he will be the one closest to you at all times. I'm talking if you take a shit he will be standing outside the door listening for it to splash or else he would be in there making sure you're okay, Do we have any issues or questions? No? I didn't think so... So this is what they making you eat in here huh?" Carmen said not even giving me a chance to speak. That was the person that Carmen was, when she said something then that's what it was.

I just chuckled at how dominant and controlling Carmen was, that was one of the reasons I was in love with her. "Now, don't you wish you would've stayed with me?" She asked smiling. One thing about Carmen was she wasn't the type to lay around crying like most women. Carmen was talking about sending her whole Puerto Rican Cartel Goons to help find and kill Big Tee and whoever it was he worked for. Carmen was one of the most Beautiful, Hustling Women I knew but at the same time I also knew that she would send that Killer cartel to kill anybody with the simple word go. She wasn't to be messed with under any circumstances.

"How would you feel if I told you I had some info on the Big Tee Vato you speak of?" She asked me. I set up asking her what was it and if she knew where he was. She looked back at Diego and he handed her a paper that she handed to me. "He has four young Pootas with him that are armed but they are easy to kill. It shouldn't be nothing to get a hold of him." Carmen told me sitting back in the chair that she pulled beside me. I sat back staring at the address where he was hiding and I couldn't wait to make the call to get them.

"Well love I can't stay long because Business call but for you I will always be around. I will be calling to check on you and I want you to call me if you need anything at all." Carmen told me and she stood to her feet and leaning down to kiss me. "I love you Jay, get healthy and stay safe. Diego, you take care of him." She told me and the Bodyguard. I told her that I loved her too and she exited the room but another surprise was standing by the door that I wasn't expecting. It was Ciara from the Mainstrip, Carmen looked back at me and chuckled, "Try not to go to jail Papi." She told me but shooting a shot at Ciara's age. I had no idea why Ciara was here but I was for sure going to talk with the hospital staff for telling people where I was staying.

"That don't look like my Cousin." Ciara said with her face turned up. I was instantly irritated by her presence, I didn't understand what made her think that we were that cool that she could come and visit me. "Neither do you but that never stopped you." I replied. She walked towards my bed when she saw Diego standing in the corner, "Who is he?" She asked. "That somebody that's going to escort you out, what's up Ciara?" I ask not wanting to kick it. "Oh relax there, don't worry because Honey is downstairs parking the car. I just was at your beautiful home in them expensive suburbs, when Honey asked me if I wanted to ride with her to visit you. Now I have a business proposition for you that I know you won't refuse." Ciara told me. I was pissed hearing her tell me that she been to my crib and the fact that she was even hanging with my girl had me even more mad. "What the fuck type of proposition you could have for me?!" I snapped at her. It amused her to see me upset, "I'm going to get straight to the point then. I want $50,000 in cash to keep our little Sex Session a secret from your Girl. If you don't pay, then I will tell her. Your happy home will be totally ruined and I know you don't want that." Ciara told me. I laughed, this had to been some type of joke, "Are you serious? I don't have time for the games Ciara, now go on and get up out of here," I told her. The Hood Rat came right out of her, "Nigga do I look like I'm playing?! You see... This is why I applied to the Mainstrip, I knew who you were from the moment I seen you and I knew I could get you." Ciara told me as she ran her fingers from my foot all the way up to my thigh heading toward my dick.

"Ever since the first time fucking you I knew I could trick you into giving me more dick and now that my mission is complete, I'm trying to get rich. I need my $50,000 or I have no problem telling my Cousin that we were fucking on a regular." Ciara threaten meand pulling out her phone to show me the tape from the big Orgy. I sat steaming hot, I couldn't believe this bitch came to me with this while I was in my hospital bed. $50,000 wasn't shit to me but it was the fact that this Bitch was trying to extort me.

"Bitch I ain't paying your Stupid Ass Shit! It's my word against yours, who you think she's going to believe?" I said with a grin on my face. An even bigger grin spread across her face, "I figured you might say something like that, that's why I bought my insurance with me." She told me as she reached down in her purse to toss me what looked like a DVD. I picked it up and ask her what the hell was this supposed to be. "That right there is my insurance. That's the DVD footage from the Boom-Boom Room that has a clear view of me sucking your Dick and you fucking my brains out. Now it would be crazy if at some point during the car ride with Honey that I just so happened To drop this in her car leaving her to see it. That will be all the way fucked up for you. So, my advice to you is that you just pay me the lil' $50,000 or risk losing your family when it could've been avoided. Your choice." Ciara told me as she paced back-and-forth around the room. I couldn't believe that this bitch had video footage of me fucking her, the rage that came over me began to fill my brain like a tumor and I was ready to kill her. If only I had my pistol she would've been dead. "You Stupid Bitch! You act like you don't know who I am! You trying to Blackmail Me?! Bitch if Honey gets hold of that tape I swear to God I will fucking kill..." I was saying until Honey stepped in the room stopping me from saying what I was going to say.

"Hey Baby, it's crazy trying to find some place to park and who are these big Men standing by the door like Secret Service? Who is he?" Honey asked noticing Diego and the other Bodyguards. I quickly hid all the anger I was l ready to release upon Ciara and put on a smile, "Hey Baby, oh they are just some New Members of the MSN who will be Bodyguards for a couple of weeks, that's all. You look good though, where you been at all day? Where are the Boys?" I asked her but honestly not caring about any of it. I was so pissed at Ciara that all I was thinking about was how can I off her and do it clean.

Honey began telling me about her day and plans for the day but with Ciara in the same room as us I only become more angry by the minute. For her to have the audacity to think that she will blackmail me and get away with it was only proof that she was one of the dumbest people walking. "Well Babe, we just came to visit you and make sure everything was okay. I love you and will be back a little later." Honey told me as she leaned down kissing me. I told her that I loved her as they walk towards the door, Ciara looked back at me with a devilish grin that made my blood boil. Soon as I walked out the door I called Rizzy, it was time for people to start disappearing...

Chapter Thirty-One
Going Home

(THREE WEEKS LATER)

AFTER BEING STUCK IN THE HOSPITAL FOR ALMOST TWO MONTHS, today was the day I was being released and I never been more happy to leave anywhere as I was about leaving here. I have passed all the test the doctors giving me and I had completed physical therapy so according to them I was ready to hit the streets again. Honey, the kids and Rizzy all told me that they will be to pick me up in the next hour so I was packing all of the gifts and things that people giving me so we would be ready to leave as soon as they arrived.

There was two knocks at the door when I looked at the time I was impressed that my family was early and not late. When I open the door there stood Alicia and E-Bo. Since my stay at the hospital I had talk to Alicia a few times and she was trying to visit me but at the time she was trying to come because she knew that Honey woul be there. I was totally surprised to see E-Bo, I haven't seen him since the time I came and pick up the guns need it for the Hustle Fam Lick. I wasn't even copping from him no more because I had found a better price and better Product so ever since I bossed up and been doing my own thing we haven't talked at all.

My unborn Son's Mother Alicia and E-Bo turned facing me and she had gotten big as a house. She look like she was ready to have our Son at any moment. She looked Me up and down when her eyes started to water at the fact that I had been shot up in the hospital fighting for my life. "Oh my God, are you okay? Are you all right? I hate that I haven't been able to come and visit you and I know I didn't tell you that I was coming this time but E-Bo called me and told me that he was coming to visit you and asked me if I wanted to ride with him. So, I said yes and here we are!" Alicia said as she wrapped her arms around my neck standing on her tiptoes to kiss me. "Yeah, you know we had to come and check on my Godson's Father and make sure he was sure he was straight even though I had to hear about this in the streets instead of you calling me. E-Bo said. I shrugged my shoulders and shook my head, "Yeah, I just been trying to get Myself together since this shit happened and I really haven't been talking to anybody, feel me?" I replied. E-Bo looked at me with a grin but that grin didn't seem like a regular grin, there was something to it. "Well it's good to see you Boy, for real. You know you made it when they start trying to kill you." E-Bo said as him and Alicia took a seat on the chairs across from the bed.

I sat across from them on the bed when E-Bo stared at me and just couldn't stop grinning. When I asked him what he was grinning for he just shook his head, "Nothing, I'm just proud of you and how you've grown up. It's crazy cause I still remember the day I picked you up from the bus stop and putting you up on the street shit. Now look at you, all grown up and doing your own thing. That's good shit." E-Bo said. I'm nodded my head remembering all the same thing, "Yeah man, if it wasn't for you I will still be a 9-to-5 working Ass Nigga like you said. Them days are over now." I added to his comment. For some reason I feel like E-Bo was on straight bullshit. For him to pop up here without calling or telling me, Then inviting

Alicia knowing I got a girl wasn't cool and made me feel some type away. "What was this Nigga E-Bo on?" I asked Myself.

"So do the police know who did this to you?" Alicia asked Me. I shook my head no and before I could respond, E-Bo did it for me. "Nawl they ain't gone catch no Nigga unless he tells who it was. It was probably somebody... Well, never mind." He said discontinuing what he was saying. My eyebrow raise curious to know what it was that he was about to say, "Nawl, gone head, What was about to say?" I asked. Acting like he didn't want to tell me, "All I was about to say was that it might've been somebody you fucked over, sold some bullshit too, or maybe you forgot about the little people that helped you come up. I don't know, that's just what I think." E-Bo answered. I had became a Man that learned to read people very well and I could tell that all what he was saying was subliminally towards me. "Hmm, could it be? Nawl it can't be... I looked up to this man for years, he's my Role Model, I know he can't be jealous of me. Could He?" I thought to Myself. It sure sounded like he was and if that was the case, for the first time in a long time I wouldn't know what to do.

The room was silent and Alicia was feeling the slight tension that had began to build between Us. "Nawl I never fucked nobody over so that can't be it. I never sold any bullshit because the shit I get it I pay top dollar for and it's imported from the West Coast so that can't be it. And little people that I forget?? They must be so little now that I can't remember them. Feel me?" I said with a grin on my face. "Sooo, I heard MSN in is making a franchise of the Mainstrip and bringing a lot of locations to Michigan? That's what's up. E-Bo said slightly changing the subject. I nodded my head, "Yeah, we're doing so good that we planning on going international with it. MSN is doing great, they say I was even making money while in that coma." I told him. He chuckled, "Oh yeah? So you should have a new Range Rover then since the last one took all the shots?" He shot back. The grinning had come to an end for the simple fact there wasn't no way for him to know I was shot up in the Range

Rover, they never reported what I was in on the news so how did he know? "Yeah, Right after I leave here I was going to go and buy that Maybach that cost $350,000 to make up for that Range. Hey, E-Bo, you've been in the game for a long time, why you ain't got a Maybach? Instead you're still driving that old ass Benz." I asked him. We were no longer at the point of a conversation but it had become a stunt battle.

Alicia seen the conversation flipping from good to bad in a matter of seconds, "Well umm, Jay we just came to visit you and make sure you were good. Would you make sure you call me soon as you get a chance?" Alicia asked me. Never taking my eye off E-Bo I told her that I loved her and will call her the first moment I get a chance. Alicia stood up and leaned over to kiss me, E-Bo stood his feet and followed Alicia to the door, "Yo Jay, don't forget... I made you, I put you in this street shit and I could end you as well." He told me. The things he just told me literally hurt my heart because this was the same guy I admired so much and wanted to follow in his footsteps. I used to respect him to the fullest but after seeing jealousy overcome him, things were different. "E-Bo I'm already passed you. I could end before You end Me and don't forget it. You're not doing what I am out here, can't you see?" I replied. Both Alicia and E-Bo walked out of the room and right then I knew that E-Bo and I business relationship was totally over. I may have gained a new enemy that I may need to watch out for...

I was released from the hospital and Honey and Rizzy carried all of my things into the cabin that I owned in Northern Michigan. I didn't trust my Mansion because Big Tee been there multiple times and knew it well and until I knew he was caught, I refuse to go there. The only people knew about this cabin was MSN so I was straight, being shot six times make you this paranoid to the point where everybody is a suspect. The kids felt right at home and began running all around enjoying themselves but Me on the other hand only wanted to get straight to business. Big Tee and whoever hired him was my main priority and I would not rest until I have them.

Rizzy and I stepped into my office when I went to sit at my desk watching the surveillance system and Rizzy went to pour us some drinks. I pulled out my medication pills and chase them with the Remy Martin, "Alrighy, tell me something good. Do you got big Tee?" I asked. Rizzy looked at me funny telling me that I shouldn't be taking my medication with alcohol, "Do we have big Tee!?!?" I yelled slamming my glass down On the table. Rizzy slightly jumped from my sudden yell, "Yea... Yeah, we got him Man. He's down at the Warehouse we got down by the water." Rizzy told me. Knowing I was out of line, "I apologize for yelling Cuzo, it's just..." Rizzy Shook his head and waved his hand, "I already know Fam, you're stressing and I feel you but things is going to get back good soon, just watch." Rizzy told me.

I took a big gulp from my glass, "Good, that's real good. What about that Bitch Ciara?" I asked. Rizzy sat back in the chair in front of Me, "I got some of the Homies watching her 24/7 until you give the word to pick her up." He answered. I'm nodded my head, "Yeah, that's good too. I guess things are going to get better sooner than expected then huh? Yeah, make that call have her picked up and brought to the Warehouse. Its time to start handling Muthafucka's!" I told him. I was home now and it was time to get things done and organized how it was supposed to be.

I couldn't wait to find out who was the people responsible for having me almost killed. "Now where the hell is D-Money at? I haven't seen or heard from him since he visited the hospital that one time?" I asked Rizzy. Rizzy shook his head, "I haven't talk to that Nigga either but the young Niggas in the Warehouse told me that he came by there trying to get in and talk with Big Tee, I told them not to let nobody in until they got word from either one of us. The young Niggas say that he even tried bribing them to get in, I think he was trying to kill Big Tee before we had a chance to talk to him. There's something fishy about that Nigga D-Money Bro, I don't know what it is but I ain't liking it." Rizzy say. Both of us had a feeling that D-money had been doing too much as of lately and we need to find out what exactly was it he was on.

"Alright, well let's get down to that Warehouse and see what this Bitch Ass Nigga Big Tee got to say. Whatever he tells us we just go from there and that Bitch Ciara might as well get handled too." I told Rizzy as I stood to my feet reaching in my desk drawer for my lemon-squeeze 45. It was finally time to go and handle the people responsible for trying to kill me.

Rizzy and I headed toward the front door when Honey gave me the look as if she knew what I was up too. It wasn't a secret that I wanted revenge and she knew that I couldn't be talked out of it. I walked in the kitchen toward her, "You know I love you right?" I asked her. Her eyes instantly began to water as she nodded yes, "I'll be back okay?" I told her as I planted a soft kiss to her forehead and walked into the living room where the boys were. I called the Boys over to me when I took a knee, "Y'all I know I love y'all right?" I asked with my arms wrapped around them. They both nodded their head answering yes at the same time, "I need y'all to protect and watch after your mommy and auntie for me while I'm gone okay?" I ask them. They both nodded their head and for the first time ever they didn't ask me to bring anything back. I think they knew that shit was real and this wasn't the time to ask. I told them to give me a kiss and being the sweet boys they were, they both kissed me on the cheek follow up with a big hug. Rizzy, Diego and the rest of my bodyguards all headed outside to the trucks, it was time to head back to Detroit...

Chapter Thirty-Two
Truth Shall Set You Free

RIZZY AND I PULLED UP TO ONE OF THE WAREHOUSES WE OWNED DOWN by the Detroit River where Big Tee was being held. It was surrounded by a gated fence and MSN owned it since we first started hustling. There was at least 50 Young MSN niggas that we made part of the team that was standing guard and patrolling the property. We pulled up to the gate when I rolled down the window and without needing to say anything, the young MSN member yelled for the gate to be open. We then pulled it all the way to the back of the Warehouse were Big Tee was being held.

When we stepped out of the truck all eyes were on us, the young MSN members stared at me as if they seen a ghost. All I was focused on was a big Tee who was hanging tied up in the air. He was bloody from the beatings he had taken and one of his eyes were so swollen that it was sealed closed. As Rizzy and I walked closer toward him I couldn't help but to laugh. Seeing his fat ass up there hanging bloody with pissy pants on and helpless as a newborn child made me feel good. I grabbed the water hose that laid on the floor nearby and sprayed the forceful water directly at him waking him up, "Jay... Jay, please Man. I'm sorry Bro. I didn't even want to do it!

Please, I'm begging you!" Big Tee begged with drool and blood dripping from his mouth.

"Nawl bitch don't beg now!" Rizzy yelled at him. I told the young MSN in members to lower him down a bit, "Calm down, calm down, calm down Big Tee... Now, you know me Big Tee and you know that I don't play no games so you know when I say something that I mean it. I want you to tell me who hired you to set me up and if I think that you're lying to me about anything, if I feel like you're holding out on any information... I will kill you. This is your only chance in making it out of here alive, who was it?" I asked in a calm and subtle tone. Big Tee instantly began crying and telling me that if he told me that he will be killed, I stepped up closer to his face staring him dead in the eye and lifted his chin. "Big Tee, I will kill you if you don't tell me who hired you." I whispered to him. The tears began to flow profusely, "It was... It was... It was D-Money. He paid me $30,000 to set you up to be killed." Big Tee cried. I looked back at Rizzy and all he could do was shake his head like he wasn't surprised but I was in straight denial. I quickly pulled out my .45 and slapped it across his face hard as hell, "Don't you fucking lie to me! Who hired you!? Who hired you!?" I yelled hitting him again. His other eye was on his way to be swollen shut now, "I swear...I swear...D–money paid me! I swear to God he paid me." Big Tee cried out.

Rizzy walked up to me pulling me to the side, "Yo Jay, I can't hold you up I think big Tee is telling the truth. Yeah he's our Brother but we both said that the Nigga been acting different lately. Think about it, he been trying to come in here and kill Big Tee Hisself, and he kept trying to put it on Mario and the Hustle Fam crew. I believe this Snake Ass Nigga Bro." Rizzy told me making the most sense. As bad as I didn't want to believe it, I had to consider that it may have been true. "Jay... Rizzy, please don't kill Me. If y'all let me live." Big Tee was saying until I turned facing him and sent three hot halo point shells into his skull killing him instantly. I headed towards the truck when Rizzy and the bodyguards follow behind me to leave the Warehouse...

"What we gon' do about the Nigga D-Money since you killed all the Niggas who put us on up on Him." Rizzy asked Me. I sat there in silence but deep in my thoughts still from what Big Tee just told Us. My own Man's who was like my Brother tried to have Me killed was a hard pill to swallow. I exhaled with a straight face I answered, "We have to kill Him....Call D-Money up and tell him to meet us at the Warehouse and that we were on our way there. Plus see where them Niggas At with that bitch Ciara. I want them there at the same time, I have a feeling that they have a few things in common." I told Rizzy. Rizzy jumped right on the phone and made the call...

(TWO HOURS LATER)

Rizzy and I pulled back up to the Warehouse and soon as we walked back inside we seen Ciara sitting in a chair Butt-Ass naked crying with duct tape covering her mouth. I couldn't help but to laugh as we approach her. I snatched to the duct tape from her mouth hard as possible, "Jay, please don't kill me! I swear I won't tell yo Girl! Please let me go! Please!" Ciara begged. I stood in front of her, "Yea, just give me 50,000 and I'll let you go!" I told her jokingly. My phone ringing interrupted my laughs, it was D–Money. I started laughing again, "What's up Bro? Shit, we are in the garage about to handle this Nigga Big Tee, we waiting on you. Alright, well come on then!" I told D-Money before hanging up. D-Money said he was about to pull up and to tell the young MSN Members to let him in. "Yo, call them Niggas at the gate and have them let that Nigga D-Money in. It's time to get this party started." I told Rizzy.

"Now, Ciara I know that I don't know you well but I do know that you're not smart enough to come up with a plan to set me up for

$50,000 by Yourself so... Who put you up to trying to Extort me? Was it D-Money? You could tell me." I asked her. She cried harder, "Do you promise to let me go if I tell you?" She asked. I looked at Rizzy then back to Ciara, "I promise Baby Girl, I'll let you go." I answered her with a grin on my face. Rizzy's phone rang, "That was the front gate, they said D-Money is coming through the gate right now as we speak." Rizzy told me after hanging up. I started clapping when I kneel down in front of Ciara whispering to her, "The truth shall set you free." I told her. Taking a pause before she answered, "Yes, it was D-Money who had me Extort you. He hired me just to set you up on tape. He paid me $5000 just to fuck you and told me when I got the $50,000 that I could keep it. I am so sorry! I'm sorry I didn't know that it would be like.." Ciara was saying until I cut her off. "You didn't know I would kill you for this shit, that's what you didn't know. Now you're begging for your life, that's funny!" I said as I became more and more angry.

D–Money walked into the Warehouse and when he seen Ciara sitting there ass naked he just shook his head seeing her tied up and in tears. I turn towards him with a smile on my face, "What's up Bro, glad you made it to the party but you're just a lil' bit late." I said as I pointed over to where a Big Tee's dead body was still on the ground. "As you can see, we couldn't wait for you but we left something for you doe." I said. Ciara looked up at D-Money, "Tell em' D-Money to let me go! I already told them everything! Come on, tell them to let me go please! I love you!" She begged him.

Hearing her tell D–Money that she loved him shocked both Rizzy and Myself while he stood there looking stupid. I guess he was surprised how quick Ciara sold him out. Ciara told him that she loved him which meant that I must've been fucking the entire time, "Bitch! What the fuck is you talking about! I know y'all ain't believing whatever this Bitch is talking about!?" D–Money asked looking back at Us. Me being the Nigga I was, I just stood there staring at him in the face. It amazed me how he could stand there in my face and lie to me.

I quickly pulled out my pistol and D-Money's eyes grew big, He was nervous as if he was worried about his life. "You kill her then if she's lying." I told him handing him the pistol. D–Money took the pistol like that was the best deal ever. He aimed it at Ciara head but before he could fire off a shot she yelled, "I'm Pregnant! Don't kill me because I'm pregnant with your Baby Darien!" She cried out. All of us couldn't believe what she just said, D–Money heard that and lowered the gun. I walked up to him, "Well, what's it gon be? Is she lying or are you?" I whispered. D-Money was deep into his thoughts but knew he couldn't allow us to think that he was the one that paid her to set me up. He raised the pistol backup aiming it at Ciara's face. Knowing that he had to kill the Mother of his child was hard to do but he rather proved to his brothers that he was solid.

Feeling the pressure of Rizzy and I over his shoulders, there wasn't any way out of this situation but to kill her. D–Money then let off two shots into Ciara's body which knocked her dead body over onto the Warehouse floor. I can literally see the pain in D-Money's face as he dropped the pistol beside Ciara's body. I gave a couple of the young MSN Members a head nod when they rushed D–Money to restrain him. "What the fuck is going on?! What the fuck is y'all doing?! Let me the fuck go!! I will kill Y'all! D-Money yelled struggling in attempts to get loose. I then walk toward him while the MSN members held him. "You paid Big Tee to set me up to be killed, you even paid this Bitch to Extort Me Darien and you so much of a Grimy, Dirty Nigga that if I paid her you would've killed Her. You are my Brother, my Family. Why would you do this? How could you do this?!" I asked as both my eyes watered thinking about the situation. "I loved you Bro, would've done anything for you and this is how you do Me?" I asked. The Warehouse grew silent and the tension was at an all-time high between us. I looked over at Rizzy and his eyes were watered with tears as well. We both were hurt by the situation and the betrayal that was bought amongst us. We all grew up together and created the MSN Movement that was supposed to take over the world. We were all Millionaires so D-Money's reason for this was something that I needed to know.

"Jay... Rizzy... Y'all were my Brothers but both of Y'all got to Clowning and getting crazy! Especially you Jay! You started getting more money than Us and began thinking only for Yourself! Then you started thinking you are the Boss?! Not only were you thinking that but you were running shit but then you went out to California and fucking with the Bitch you knew was mine?! Fuck you Nigga! Fuck you! Fuck MSN! And Rizzy you were next too! Kill me! I ain't got shit to live for anyways!" D–Money yelled with tears falling from his face. I could tell that everything he was saying been on his mind For a very long time. D-Money was hurt and he was only hurt because his mind was messed up. How could he be mad at me for wanting more and more money? How could he be mad at me for fucking a woman that didn't even like him? How could he be mad because I was leading MSN into the legit direction? It was clear that D-money then gave up on the MSN so why should I continue to love him as a Brother? With nothing to say to his ignorance, I walked away pulling out my phone and making My way to the car. Rizzy could no longer stand to look at him because he walked away as well.

(THIRTY MINUTES LATER)

Rizzy and I sat at the table across from the Warehouse staring at our use–to be Brother when my phone rang, "What up doe? Alright let em' in." I said hanging up the phone. Rizzy gave me a look and asked me what was going on, I just shook my head telling him that I couldn't kill D–Money Myself nor could I see it. Rizzy didn't know what I had up my sleeve and when he saw the two suburbans pull in he was really confused.

. . .

D–Money, Rizzy and the rest of the MSN Members were all curious as to who this was pulling up. When Rizzy seen them hopping out of the truck he quickly clutched his pistol. It was Mario and his Hustle Fam Crew. I stood in between both Organizations making sure nobody from either side did anything stupid. Mario walked towards me sticking his hand out to give me a play. Rizzy was totally confused as to what was going on, "What up Jay, you good?" Mario asked me but looking at the D-Money with the meanest stare down. "Yeah I'm good, you?" I returned the question. Never taking his eye off of the D-money, "I'm good now doe, bets Believe that!" Mario replied with a devilish grin on his face. I walked over to one of the Little Homies and gave him orders to grab a bag from the back. Once he returned with it I then gave Rizzy a head nod signaling that it was time for us to go. "Hit me up Dog, I got you." I told him as a Rizzy, my Bodyguards and I headed towards the trucks. D-Money was far from stupid and it wasn't hard to put two into together, "Oooh, this is how you gon do it?! You couldn't kill me Yourself so you had this Pussy Nigga come do it?! You're a fucking Pussy! You a Bitch, fuck you! Fuck you Bitch!" D-Money screamed. I looked at Mario one last time, "My young Dawgs got something for y'all Boys before y'all leave too." I told him. Mario gave me a head nod and had his guys grab up D-Money. I took one more look at D-Money and I was disgusted with him. Just when we were loading up in the truck, D-Money yelled some shit that really caught my attention, "Fuck you! That's why E-Bo paid me to have you killed! Don't nobody like you! You are a Bitch and your world will be falling down soon!" D–Money screamed before the Fam went across his face with a pistol knocking him down. We then hopped in the truck and pulled away from the warehouse when I couldn't help but to think if what D-Money just screamed was true. D-Money and I wasn't on good terms so I couldn't put it past him.

Pulling away from the Warehouse the truck was in pure silence and neither Rizzy or Myself had anything to say. We cruised down

Jefferson Avenue when it was burning Rizzy to know, "Yo Bro, how did you end the beef with Hustle Fam and MSN?" He asked. I could tell that he was bugged out over what just happened, "I called Mario and met up with him privately and told him the whole deal. I told him that it was us who hit his Stash House, I told him why we did it, who turned us onto it and with him being the Hood Nigga he was, he understood. Now don't get me wrong he only understood after I offered him an offer he couldn't refuse and Would only profit off of it." I told him. Rizzy was all ears, "The offer was that we reimburse him the majority of the things we took and since he was being taxed on the bricks of Dog I offered him a 25% discount and better quality. He was with it and now he buys from Us. We are now officially the Providers of the entire state of Michigan. We do business with them now, everybody in his camp agrees to a truce like we do and all we had to do was give up that Grimy ass Nigga D-Money." I told him.

Rizzy exhaled like he just watched a good ass movie, "Damn... So do you believe what D-Money just said about he was paid by E-Bo to have you killed?" Rizzy asked. I sat there in my thoughts, "You know what, I can't even chance it or prolong it anymore. It's time that I kill him before he tries to kill me. It don't even matter if he did pay him or not, I want you to put Niggas on his head ASAP." I answered. After my own Brother betrayed me I was no longer trusting anybody but my blood cousin Rizzy, my family which was Honey, Alicia and the boys. Too much was going on in the streets, how dare I trust anybody?!?!?

Chapter Thirty-Three
Life Changing

(ONE WEEK LATER)

MEANWHILE, THE SEARCH FOR E– BO WAS STILL ONGOING AND NOT even me could find him. I had the entire MSN Crew looking for him on a daily and nobody could find him. I had MSN Members post at both his restaurants and the Titty bars he like to trick At but there wasn't any luck. I had Dancers at everyone of his Spots that was supposed to call me whenever they seen him so it wouldn't be that long before my next time seeing him. He had changed his phone numbers and everything, I was sure that he knew that I was looking for him and like the smart man he was, he was laying low and out of sight...

Rizzy and I were riding in the back of our sprint Mercedes Benz van while the Bodyguard chauffeured us taking us out of the city when I decided to call Alicia to check up on her. Our little boy was due any day now so I tried not try to not roam away too far from her just in case the time came. I dialed her number three times and wasn't getting an answer. Alicia never missed my calls as long as I known her so for her not to answer was unusual. Something wasn't right and at that moment I had a feeling that I should call and check up on Honey and the boys. I called and it was picked up on the first ring, "Jay!!!" Honey screamed into the phone before it was snatched away from her. "I told you that I put you in this game and could take you out, didn't I?" E-Bo said. My stomach literally dropped down to my balls when I heard E-Bo's voice behind Honey's phone.

How the fuck did he know where I was staying? How did he get past the security that I had patrolling the house? I heard him laughing, "I bet a million questions are running through your big ass head like how did I know where you were staying and how did I get past your weak ass security? Well, I have my ways, if it makes you feel better it wasn't easy to find you." E-Bo said.

At this point I was beyond mad but more so worried about Honey and the boys safety. Rizzy seen the look and worry on my face and kept asking me what was going on so instead of being able to tell him I just put the phone on speaker and told the Bodyguard driving to get to the cabin as fast as possible.

"Now let's get to business, I know you probably tried calling your Baby Mama Alicia but she won't be answering the phone again for anyone for now and forever. The bullet I put in her head and her stomach won't be allowing her to do anything in this lifetime again." E-Bo said to me. Hearing that the Mother of my unborn child as well as my child was killed hurt like no other pain has ever. Rizzy yelled for the Driver to get out to the cabins fast but the cabins were two hours away from the city. "Alright, alright....What is it that you want E-Bo? Do you know if you touch my family what I would do to you?! I swear you would suffer from the worst death ever known to Man!" I promised him.

"I know you're not threatening me?! I am still the Boss! I'm the one with a gun pointed to your family heads and you still want to talk shit and threaten me?! You know what, as a matter of fact..." E-Bo was saying before he walked away from the phone. I then heard

Honey screaming in the background, "Get us to the fucking cabins!!" I yelled at the driver. Hearing my Baby Honey crying was breaking my heart, "Yo Jay! Jay, listen to your Bitch scream! Boom!" Was the sound of a loud gunshot fired. I dropped the phone in disbelief as to what could've just happened. Right then I felt my heart crush, my eyes immediately watered up from the thought that Honey was hurt. With the phone still on speaker we heard E-Bo through the phone, "Jay! You did this to your fucking self! You killed Honey! Now you know I ain't playing with your ass! I want two million sent to my account or the boys will be next! I'm sending you the routing numbers and you have a hour to get it there! Oh yeah, I meant to tell Y'all. If I were y'all I wouldn't be on any main street and far away from any police possible." E-Bo said before hanging up the phone. Rizzy put his hand on my shoulder feeling the pain that I was in, he knew I was hurt and at the moment couldn't go through this by Myself. We had no idea what E-Bo meant when he said we should stay off the streets and watching out for police but when we heard the police sirens coming from behind us, I was sure we were about to find out. When we looked behind us there was at least 10 police cars and even seen the detectives Brown and Gordon. "What the fuck is going on here?" Rizzy asked.

My bodyguards pulled the van over and both Rizzy and I slid our pistols up to them since they were certified gun handlers. "Get out of the truck! Step out the van with your hands up!" The Federal Officers yelled at us as they surrounded the van. Everybody stepped out of the van and when I seen Detective Brown I asked him what was all this about. The officers began placing their cuffs on Rizzy, "What the fuck is going on?! Why are y'all putting cuffs on him?!" I was yelling. The officers stood there telling him his rights and when they told him the charges he was facing I heard them say multiple cases of murder and armed robbery of a federal vehicle. Hearing the charges I still didn't quite understand what was going on. Detective Gordon and Brown approached me trying to call me down, "Look... We were tipped by an anonymous caller that he was responsible for the robbery of that armored vehicle downtown where the officers were killed months ago. We even have somebody willing to testify on him, if I were you I would be looking for the best lawyer in the world because he will need it." Detective Brown told me as they walked away with Rizzy in cuffs. "Don't say shit bro, I'm about to send the best lawyer team down there to get you out!" I yelled at him as I watch them load him up in the squad car.

I couldn't believe what just happened, too much shit was going on and I had no idea how to handle all of this at once. In the last twenty minutes I may have lost Alicia and my unborn, possibly lost Honey and the Boys then I just lost my right hand Man, my cousin Rizzy. Shit had just gotten more real than it's ever been, it was clear that E-Bo was the anonymous tip that ratted Rizzy out for the Armor Truck Heist we done. Crazy thing was that he only told on Rizzy and even found some wack ass person to testify on him. E-Bo was one of the smartest men that I ever met, he didn't Rat on me because he wanted me to feel every bit of the pain that he sent my way an indeed I was. I needed help with all of that was going on and there was only one person that I knew would be the best help possible. I then made the call to Carmen, she would know exactly what to do.My Bodyguards and I got back inside the van and headed out to the cabin where I was living at. I jumped on the phone and had two million wired to E-Bo for the boys…...

CHAPTER-33 E-B0

(WEEKS LATER)

The search for E-Bo was still ongoing and even though I was a very impatient Man, I had no choice but to wait it out until I could catch him slipping. Today was the day that I was determined to catch him and I didn't care what had to be done to do so. My Bodyguard Team and I all got rental cars and planned a Steak-Out at his breakfast restaurant where I was sure that he still often visited. Diago and I was parked across the street in the bank's parking lot while my other Bodyguard Sadi who spoke English was parked in E-Bo's parking lot with hopes to catch him.

After hours of waiting on any sign of E-Bo Sadi radioed through the walkie talkies we had that an all Black Audi A8L was pulling in that could possibly be E-Bo. It had the darkest tint and pulled up directly in front of the restaurant. Pulling up directly In front made it easy just in case they needed to move quickly to get away. I used the binoculars to get a closer look and even though I couldn't see anything inside of the car, I had a gut feeling that it was indeed E-Bo. A Waitress stepped out of the restaurant and walked up to his passenger side to lean into the window. The many times that I been to this restaurant I never seen nobody pull up and post in front of his business and that's why I was sure that was him. I radioed over to Sadi telling him to move in closer but to do it smoothly so he isn't detected. I then told Diago to also move us in slowly toward the black Audi just in case it was E-Bo that we could attack quickly.

My mouth began to water and heart was beating at a thousand miles a minute. Just the thought of thinking that this moment had finally come had me excited and anxious to see his blood splatter all over his dashboard. Watching the Waitress hand a carry-out bag inside the car I just knew that it was E-Bo who had come to make a pick up. The Waitress he was talking to was very observant of her surroundings so when she seen Sadi's truck moving in closer to her I could tell that she was becoming suspicious, "Yo Sadi, slow down. Your moving in to aggressive, she's on to you!" I radioed him. The smile that was on her face had changed to a worried look, "BOSS She's on to us, I got to move in!" Sadi yelled through the radio. At that very moment, I told Diago to move immediately. The black Audi's brake lights turned on being the clear indicator that he was putting his car into gear to get out of there. The Audi stabbed off leaving nothing but tire smoke. "Get him Sadi! GO! Everybody

GO!" I radioed. He was on us and now all three cars were in full pursuit to get him. All of us were swerving from lane to lane hawking E-Bo's ass down through the Suburban area. I smiled yelling for Diago to get his ass while I sat in the passenger seat making sure my pistol was ready to be fired.

I looked over at the speedometer and Diago was pushing the truck and ninety miles an hour when we all finally caught up with a E-Bo. We all were right on his ass when I rolled down my window ready to shoot as soon as I got a clear shot. Up ahead, was the last light before we were back in Detroit and one thing that was for sure was that if we allowed E-Bo to get back on the Detroit side there was a big chance we wouldn't be able to catch him. In the city was to many outlets for him to get away so we needed him caught in the suburb we were currently in. That last light was a four way intersection and a Grosse Pointe police squad car was right there posted waiting for anything to happen. Diago was bumping the truck against E-Bo's bumper trying to get him to spin out of control but it wasn't happening. "Don't let him get away Diego!" I yelled. I then radioed over to Sadi who was right behind beside us telling him that when we got to that light that crossed over to Detroit to not stop and we all running through it. Sadi copied my order and that was the plan. I didn't care if the police was a witness to E-Bo's murder, I just needed him dead or caught.

All three of our trucks were swerving through traffic but even E-Bo was having a hard time trying to maneuver. There were two cars ahead of us that was preventing us from staying on E-Bo's ass, "Move! Move! Move! Slow ass Bitch!" I yelled damn near hanging out the window at the car in front of us. I was pissed what was just a close catch was now slipping away from us. I still refused to let E-Bo get away from me and I was determined to make the day that he paid for what he done to my family. The light then turned green which was the greatest advantage for us because now he was blocked in. He had two cars in front of him that was blocking him from running the red light. All three of my crews cars were two and three cars away from E-Bo and I couldn't stand it. "Fuck this!" I said stepping out the truck determined for my street justice. I began jogging towards E-Bo's car when all of a sudden he started ramming the cars in front of him forcing them into the upcoming traffic. Cars began crashing and causing some big accidents but E-Bo made Hisself an out soon as there was a brief clear opportunity He stabbed off into Detroit getting away from us. I stood in the middle of the street with pistol in my hand livid that I didn't make it to him. Diago pulled up so I could hop in, E-Bo had slipped away this time but I promise he won't get away again.

Chapter Thirty-Four
Pulling it together

(TWO HOURS LATER)

AFTER I WIRED THE $2 MILLION TO E-BO, I THANKED GOD THAT HE held his word and didn't touch them. When I finally made it to the cabin he had the boys tied up in the bedroom with the door close but the most hurting part was that Honey was truly dead. He left her body in the bathtub and moving her was so hard to do that I couldn't, instead Diago and the rest of the bodyguards had to do it for me. E-Bo went on a killing spree killing my Security Detail and both of the most important women in my life. For that he was going to pay for it to the max. I asked the boys What did they see and they said that they didn't see anything, but just heard the gunshots going off. Lil K told me that he knew his mother was killed and surprisingly he was handling it well. Maybe because he didn't know just how real the situation of losing somebody close to him was.

My Bodyguards and I took the boys to a hotel because staying at the cabin would be too hard to do, knowing that we lost somebody so important to us there. I already had so much to do and one of the things I did first was called the Lawyer Team that MSN had on thePayroll. The lawyers that we had were the best in Detroit, Michigan but with the situation that he was in we needed the best in the world. I called an high profile Jewish lawyer that I was recommended to before so they could team up with the lawyer team I already had and off top I knew I was going to be charged an arm and a leg. The Jewish lawyer told me that he needed 50,000 just to retain him but for my family there was no limit. I tried posting a bail for him but when there is a murder charge involved there isn't a bail. I was stressed out and badly needed some rest. Things were about to start adding up and after wiring that 2 million to a E-Bo, I would be lying if I said I didn't feel it. Then I had all types of upcoming events that I would be responsible to pay for so I had to go and make/pick up every dollar owed to MSN, even D-Money's Money.

(TWO WEEKS LATER)
   The boys and I were still living in a hotel and after burying Alicia and Honey, I was at my lowest point in life, all I was doing was laying up in the hotel chillin with the boys, from time to time I would make calls to make sure the Mainstrip's was doing okay. I would make calls to all the MSN captains we had in control to make sure things were good but I wasn't my old self. I was looking rough and not even the same clean cut nigga I would was known to be. The 2 million that I had sent E-Bo was a nice hit but with all the income MSN had coming in I was still straight and was still working with a few hundred thousand. It had been two weeks since Rizzy had been picked up and the lawyer tab had already been shot up to a hundred thousand and fifty thousand dollars. Fighting all them murder charges was what was costing the most. Rizzy called me and gave me the codes of his safe in case I needed some extra money, but how I was feeling I never wanted to leave the hotel.....
   Two knocks on the door snapped me out of the zone of watching the boys play their video game. Like every time that I answered the door the Bodyguard Diago got up and followed behind me. When I opened the door I was shocked to see who was standing in front of me, "Hi Papi? Whew. . . You looking rough," Carmen told me as she stepped closer to me placing a kiss on my cheeks and giving me a big, warm hug. Hugging her was so

comforting and actually made me feel better than I had in weeks. I never would've thought a simple hug could make me feel so good but Carmen has an affect on people.

Carmen was looking good as usual but I was sure her visit was deeper than what she made it to appear. I had the bodyguards that was assigned to me to stay in the room with the boys while Carmen and I went down to the hotel's restaurant to talk. When we stepped outside the room. Carmen had more bodyguards patrolling the room than usual. I guess after hearing about all of the shit I was in she made sure she was prepared for anything.

We took a seat at the bar when the waitress came and asked if we were ready to order, Carmen told her to just bring us a bottle of 1800 tequila and that would be it for the time being. Diago Carmen's bodyguard had updated her on everything going on so I knew she had a million of questions. The Waitress had returned with the 1800 and before discussing anything we both had to take some shots. In these past two weeks, alcohol had become my best friend, "Sooo, you wanna' talk about it Papi?" Carmen asked me. I couldn't even look at Carmen in her eyes I was so down and embarrassed with Myself, "Ain't nothin' really to talk about. Shid, it is what it is, ya know?" I said nonchalantly. "What do you mean it is what it is. No, it's not what it is. It's whatever you make it. Now you have my deepest sympathy, you do but you need to get your stuff together and get back on the right track. So what are you going to do now?" Carmen asked. I didn't understand what she really meant. "I'm going to find him and kill him," I responded. Carmen threw another shot back of the 1800. "What's understood don't have to be explained. I'm going to make a call and find out where this Vato E-Bo is at and in the meantime I want you to get back on your hustle shit! Get back the hustler I knew and fell in love with. We all know that beefing and getting money at the same time is damn near impossible but I need you to get back in the streets and get your money Babe. Let these City Vato's know that you're still out here and can't be stopped! Keep flooding the streets and discipline anybody that gets in your way. If the streets see that you're not the same MSN Jay you once were, they would eat you alive and your street cred will be dead and E-Bo's live. Stay focused okay love?" Carmen motivated me.

Carmen slid over to me an wrapped her arm up and under mines leaning in and kissing me on the cheek , "You took a big loss but you also took a big gain, you have two little boys upstairs that love and need you, and what they don't need is to see any softness." Carmen spoke as . I sat there taking another shot of the 1800 and was actually amped up and motivated from her encouraging words. I never take advice from a woman but Carmen wasn't just a regular woman. She was a BOSS that been down the same similar row before. I turned to her and gave her a big, tight hug thanking her for everything. She told me that it was nothing. If the shoe was on the other foot she knew I would be there for her. "Ummm another thing. . . I want you and the boys to go and pack up y'all things and come back to California with me until we find that fucker E-Bo. Once we catch him, which won't take long long then y'all could move back if y'all want to." Carmen told me. Talking to Carmen was much needed and appreciated, but I was far from a Bitch and just like she just said, I needed to hit the streets and show them that I was still here getting money and running the streets. I refuse to let anybody think they ran me out of Detroit.

"I agreed with everything that you said but, like you just said. . .I have to hit them streets and show them that I still run shit and MSN is still here. I appreciate your help in finding him but I won't go anywhere until I catch him and kill him!" I told her. Carmen smiled, "Okay, I understand totally. I kinda knew that you would say that. I just wanted to hear it. Now I know you're on point and ready to get back out there." Carmen said nodding her head like she was impressed with my response. We both downed another shot realizing that we drank the whole damn bottle. I know that you're not going to like this but. . .just until we find that E-Bo fucker I'm assigning six more bodyguards to stay by you and your boys side wherever y'all go. Only two of the six speak English, so you have to be patient with them. Sadi right here and OC is right there." Carmen told me. Just when I was about to respond about all of this security she kept putting around me, she stopped me. "Before you say anything. Let me remind you, I'm not only putting these body-guards around you because we have a lot of business together but because I honestly love you and care about your well-being. That's all." Carmen told me. I sat back and relaxed, It felt good to know that she cared for me the way she did. You just have to always have your way don't you?" I asked rhetorically. Carmen just laughed and nodded her head, knowing that I was right. . . .

Chapter Thirty-Five
Flooding the Block

(ONE WEEK LATER)

CARMEN HAD ALREADY RETURNED TO BACK TO CALIFORNIA AND WITH all of the bodyguards she had left me, we were riding around in three suburban trucks that were bulletproof and tinted with a 5% shade making it unable for anybody to see from the outside. After being shot up and people dying, all over the place I was more cautious than ever. I had taken Carmen's advice and decided to hit the streets harder than ever providing them with the best drugs that the city has ever seen.

I called my young Dawg Gutta and Rizzy's young Dawg J.T who were not only our Protégé's but the Captains we left in charge of the MSN organization. Gutta and J.T were friends since they were kids and they both reminded Rizzy and I of Ourselves when we were younger. They both had the hustle and ambition to be successful in this street life and by any means, had the plans to do it. Rizzy and I met them at the beginning of the MSN movement when they were at a liquor store slanging crack rocks and nickel bags of weed. They ran not only the block they were on, but the entire neighborhood. When we seen that we have to add them to our team, and they've been with MSN since then. .

When I called them so I can meet up with them, they told me to meet them off of Jefferson at the Trap house they had their Workers slanging almost everything out there. It had been so long since the last time I pulled up at a Trap-house it made me laugh when I seen that shit didn't change. Crackheads feigning, Weed Smokers need their weed and the Strippers and Freak Bitches needed their e-pills and cocaine. Gutta pulled up at the same time in his all white Magnum. Seeing that he had one of the same cars that I had when I thought I was getting money was also funny.

My Bodyguards stepped out of the surrounding trucks and came over to open the truck door for Gutta to get in with me. Gutta hopped in like a spitting image of me back in the day. He was still so hood that he wore the average Detroit Doughboy gear that we were known to wear. He wore his Cartier Frames on his face, a Rolex on his wrist, and Timberland boots on his feet. Gutta hopped in giving me a play, "Whasup Big Homie, good to see you. It's been a long time since I got you to come down here." Gutta said with a smile on his face happy to see me. "Yea, I'm good. . .I know, it's been a minute since I been down this deep into the hood. I see you doing yo' thang doe with the all white Magnum and all. I had one just like it." I told him admiring his style in cars. "Awww Man, If it wasn't for you fuckin' wit' me how you do I wouldn't have none this shit that I have. I owe it to you." Gutta told me as he reached in his pockets. He pulled out rubber band stacks of money and handed it to me, "That's a hundred thousand right there. That's from the last package was dropped off on me." He told me. I looked at the band of money and looked back to him. "Damn you riding around wit' a hundred bands on you? You trippin, You know Niggas be hating out here so you don't need to give them any reason for them to try you, feel me?" I told him. Gutta reached under his shirt and pulled out his 9mm from his waist. When he did that my bodyguards quickly drew their pistols and directly aiming them at Gutta.

"Whoa! Whoa! Whoa! Hold up!" I held my hands up toward my Bodyguards. Gutta didn't know what the hell was going on and with the guns pointed at his face so he knew not to move. "Gutta, give me your gun, Give it to me for a few minutes." I told him. Gutta handed it to me and I handed it over to the bodyguard that was sitting in the front seat, "Bueno Si Manatobo, No!" He said. Gutta and I looked at each other and I could tell that he was mad but also confused, "Don't trip Bro, you'll get yo' gun back when you get out. They are just super cautious for my safety and doing their jobs, that's all." I told him. Gutta exhaled. "Damn, I was just telling you that I'm strapped for any stupid Nigga that want to try their luck so I wasn't worried about shit. And I knew that I was bout' to meet up with you so that's why I had all that money on me. I usually don't carry that much money on me." Gutta replied.

"Cuma el Nacho Bueino." said the bodyguard sitting in the front seat. I looked behind us and seen a Cranberry Charger pulling up behind the bodyguards truck that was behind us.

It was J.T, he hopped out of his car and was headed up the sidewalk that led to the Trap-house when Gutta rolled down the trucks window and yelled for J.T's attention telling him to come and hop in with Us. My bodyguard stepped out of the passenger side to give him a seat while he stood guard outside. Before letting J.T in he patted him down and removed his pistol that he had on his waist. When J,T got in I told him that he would get his gun back when we both get out.

With the blunt in rotation, J.T Fat Black Ass turned around giving the both of us a Play. "Whasup Jay?! Long time since I seen you down this way, you good Fam?" He asked. "Yea, I'm good. Yea I know it's been a minute since I been down here, y'all know a Nigga been busy doe'. I see y'all still doing y'all thang and holding the hood down doe', that's whasup." I said admiring his little MSN chain that Rizzy gave him. "C'mon Man, if it wasn't for you and Rizzy we wouldn't have this hood like we got it now. How is that

Nigga Rizzy by the way? I'm pose to go up there and visit that Nigga this weekend?" J.T asked. "Aww Man, you know that Nigga is in there maintaining and holding this MSN shit down to the fullest. I'm bout' to get him up out of here and get them hoe ass charges off of him soon." I told them as I hit the blunt that they passed back around to me.

"Oh yeah, before I forget. Here's the fifty thousand I owed Rizzy and here is an extra twenty thousand from me. I still got some Work left so I'll give you the rest then." J.T said handing me a total of seventy thousand dollars the long way. It felt good to know that both Rizzy and I had picked the right guys for the MSN Captain position. Neither one of them were even 18 years old yet and they were already on the Street Road To Stardom. I took the money, "fasho Fasho. . . So look, another reason why I came down here personally is because I wanted to drop this Work off to y'all and assure y'all that it ain't no paper shortage, ya feel me? I know the streets probably think that with all the shit that's been happening that MSN had fell but I'm here to tell y'all that we strong as ever!" I told them before hopping out of the truck and telling them to follow me.

We all walked to the bodyguards truck where I had them all stashed.I pulled out a big ass package that held sixty pounds a weed and handed it over to the both of them. I reached in the backseat of the Truck and handed them two duffle bags that held bricks of Cocaine, Heroin and over a thousand E-Pills.the street value for everything that I just given them ranged from anywhere between 200-500 thousand dollars. Gutta and J.T had the hood on lock so I knew they were perfectly capable of selling all of the stuff I was given them in the next couple of weeks, if that.

They both carried all of the packages inside of their Trap-house and when they came back outside they both gave me plays, "Good looking Jay, forreal. We bout' to go in there and take care of all that shit. We should be done in about four days to a week. Yo, be smooth out her big Bro. If you need any help what so ever just give us a call and And we riding wit' you." Gutta told me being as sincere as he could be. "Fasho then, I like to hear that. I should be straight wit' these guys wit' me but if I need y'all I fasho would let y'all know." I told them. My bodyguards then handed them both of their pistols and we went separate ways......

Chapter Thirty-Six
Wayne County Jail

(THREE MONTHS LATER, EARLY DECEMBER)

RIZZY HAD BEEN IN JAIL FOR MONTHS NOW AND EVEN THOUGH IT WAS freezing cold outside I wasn't going to let the Detroit weather stop me from visiting him. Every other Thursday I would go and visit him to make sure he knew he had me in his corner no matter what. Rizzy wasn't only my Cousin but he was the closest thing I had to a Brother, my Best friend and Right Hand man that I was missing out here in these streets with me like crazy. I stay on all of his lawyers asses making sure they were on their jobs and trying to get him out of there but they would tell me all the time, They were going to do the best they can do but cases such as these would take a lot of time.
. .

    I ran inside of the Wayne County Jail in attempts to dodge the freezing cold weather and the flowing snow that was falling from the sky. There was a bench sitting from one side of the wall all the way down to the other side where I seen a woman laughing at me. This particular female I would often see here when she would be visiting one of her Male friend who I assume was her Man. This Woman was here every other Thursday and didn't miss a beat. She was a short brown-skinned cutie that was very attractive. I couldn't really tell how good her body looked because she always wore a coat that would cover her but from what I could tell she had a little ass and even a little gut. Me being the Hustling Nigga that I was I just couldn't allow myself to holler at her in this particular place. She was either visiting a boyfriend or a baby daddy and if I was in their situation I wouldn't want anybody trying to holler at my girl when she came to visit me so I just left that thought to remain only that.

The wait to visit your people was a long wait so I sat right beside the attractive Woman who was laughing at Me. This Woman and I had never spoke before but I was curious to know just exactly what it was that she was laughing at so I asked her with a smile. It seemed that me asking her that question made her burst out laughing even harder, "I'm sorry for laughing but. . .But, Boy you know its cold as hell outside and you only have on a vest? Where is your coat?" She asked. I looked down at my vest and chuckled lightly as well, "Well, I do have a coat but I just never wear it because I'm always in a heated car." I answered. She then turned toward me and looked me up and down. "Ohhh, excuse me Mr. Heated Car, I see you. . .big shiny watch, glasses and chain." She told me being Sarcastic. I could tell that I was dealing with somebody that was argumentative so I asked her what was her name. She looked me up and down again, "My name is Shanice, yours?" I looked her up and down as she did me, "I'm Jay." I answered. recognizing my being sarcastic we both laughed.

"So, if you don't mind me asking..Who are you visiting?" I asked her making small conversation. Her eyes rolled before answering, "I don't mind you asking, I'm visiting my stupid Child's Father. You?" She answered and returned the question. I exhaled, "I'm visiting my Cousin who is as close as my Brother. So why your Baby Daddy gotta be all of that doe'? He must not be that stupid since you come and visit him every other week." I said to her. "NEXT TWO PEOPLE!" The County Guard yelled. There was still two more people in front of us, "yes I do love him but he's just stupid! Stupid for killing somebody and not thinking about his family first."

Shanice responded. I nodded my head feeling for her. "Ohhh, y'all have a family and everything huh?" I asked. She opened her coat up, "I'm six months pregnant." She told me, My eyes grew big, "WOW, I didn't know you were pregnant. I just thought. . ." I was saying then I caught myself before saying something mean. She knew exactly what I was about to say, "Oh what? You thought I was just this fat from eating?" She asked. I was confused on what to say until she burst out laughing from fucking with me. "It's okay, calm down and relax. I was just messing with you." She said making the both of us laugh.

"So what is your Cousin in here for, something as stupid as my Child's Father?" Shanice asked. "Awhole lot of bullshit that I'm actually trying to get these blood sucking Lawyers to get him off of but it seems like every time I turn around that they are asking for more money." I answered. "Well at least y'all have money for a Lawyer instead of having to accept a Court Appointed one like we have too." Carmen replied.

"NEXT TWO PEOPLE!" The Guard yelled. Shanice and I were up next and I could see the discouraging look on her face from talking about her and her Mans situation. "Hey, it's gon' be okay. He's lucky to have a good woman like you that is taking the time out of your day to come and visit him. I'm sure he's going to be happy to see you no matter what y'all are going through. That's real encouraging on your part and the City need more women like you." I told her trying to be encouraging. She smiled which was a clear indication of what I just told her made her feel better. "You and your Cousin must be really close as Brothers because you come visit him a lot too. I don't see too many guys coming to visit their family or friends." Shanice told me. I smiled, "Yeah, that's my Dawg. I gotta hold him down." I replied. "NEXT TWO PEOPLE!" The Guard yelled. Shanice and I both stood up, "Here we go again." I said as we followed the guard to the elevators.

We made it up to the visiting floor and one thing I hated about coming to visit my Cousin was that I had to stand up and talk to him through a glass that only allowed a face to be seen. I also hated how it takes so long before who I'm visiting makes it to the window. Wayne County Jail was the slums and might as well already been a prison.

"TO SEE INMATE HARVEY STAND AT WINDOW SEVEN. , ,TO SEE INMATE DAVIS STAND AT WINDOW SIX. THE VISITS ARE ONLY THIRTY MINUTES LONG, BEGINNING NOW. ." The Guard announced and telling both Shanice and I what windows to stand at. As we both stood there, waiting on our people to arrive Shanice asked me if it was just her but do I have bubble guts during every visit? I told her that she was not the only one and that I had them at that very moment. It was just something about seeing my Cousin behind bars that didn't sit right with me. This place wasn't for him and it was totally out of his element. Jail and prison was for Niggas that made some dumb mistakes out there, robbing liquor stores and taking old lady purses. Rizzy was a Multi-millionaire. He had no business being locked up and I had to get my family out of there. Just months ago, Rizzy and I were blowing money and fucking some of the baddest bitches and now we were talking behind the glass of a jail visiting window. I know if I was sick to be visiting him in jail that he was sick to be getting visits in jail.

Shanice Baby Daddy arrived at her window first and the first thing I heard him do was go off on her, "Damn Bitch why you didn't send me that money yet?! I'm in dis' Bitch hungry as shit and can't even go to the Commissary because you out here bullshitin!." He yelled at her. Embarrassed from how he was speaking to her she tried talking in a low tone trying to explain that she didn't have the money to send him at the time. Rizzy finally arrived to the window, "Whasup Cuzo?! Whats good Boy?!" He asked me in an excited tone happy to see me as he always was.

I heard him speaking to me but I was still tripping on how Shanice Man was talking to her directly beside Me. Rizzy seen that

I was distracted when he called my name snapping me out of the daze that I was in. "Oh shit, my fault Cuzo I'm tripping on that Clown next to you." I said referring to Shanice Baby Daddy. Rizzy looked who was besides him and sarcastically chuckled at him, "Yeah that Nigga is most definitely a Clown. . .Anyways, what's good Fam? Tell me something good, I miss yo' Big Head Ass Dawg!" Rizzy told me like he don't call and talk to me damn near everyday. "Shit's the same ole' same ole' out here Fam. All I do is work the Streets and watch over the boys. I just recently pulled down on the protégé's and they doing good down there. We made some good picks recruiting them Niggas." I told him. Rizzy just smiled, "yea that's whasup Man, I'm glad we got them hustling ass niggas too. They good peoples." Rizzy said. I nodded my head, "yes we did. They just like us too. That nigga G pulled up in the same color Magnum I had when we first started and that nigga J.T pulled up in a cranberry charger just like the one you had back in the day." I added. While Rizzy and I were kicking it about some of every-thing, I couldn't help but to over hear Shanice and her Baby Daddy arguing. "Why do you keep hollering at me? You not happy to see me?!" Shanice asked him. He snapped back, "Yes, but I gotta' get outta' here Shanice! You just don't know, This shit is crazy and I can't do it! Did you holler at that Lawyer like I asked you too?" He asked her. Shanice looked down to the floor like she was embar-rassed to answer him, "I talked to him but he wants fifty thousand just to be retained and you know that we don't have that. I been working at getting it though by working extra hours and in February when I get my taxes I know that I could get it." Shanice was saying before her Baby Daddy started back yelling at her. "I'm not trying to hear that shit! I need that fuckin' money and I need it now! Talk to yo Mama bout putting her house up or something and I promise I would pay her back!" He told his Woman.

For the second time Rizzy snapped me out of their business. "Yo' Cuzo, How much did you pay for my Lawyer again?" He asked me being louder than what we were normally speaking. I just knew that I told him before, "Ummm, I done already gave them Mutherfucka's close to one hundred and seventy thousand dollars already." I answered. When I answered him I noticed thar Rizzy would look over to Shanice's Baby Daddy to see if he heard it. I looked over at Shanice and she was already looking at me, I guess hearing the amount that I paid the Lawyer had caught her attention.

"So Cuzo, is that a new MSN chain? How much that one run you for?" Rizzy asked me. I laughed because I knew exactly what he was doing but at the same time this type of shit excited him. He wanted Shanice's Baby Daddy to hear how we were doing it and I childishly played along. "Oh this? I only paid sixty thousand for this. I got you one too. When you beat this case I'm giving it to you soon as you are released." I answered him. "What the fuck you lookin' at that Hoe Nigga for?!" Shanice Baby Daddy yelled at her. I looked over at her when she tried to turn her head. She jumped scared when she heard him yell at her, "What?! You wanna fuck that Nigga or something?! Go and fuck that Bitch Ass Nigga then!" He yelled at her.

Rizzy and I gave each other a crazy ass look, he shook his head and me knowing him like I did I knew that he was going to do something crazy. "Ummm, yeah so you don't even gotta' come see me for the next visit Bro. Be smooth out there and I love you Fam." Rizzy told me as he began pulling up his pants and getting ready to walk away from the window. I was totally confused in what it was Rizzy was about to do but I knew it wasn't going to be good. "Bro, what the fuck you mean? What the fuck you bout' to do?!" I yelled through the window but it was already to late. Rizzy done walked over to Shanice's Baby Daddy and without hesitation he went dead in his shit throwing some of the hardest punches to his face until he got him on the ground and continued the beating on him. "No! No!" Shanice yelled not wanting to see her unborn child's father getting beaten. The County's sirens began going off and Guards came from everywhere to break it up.

It took four guards to stop Rizzy from beating Shanice's Baby Daddy face in. "ALL VISITORS, VISITS ARE OVER AND REPORT TO THE ELEVATORS IMMEDIATELY!" A man on the intercom announced. A guard yelled at us while holding the elevator door opened for Us to leave the visiting room. Both Shanice and I were demanded to get on the elevator and while we were on our way back down to the main floor I couldn't help but to see her wipe the tears from her eyes. When we got off the elevator she sped off heading toward the Wayne County's Exit when I caught up with her outside in the freezing cold. "Shanice! Im. . Im sorry for what just happened up there. I didn't. . .Shanice cut me off, "You don't need to apologize Jay, Im just tired of all of this shit! He actually deserved it how he talks to me!" Shanice said sniffling from the cold weather and the tears that she shedded.

Four of my Bodyguards who were already standing outside waiting had approached me, "Who are these guys?" Shanice asked looking at all of them. I looked back at them then back to her, "These are all of my Security Detail. . .Again, I want to apologize for. . ." I was saying until she cut me off again, "Again Im telling you that you don't need to apologize, seriously. He's stupid and deserved it!" Shanice told me and began started laughing. Seeing her laugh made me laugh too, She was sick of her Nigga shit so seeing him get his ass whooped made her feel good inside. "So you must be a pretty important person since you have a Security Detail and all huh?" She asked. The Bodyguards trucks pulled up in front of the County with my Benz in the middle of them. "Nawl I wouldn't say all of that, these guys just don't want to see me get hurt that's all." I responded. She nodded her head, "And Im guessing It takes two trucks of Security to do that as well?" Shanice asked. I looked over, "Umm.....kinda, that's just their rides and mines is in the middle. I like to drive Myself and they like to follow me." I told her.

Shanice gave me a look like she knew things were deeper than I was making them seem but there was no need for me to tell her my living situations since I didn't know her. Even though I didn't think hollering at somebody girl at a place such as this was the "real" thing to do, but being that her Baby Daddy was such as Sucker Ass Nigga I threw all them rules out of the door and now I figured she was fair game. "Umm Shanice, I wouldn't normally do this but I was just wondering if I could call you sometime, maybe take you ouy to eat or something?" I asked. Shanice smiled showing me her pretty dimples, "Even with a big ole' belly like this you want to call me and take me out?" She asked me like she was surprised. I nodded my head answering yes, "I am most definitely flattered, you seem like a nice guy and all too but. . .Anywhere but here I would consider giving you my number. I know that my Baby Daddy is a piece of shit but I cant be totally disrespectful to him even though he is to me. Ya know?" Shanice explained. Totally understanding where she was coming from I dropped my head looking down at the ground, "I tell you what though, if I were to bump into you anywhere else but here I would give it to you." Shanice told me with a smile on her face. My head lifted, "Aight bet, Im gon hold you to that." I told her as I smiled back. "Nice to meet you Shanice." I Said to Her. "Nice to meet you as well Jay with Security Detail." She said back to me. The fact that she still respected her Man even when he didn't respect her was a major turn on to me and I could tell that she knew the meaning of what being loyal to her Man no matter what. Shanice and I both went our different ways, I was sure I would see her again soon. . . . .

Chapter Thirty-Seven
Its Mine, I Spend It!

(MONTHS LATER)

BUSINESS WAS DOING GOOD AND THINGS WERE FINALLY BACK ON THE right track financially. Gutta and J.T. were calling every two days for more work and to pay me my money. Every time I pulled up on their block their Trap-house was doing numbers. The MSN money was flowing and everybody on the team was eating. Gutta and J.T bossed up so much that they both moved out of the hood into the suburbs, they even bought Themselves new cars and more jewelry. Watching how Gutta and JT were splurging letting it be known that they were getting money, I figured it was only right for me to go on a shopping spree Myself.

It's been along time since I had been on a shopping spree and after all of the things I've been through lately I most definitely deserved one. The first place I wanted to go was straight to a car dealership and get whatever the hottest car or truck that was out. My bodyguards Diago, Sadi and Oc were all behind me as we walked into a Rolls-Royce dealership to see what they had. "How are you fine gentlemen doing today? My name is Finch, is there anything that you guys may be needing help with today?" The car Salesman asked approaching us introducing Himself. I circled around an all black Phantom admiring all of its features, "In fact there is something that I would be needing your assistance on today. What is the newest model of car you have in this dealership?" I asked. Finch smiled, "Follow me to the back and I will gladly show you." He told Us as he led.

We followed Finch all the way to the back of the building into a disclosed area where my mouth dropped looking at an all white car that was a better version of the Phantom that was in the lobby. "This is the latest model they recently just came out, it's similar to a Phantom but it is indeed not a Phantom at all. This is the Ghost, Rolls Royce newest addition to the family." Finch said proudly. I circled around it and was already in love with it. This Ghost with something that I never seen on the street and I knew that the moment I dropped this I would shut the streets down. I desperately needed this car and could care less whatever the price was. "But. . ." Finch froze, "Its a ninety day wait approval for it." He told me. I looked over at the Bodyguards with a smirk then back to Finch, he had no idea that I waited for nothing. "Y'all think Carmen got this yet?" I asked them with a competitive grin on my face. They all grinned, "Pretty sure she does Boss." They answered me. I opened the back door to it and took a seat while rubbing on the leather seats, "Umm Sadi, I need you to call our Guy so we could get this bullet-proofed immediately. Have him put the darkest tint in all of the windows as well, I want peanut butter seats and a camera put into the license plate so I can see any car coming from behind me." I told my Bodyguard. Finch stood there listening through all of the orders I was placing. "Did you hear me? I said that there is a ninety day wait-approval before you could get this car out of the building." He repeated. I lifted my head looking Finch into his face and asked him how much. Finch paused. "This car being that it isn't supposed to be released to the public for another year, it cost four hundred and twenty five thousand dollars, without taxes." He answered. I shook my head, "No, no, no. . .The price of the car doesn't matter. What I want to know is how much would it cost me to get passed the ninety day wait-approval?" I asked. Finch then looked around like there was somebody else in this room besides us, "With all of the paperwork I would have to do, getting it registered an entire year early, let me see. . .It would cost you close to five hundred and forty-five thousand dollars to get it out of here." Finch told me. I stepped out of the backseat of the Ghost and gave Oc a head nod. He nodded back and walked out of the disclosed room.

A few minutes later Oc walked back into the dealership with a Louis Vuitton suitcase filled with cash handing it to Finch. When Finch opened it up his eyes grew big and wide shocked by all of the money he was looking at. I was sure that he had never seen this much money in cash in his entire life. "I'll go and get started on the paperwork. Oh, umm who's name am I putting this car under?" He asked. I looked back at the bodyguards then back to Finch telling him to put it under Diago's name. With a car this expensive I didn't need any reason for the Feds to investigate so I put it in Diago's name since he wasn't from America anyway.

Oc stayed at the dealership with the car until our car custom designer arrived to take the car with him so he could do all that was needed. Meanwhile the rest of us went to Somerset Mall, I was by far done with my shopping spree and now it was time to start on my clothes. We all went inside the mall and tore damn near every store up there we went inside. I went inside a Footlocker spending over twelve thousand dollars on me and my boys, I went to a Nordstrom's spending over ten thousand dollars on me and my boys, spent over twelve thousand dollars at the Gucci store, six thousand dollars at the Louis Vuitton store, two thousand dollars at the Neiman Marcus store, nine thousand dollars at the Cartier store and a thousand dollars at the Polo store. When I got home I sat in my office documenting what I had spent for the day and it all came up to a little over fifty-thousand dollars. Then to get my Ghost bulletproofed and customed the way I wanted, I was sure that it would cost me close to a million dollars. It felt good to go and treat the boys and I. . .

Chapter Thirty-Eight
Court

I HAD RIZZY'S LAWYERS KEEP POSTPONING HIS COURT DATES WHILE I had my people looking for the witness that E-Bo paid to testify against him but she was on a 24/7 watch in protective custody. She couldn't be touched and the judge had enough of procrastinating. He was ready to get this high profile case moving and finished. We had postponed his court dates four months longer than the minimum which was nine months.

Rizzy walked into the court room wearing the three-piece suit that I had just got him and was sharpe as a knife. He had on some black reading glasses that made him look like a sophisticated intelligent black man that was ready to fight for his freedom.

Before the court room was ready his lawyers had just came from talking to the prosecutors and they told Rizzy he could either cop out to eight year plea or fight it in trial and risk going to jail for the rest of his life. Rizzy turned to me and without hesitation told me that he was going to accept it. I was a bit disappointed because I felt that he had a good chance at beating all of his charges and not having to do any time but his lawyers came to me and explained that the Plea agreement was the best choice for him. They told me that a second Witness had come from out of the blue and it was the best just to not risk it with all the Jurors being white anyway. With all the charges that was filled against him he most definitely would have been facing 25 years or better if found guilty.

Rizzy turned back to me again and just shrugged his shoulders knowing that this was the best decision for him. I was livid, E-Bo wanted to make sure that he was found guilty so bad that he hired a second person to testify against my Cousin, that was crazy. Being that Rizzy just took the plea deal there was no need for a big court session so the judge told Rizzy to step to the front of the court room and sign the papers that said he agreed to the terms. Before they took Rizzy back to the back of the court room he turned to look at me, "Hold it down Fam! Hold it down out there! MSN Nigga foe' life!" He yelled with a smile on his face. Even though I was feeling down, hearing Rizzy scream MSN lifted my spirits back up. "MSN foe' life Fam! I got you! Don't worry about Shit!" I yelled back as he was being escorted out.

Walking out of the Courthouse I exhaled knowing that I was going to miss my Cousin by my side. I was truly Alone now and had to run MSN all by Myself. Right then I made a promise to Myself that I would hold our name, our business and our hustle down and by the time he came home the MSN Movement will be the biggest movement worldwide......

Chapter Thirty-Nine
Been a Long Time

LEAVING THE COURTHOUSE I BADLY NEEDED A STRONG DRINK SO I decided to hit one of my favorite restaurants which was Southern Fires. Besides the drinks that they served, they also had some of the best soul food in Detroit. Now that Rizzy was gone I had to make the adjustments to make sure I kept all three hustles going on as well as our legit franchise of Mainstrip's going good. With Carmen being the primary source for the Work, I wasn't going to be able to pick up the shipments and go out there to wire her the money in person. I was going to need a more convenient Plug that I didn't have to travel far to buy from. The question was who would I buy from????

I ordered Myself a 16oz Porterhouse steak that was well done and came with the baked potatoes and macaroni and cheese. I had a sprite to wash it all down with and I had shots of Patron to wash the drink down with. The Waitress came over to my table and asked me if there was anything else that she could get for me, before I had a chance to answer Her, a familiar voice spoke from behind me, "Can I have what he is having please? It looks delicious." I turned around to look who it was that was ordering the same thing I was and I couldn't believe who it was. "Well, well, well... how are you Mr. Jay with the Security Detail?" Shanice asked with a smile on her face standing over me. I looked her up and down and couldn't believe just how good she was looking. The last time I saw her she was pregnant and her Baby Daddy just got his ass whipped by Rizzy "Wow! Shanice? I am fine and how about your self?" I answered her question with a question. She nodded her head "I'm doing fine, I'm fine. I hate to interrupt but is it OK if I join you?" She asked. I was unable to take my eyes off of her and insisted that she join me. Shanice looked amazing and totally different than she did last time I seen her at the County.

Shanice sat across from Me at my table and for the first time in a long time I didn't know what to say to a Woman. "So when I pulled up outside and seen three black trucks with what looked like bodyguards posting ,I asked Myself... who could it be that has bodyguards and only people that I knew that had bodyguards were the President and You. I know the President wasn't here so when I came in and saw you over here in by Yourself with that Guy standing right there I just knew it was you. It's been along time since I've seen you, how are you? How is your Cousin that you used to visit all the time?" Shanice asked "Wow, that is crazy that you remembered that, that was a nice minute ago. Ummmm Yeah, I'm doing good and my Cousin who I used to visit, well I just left his last court date. He was sentenced to eight years today." I answered her. "That's crazy because I just left my child's father court date today too he was sentenced to life without parole so. Yeah, that's just what it is." Shanice said.

After talking about the court dates that we just left from Shanice and I sat there eating and enjoying each other's company. We sat there talking about everything like we were the best of friends that just been reconnected. She told me that Her and her Baby Daddy were finally over and been over since the fight he had with my Cousin. She told me that she was living the single life and just enjoying her life with just her child and Herself. I commended her for that and told her leaving that lame was a good decision for her and her child. When she asked about me I told her that I was a single father as well. And enjoyed the single life too. When we both told the other that we were single it seemed like the flirting between us was at a all-time high and became nonstop. I reminded her that she told Me that any place but the County she will give me her number and she told me she remembered so that's why she came over and decided to join me for lunch. Shanice wasn't only looking good by her appearance but I can tell from the way she carried Herself that she was in a better position than she was months ago. Shanice was a stress-free soul now and being as beautiful as she was she deserved it.

Shanice looked at her watch "Aww man, I'm sitting here with you having such a good time that I forgot that I had to get to the grocery store before they close so I could pick up all the Fourth of July food. Speaking of, I'm having a small Get Together with just a few friends and family at my house and if you're not doing anything you're more than welcome.I would love to meet your boys and introduce them to my kids." Shanice said inviting me and the boys over for the holiday. I sat there kind of in shock that I had been invited to something that was family oriented. " Ummm sure, do I need to bring anything?" I asked. She reached in her purse pulling out Two-Hundred Dollar bills placing them on the table "No silly, you do not need to bring anything but you and your boys appetites. And I don't want to hear nothing about it but lunch is on me." Shanice told me before asking me to walk her outside.

We stepped outside with all four of my bodyguards behind us and two posted at the trucks, "Whew... I forgot that your escorts are Presidential and always have protection follow behind you." Shanice said looking at me with a smile. I was still amazed at how good Shanice was looking and admired how her body was looking in her business suit. "Now all I need is a first lady and I will really be Presidential." I told her with a grin on my face. She smiled handing her valet ticket to the valet, "Well I guess we gon' have to work on that then aren't we?" She replied.

The valet pulled up in a all white Lexus 360 "That's your car?" I asked. She looked back at it and back at me, "Of course, who else car would it be?? Your not the only one balling out here Mr. Jay, give me a hug before I go." We hugged each other tightly when She told me she she would call me with the directions to her house. She then walk to her car and waved before pulling out of the restaurants parking lot. Shanice had done a complete 360 from the last time I seen her and now she was in a car that cost over a Hundred Thousand. I didn't know what it was she was into but all I knew was that it was a great look for her and made me even more attracted to her....

Chapter Forty
Got You!

I GOT A CALL FROM ONE OF THE STRIPPERS THAT WORKED AT THE Crazy Horse telling me that she just seen E-Bo walk in and was getting pissy drunk at the bar throwing money. At the time I just so happen to be in the area and for no reason in the world would I miss this opportunity to go get that Bitch Ass Nigga. It has been a year that passed and how I just seen it, he wasn't even supposed to make it this far into the year.

I had all six of my bodyguard with me and we posted across the street from where the Crazy Horse was until they closed down at 2:30 AM. I was so anxious and excited that I had to Piss but didn't want to miss the chance to catch E-Bo slipping. For a entire year I dreamed and imagined how or where I would catch him slipping and now the time had come I was more ready than I ever been to squeeze my trigger. "Boss, so how do you want to do this?" Sadi asked me, for the first time in a long time I actually didn't have a plan, "Boss, may I suggest something?" OC asked from the passenger seat. "Wassup OC?" I asked him. "I suggest that we follow him and hope that he leads us to his house. Once he leads us there we get him to lead us to his safe. Once he does that we start the torturing process, burn him alive to a crisp then put a bullet in his head." OC answered. the plan that he had sounded gruesome, mean and a bit crazy and thats why it made the most perfect plan. I was with it and agreed that we would do exactly all that he just said.

"He's Leaving right now With my Girl and he has his body-guards with him too" the text message from the Stripper said. All of us checked our firearms and was ready. E-Bo stepped out of the Titty Bar stumbling drunk with his arm around the Stripper and two bodyguards followed by them. I chuckled, I couldn't believe this Nigga was out at the Titty Bars getting drunk like she was sweet in the Streets. It was also funny that he had bodyguards now, I guess after that time we were chasing him he had to smarten up. All four of them made their way to an all black BMW 745 and swerved onto Michigan Avenue. We followed them from a distance all the way to a suburban area of Dearborn Heights to a Holiday Inn Hotel.

We parked outside of the hotel outside of the surveillance system view so that we couldn't be identified after killing him. I sent one of the bodyguards that couldn't speak English in to the hotel after E-Bo to try and get his room number. The bodyguard ran back outside to the truck we were in telling us, "C'mon Monde' Pe' see room C35." Sadi translated it, "OK boss let's go, that Fucker is in room 335 on the third floor." Sadi translated what was Sadi. All six of us got out of the truck and moved in on the hotel like we were in the Army, strapped and loaded.

We walked inside the hotel and the first thing we did was went behind the counter pulling the cashier into the office shutting the door behind us. "So listen, we could do this the easy way or the hard way. We are not here for you or your little petty ass hotel money. Here, take the thousand dollars and all I want you to do is continue working like nothing ever happened. Also need the surveillance tape when we are done, can you do that for me?" I calmly asked him. The cashier was a Young black Nigga who's face went from being scared to totally relax when I put the money into his hands. " Hell Yeah we gotta' deal and I don't know shit and I don't wanna' know shit!" He answered. We all smiled "Aight bet, we need the key to C35 too" I told him.

He gave us the key without a problem and just like I said he went back to work as if nothing happened. I left my bodyguard with him just in case But I was almost sure we could trust him. The rest of us took the elevator up to the third floor and went straight to C35. We all surrounded the door with guns drawn while Sadi opened the door with the key. We burst in like the SWAT team immediately shooting his two bodyguards in the chest killing them dead.

I told the Stripper Bitch who was snorting the cocaine off of the plate to get the fuck out and told her that she better not say shit to anyone about this. E-Bo sat on the bed looking scared to death with cocaine all over his face, The face that he had was the one I've been eager to see for the past year and finally the time had come.

"Damn.... wassup E-Bo, long time no see. Good to see you!" I told him with a smile on my face sitting at the end of the bed. He was still in total shock that I was right in front of him and when he seen his bodyguards on the floor dead he knew that shit was real. I stood up walking closer to him and couldn't help Myself from slapping my pistol hard as I could across his face. His entire right side of his face begins to swell up and the moaning and screaming he was doing you would've swore he was already dying. "Jay, please! don't kill me, I got money! Over Six million dollars if you spare me!" E-Bo begged. I laughed, I couldn't believe this Nigga had the nerve to try and beg for his life after we had already done to my family. "Boy there ain't a price in this world that could keep me off yo' ass you hear me?" I told him. "Yo' pick this Nigga up, we taking him with us!" I told my bodyguards. Before Oc and Sadi picked him up they pistol whipped him some more to keep him from resisting his capture. After so many hits to the head and face he became unconscious how we wanted him.

Sadi and Oc took E-Bo Out of the hotels backdoor and I walked back to the front where the cashier and one of my bodyguards were. The bodyguard gave me a head nod signaling that everything was good there, I told him to head back to the truck while I hollered at the cashier personally. Before I could say a word he handed me the surveillance tapes. I could tell that he was just a young Nigga that was only working here trying to stay out of trouble. "You straight Homie?" I asked him. He nodded his head answering that he was good. I gave him a head nod and told him good looking as I headed towards the exit. "A big Dawg. You hiring?" He asked. I chuckled remembering the 9-5 job I use to have back in the day. I walked back towards him handed him my business card, "Call in two days and I might have something lined up for you." I told him before leaving out the front door and hopping into the truck with my bodyguards and E-Bo.

We pulled up at the same Warehouse that Big Tee, Ciara, D-Money and many other people took their last breath. The only time I even came here was when it was time to body somebody. Sadi, Oc and Diago hung E-Bo's Naked body up in the air and the pain that he was going to endure would be the worst torcher that was known to man. All of the bodyguards gave me a play And congratulated me on capturing the Nigga that killed my family. I was indeed proud and felt like a big boulder with taken from my shoulders. I exhaled stepping out of the warehouse when I looked up at the stars in the sky, "Don't even trip Honey Imma' take care of him!" I whispered to my woman Honey...

Chapter Forty-One
Fourth of July

"SHANICE? WHAT'S UP MY BABY. YEAH I THINK WE ARE OUTSIDE OF your house. Are you coming out? OK, see you in a minute." I said before hanging up the phone. I stepped out of the car with Lil'K and Lil' Dez when I kneeled down in front of them making sure their clothes were straight. They were almost seven years old now but they still knew how to get dirty fast as hell. Diago, Sadi and Oc all hopped out of the trucks and stood on each side of us. Though I had E-Bo captured already Carmen insisted that they stay by my side at least until I made my way back to the West Coast where she assumed I was safe…

Shanice walked down the driveway of a big ass mansion that had all types of exclusive cars parked in front of her house. When she seen us standing in front of my all white Rolls Royce Ghost and the Range Rovers behind it her mouth dropped. She had to know that I was all the way financially stable but the Ghost proved that I was doing better than the average 'OK' hustler. She walked straight up to me looking beautiful as ever wearing a yellow strapless sundress with her hair in a ponytail and jewelry shining when she greeted me with the tightest and heart felt hug. "So glad that you could make it!

Oh My God, and these are your boys you were telling me about? They are so handsome!" Shanice said leaning down to hug them. "Boys, this is my friend Shanice. Shanice this is Lil'K and Lil' Dez. Of course you met Diego and the crew before." I introduced everybody to each other. The bodyguards gave her a head nod and the boys said hi at the same time, "Aww Jay they are so cute! They look just like you too!" She said. I never told her the stipulation as to how and why the boys were really mine but how I seen it was that they were mine anyway so it didn't really matter. "Okay then, y'all following me to the backyard where the kids are playing in the bounce house and my family is sitting back chilling waiting on the food. Umm Jay, is it really necessary that all your bodyguards come? You gon have my family thinking Im dating some type of Mob Boss or something." She whispered to me. I looked back at them then back to her telling her that I understand but explained to her that one of them will be with me no matter what and that we would just have to tell people that Diago is my friend. Shanice said one is fine and Diago sent the rest of them back to the trucks.

When we all stepped into the backyard it was huge. The music was loud, food was smelling great and the weather was beautiful. It had been a very long time since I been at a family event such as this one but it was nice. The boys didn't waste no time and ran right over to the bounce house. Across the yard I seen what looked like an open bar, people dancing, playing spades and dominoes having themselves a good time. As Shanice and I walked through the backyard with Diago behind us at a distance I noticed all eyes were on us "Is it just me or is everybody staring at it us?" I asked. She laughed, "Well no they are all staring at us for the simple fact some of them are my child's father's relatives and the other people are only staring at you wondering who you are." She told me cuffing her arm up under mine until we made it to the table for us to sit.

"So... I'm glad that you came, I actually didn't think that you would, I thought you would probably be too busy or something." Shanice said to me with a smile. "Yea I'm glad I came too, thank you for inviting me. You have a beautiful home." I told her as I looked around observing not only her home but the different sets of people that were here. "Thank you, I worked hard to get this house looking this good." She replied. "What is it that you told me that you do for a living again?" I asked, she grinned. "A little bit of this, a little bit of that." She answered. I nodded respecting that she didn't want to tell me. "Can I get you a drink or something?" Shanice asked. I looked around realizing that I wasn't comfortable with the unknown people that was around me and I was out of my element which meant that I needed to be on point, "just a water for now." I answer her. She looked at me surprised and asked me if I was sure. "I'm sure my Baby." I answered.

When Shanice went to go get me a water there was a group that was across the yard that I been watching and now they were walking over towards me. I smoothly reached down to my waist where my desert eagle was and when I looked behind me I seen that Diago was already ready to clutch if needed. When the group of four made it to the table one of them stood in front of me, "Yo' Cuz', you MSN Jay right?" The tall black ass Nigga out of the crew asked me. "Who wants to know?" I returned the question. The black Nigga looked at Diago who was behind me then looked back at me when he reached behind him. Being fast on our feet, both Diago and I pulled out our pistols Aiming directly at him telling him not to do it. The rest of his crew jumped back at our quick reactions, "Calm down! Calm down! Calm down Homie, I'm only going for my business card that's in my back pocket!" He said with one hand up and the other hand slowly pulling out a business card out of his back pocket. Diago and I lowered our guns, "Your card? What I need your card for?" I asked breathing hard from the adrenaline rush. "Woah Man, just relax okay. I know you but you don't really know me. I use to work for Mario not too long ago but i ain't with the Hustle Fam no more. I'm doing my own thing now with the Work now, I fucks with it all." He told me. I looked around the backyard and it was weird that even with guns drawn nobody was paying us any attention. Diago and I then put our pistols away and I told him to have a seat. Shanice came back to the table with my water in one hand and her drink in the other hand, "Ohhh, I see you met my cousin Terrance huh? Here's your water Jay." She said handing me the water. "Cuz what did I tell you about calling me by government name!?" The tall black Nigga asked her in an annoyed tone. Shanice laughed, "Boy please! that is your name and I'm not calling you with those Niggas be calling you." She replied I couldn't help but to laugh at the family members. "Whatever Man, Ummm Shanice, do you think I could have a few minutes alone with your friend here?" Her cousin Terrence asked her. Her face turned up, hand was on her hip and just before she was about to check into her Cousin for asking such a thing when she looked at me and I gave her the head nod letting her know that it was fine. She then turned her attitude down a few notches, "Hmmm, yea and that's all you're getting with him too. You get a few minutes and then I'm coming back." Shanice told him. I usually wouldn't even give somebody like him the time of day but I figured I would at least see what it was there he had to offer. Shanice left us to Ourselves while she walked over to a group of women that was at the open bar across the yard.

Diago stood over me and Terrence's friends stood over him. "Soooo, I take it that they are your Bodyguards or something?" I asked referring to his Buddies behind him. "Nawl, just my Home-boys." He answered. Being that you came over here to talk to me I refuse to talk in Front of all of them. If you would have them step a few steps back then I can talk." I told him. Terrence looked back at his Buddies and told told them to come back in a few minutes. "Now for starters and to get things clear, Shanice is my Cousin and my family will be family no matter what. Saying that to say, yes Terrence is my government name but call me T-Dot." Terrence told me, I nodded my head in agreeance and drinking my water. "Now let's talk business. . .I got a crazy connect on the Kush, Cocaine, Heroin and the E-Pills that I have unlimited access to. I guess my next question to you is, if you don't mind telling me what is your price these days? Maybe I could get you a better price?" T-Dot asked me. I never would've thought the price could get better than what Carmen was Charging but now I was more curious than ever as to what his price was and if the product was just as good as Carmen's. "Well I'm paying Sixty- Thousand for the Kush Bell of Thirty , Twenty- Four Thousand for the Bricks of Coke, Forty-Five Thousand for the Bricks of Dog Food and a dollar a pill for the E's. I don't think it gets any better than that." I answered him proudly. I was actually paying a lot more than what I told him but I had to lie in order to get him to give me a sweeter price then what I told him.

T-Dot gave me a look like he knew I was lying but I could tell from his body language that he still badly wanted to do business with me. MSN had the streets on lock as far as the best Product and the best delivery and if you wasn't a part of the MSN movement then your chances of hustling successfully was slim to none. T-dot looked back at his buddies then back to me with a grin, "Well, those are pretty good prices but what if I told you I could do better? I'm talking Kush for the price of Thirty-Five Thousand for a bale of Thirty, Twenty Thousand for the bricks of Yay and Forty Thousand for the bricks of Dog food." T- Dot asked me. I gave him a look as if I didn't believe him, "What would I say to them price you ask? I would say either you the feds trying to set me up or you must know Pablo Escobar Himself and therefore you will become my Best Friend." I Said to him with a laugh. T- dot chuckled, "First off let's get this straight, ain't shit about me any type of a Fed, Police Officer or anything in that nature so I asked you to never compare me to anything like that again. Secondly, if you think that I gotta know Pablo Escobar to get them prices then wait to I introduce you to Big Meech, Marvin Gaye, and Tupac" He replied making all of us laugh.

The prices that T-Dot was telling me was great but I was more excited about him being more convenient for me instead of me having to go all the way out to California. Plus with the extra thousands I was saving if I dealt with him I could still cop from Carmen from time to time and not miss any Money or end any business arrangements. "Well I'm sold T-Dot, if your Work is as good as you explained then I'm looking forward to business with you." I told him standing to my feet to give him a play like respectable Hustlers did.

We exchanged numbers and I told him that he would be hearing from me soon.

Shanice walked back over to our table seeing that we were done discussing business. "Well it's about time you're finished up, can I have my Company back please?" Shanice sarcastically ask her Cousin with a smile. "Yeah, he's all yours Cuzo I actually have to go so I'll holler at you later all right?" T- dot said before kissing her on her forehead. He then gave me a play and left from the Get Together. Meanwhile Shanice and I had taken a seat and we finally had time for Ourselves to talk. We sat there for hours watching people enjoy themselves until they were all partied out and started to leave. We sat there so long talking that now it become dark and the boys ran to us all tired out and covered in dirt from a long day of playing.Shanice and I couldn't help but laugh at the fact that we could see just about everything they were eating, "oh my god boys, how did Y'all so dirty?" Shanice asked. I just shook my head at the Gucci and Louis Vuitton that was unrecognizable, "Aight boys, we bout to go home shortly so be ready." I told them. They both awed the fact that they had to go home so they stomped away. "You are so good with Kids, I like that." Shanice told me with a smile on her face. Shanice was a very attractive woman and I couldn't lie if I wanted to, I was really feeling her. She was so cool, have a good personality and down earth. I haven't been this attracted to a woman since Honey. I just feel so comfortable with her and I actually feel like the boys and I didn't want to leave.

"Wow, I can't believe it got so late so fast. As usual I really enjoyed your company. Maybe we could do this again someday, just Me and You." Shanice said to me. I nodded my head, "I really enjoyed Myself with you too and most definitely we could do this again just Me and You. I swear I feel like we known when each other forever." I told her as we both stood up. She walked up to me reaching for my hand to hold it, "I feel like I've known you forever too. Who would've guessed that we become close friends visiting our people at the County jail." She said as we headed out to the backyard and down the driveway. The boys were racing in front of us, "Yeah that's crazy but I'm glad that we met." I replied. It was crazy because we were both feeling the exact same way and from the look in her eye I could tell she didn't want the night to end either.

"C'mon boys, get in the car." I yelled standing in front of the car. I leaned against the drivers side door when I pulled Shanice body closer to me. I put my hands on her Waist and she wrapped her hands around my neck, "So When is the next time you're free?" I asked staring down into her pretty eyes, "Hmmm, let me see... You know I got a busy schedule, you know how that goes but I guess I could slide you in, in a couple days. just make sure you call me. " she told me. I nodded my head . "I'mma call you then." I replied leaning down placing my lips onto hers. When I kissed her lips I swear I felt chills shoot through my body. "Oh, we see you! We see you!" Both boys laughed and pointed at us. Shanice and I just laughed at the childish amusement . I told them to get in the car and before I got in with them I gave Shanice another hug and kiss. As we pulled away from Shanice's house she stood in front of it waving. When I looked in the backseat the boys were rolling down the window waving back to her. Seeing the boys interact with Shanice was a good feeling it made me feel like I was making the right decision by dealing with her. The type of relationship that Shanice and I were building we're both rare and new to me. As bad as I wanted to fuck Shanice I didn't want to rush things and mess it up before it started, There was a lot about me that she didn't know......

Chapter Forty-Two
Finish Him!!!

I WOKE UP EARLY MORNING WITH SWEAT BEADS ON MY FOREHEAD from the nightmare that I often had. I often had dreams that I could've saved Honey and Alicia if I had only done something different, was a bit faster or if I had just moved first on killing E-Bo instead of him getting the upper hand on me. Things were going good for the MSN movement legally and illegally but I couldn't escape the fact that I felt totally alone. I missed Honey, Alicia and Rizzy like crazy and thought about them every single day only regular. I was so alone that I was even missing D-Money. I looked outside the door that led to the balcony of my new Mansion and the sky was dark with heavy rain falling down hard. Today was one of those days I was feeling down because I wasn't sharing my life with the people I loved and called family. The MSN movement was doing great but it really wasn't worth a shit to me being that I couldn't share it…

I got up getting Myself together only throwing on a Polo jogging fit and some Jordans. Wherever I planned on going I didn't need to get fresh to death. When I hit down the stairs the sound of video games echoed through the living room and there was the boys sitting on the couch with bowls of cereal in front of them. I walked into the kitchen pouring Myself some orange juice when Lil'K walked into the kitchen noticing that I was dressed, "Hey Jay, you about to leave? Can we come?" He asked. I shook my head," Nawl, not this Time Son I got to go handle this business real quick then I'm coming right back here so hang to with y'all." I told him. He smiled, "Are you coming back and staying with us?" He asked in a excited and surprised tone. At that moment I realized that I had not been spending as much time with them as I should. Most of the time I would just leave Sadi the bodyguard to watch them and then go and hit up the streets. I know that I was a business Man but I accepted the responsibility to be a Father to the boys so I should be around a lot more."Yes I would be right back and i'm chilling wit' y'all so make sho' I got next aight?" I told Lil'K. He was so happy to hear that I would be back to chill with them he ran back over the the couch telling Lil'Dez. They were both happy as hell and eager for me to hurry back. I told Sadi that I needed him to stay with the boys while I shot down to the Warehouse to handle a certain situation. Already knowing what I was talking about he agreed to keep a eye on them while I was gone. I told the boys that I would see them shortly and walked out of the front door where Diago and the rest of the bodyguards were. I gave them all a head nod before hopping in my Corvette. It's time to go and take care of that Nigga E-Bo. I told them. They all hopped in their Range Rovers and followed me all the way to the warehouse that was in the city....

E-Bo had been getting torchered for days and as far as I was concerned it was only just beginning. I had the young MSN Members lower E-Bo down from the ceiling and as he was lowered I seen that all the tips of all of his fingers and toes had been cut off and burnt. Both of his eyes were swollen shut and his jaw was broken enabling him to speak. "E-Bo, Yo E-Bo Man. Can you hear me?" I asked enjoying every bit of his pain. All he could do was moan from the pain that he had endured. I pulled my Swiss Amy Knife and I slowly began slicing into his flesh leaving open wounds that made more and more of his blood pour out. Barley able to open his mouth was the loud muffled scream which let me know that he was feeling the worst pain that he ever felt. I know the pain that he was feeling was excruciating but no way, no how was I ever showing mercy to him.

I walked over to the corner where the Warehouse winter supplies were kept and I grabbed the shovel and salt that we used for ice on the ground. After being sliced up with my Knife, E-Bo was wide awoke now and with the little bit of sight that he did have allowed him to see what I was doing he began pissing himself again. There wasn't enough blood or piss that would make me stop the torcher that I was going to put on E-Bo, My adrenaline was pumping and I couldn't wait to continue. I put the salt on the bloody and pissy ground underneath him with a shovel in my hand, "Drop him!" I told the young MSN Members. They then released the chain that E-Bo was hanging from causing him to fall directly on top of the salt. when he fell down and felt the salt enter his wounds I couldn't have been more happier with the pain that was across his face. His broken jaw wouldn't allow him to scream so he would moan loudly and I was laughing at the same time. I looked at his cut off Tip-Toes And fingers and they looked terrible and Painful.

I started beating E-Bo in the head with the same shovel and making sure that the salt was filling his open wounds. I had beat him so bad that I quickly Became exhausted from the swings I took at him. E-Bo wasn't dead yet but I was sure that he wished he was, "Go get the battery acid and the gasoline Diago" I told him. While waiting on Diago I walked to my Corvette and grabbed the blunt that I had already rolled. I then lit the blunt while Diago carried the battery acid I asked for over to E-Bo's body on the ground. E-Bo was barley able to move when I picked up the hot battery acid and began pouring it all over his body including his penis. Before doing this to him I thought this was a great plan but while doing it I was watching his skin melt instantly. I watched his Penis damn near burn off and not even I could take all the pain that I was performing on him. This torcher was so gruesome that I began to think that I needed psychiatric help from how I was enjoying it.

· · ·

For the finishing touches I poured gasoline over his entire body, "Yea Nigga, this for killing my girl Honey and Alicia! This shit is for getting Rizzy locked! You bought this for Yo self! So fuck you!" I told him as I stepped back sparking my blunt. I had to be tripping because I could've sworn I heard E-Bo laughing. I kneeled down and indeed it was this nigga laughing after all that had been done to him. I was amazing that after all that happened that he could still find the time to laugh. "What the fuck? Could y'all believe this shit?! This Mutherfucker is laying his on his deathbed laughing! What the fuck are you laughing for?!" I asked him. E-Bo lifted his head from where he laid, "No matter what you do to me....they are both still dead, Fuck you and fuck yo dead lil Boy I killed!" E-Bo managed to say with a broken jaw. I stood back up, the fact that he knew that Alicia was pregnant with my Son made me even more furious. I nodded my head, "No, fuck you! You a Bitch Ass Nigga! I told him when I threw half of my blunt on his body causing him to burst into flames. I stood there watching his body burn and listening to his dreadful moans and cries for twenty minutes straight. When his body was no longer moving I had Diago use the fire extinguisher to put E-Bo's burning body out and the smell it had left was the worst smell I ever had to smell. The revenge for Honey and Alicia's death and Rizzy's incarceration had finally been accomplished after a long year of searching for him. I told the young MSN Members to dispose the remains of E-Bo's body and my bodyguard and I exited the Warehouse. I thought i would feel good after killing E-Bo but for some reason i didn't feel any different. I was still hurt that my loved ones were gone and what E-Bo told me before I killed him made all of the sense in the world. They were still gone and wasn't no way for me to bring them back. I had to move on and that I planned to do, it was just going to take me some time to do.......

Chapter Forty-Three
J-Dot

(WEEKS LATER)

IT WAS WEEKS AFTER KILLING E-BO I THINK I FINALLY BEGIN TO GET back to normal and I was back on track focused on MSN and it's ventures, I was low on Work so I called Carmen and she said the next shipment won't be ready until next week. Carmen was the best Business Women I ever met so I could never blame her or get mad at her if she tells me she won't be ready for another week. Carmen and I had a rare relationship when we were Together, enjoyed each other's company and going out like a normal couple would. The crazy thing about our relationship was with the both of us being Hustlers, it was hard for us to adjust to each other free time and the scheduling around the other is damn near impossible. We both had the feelings for the other but at the end of the day we were both committed to our Hustles more than anything and that's why we couldn't be in a relationship together. Carmen wanted me to quit my hustling and bring the boys and Myself out to California so we could live with her. Me being the grow man I was, I couldn't accept her offer and declined so I can stay in Detroit to expand the MSN Movement and Strip clubs...

Badly needing some Work to flood the streets with at lease until Carmen packages arrived, I remembered that Shanice had a Cousin that swore he had a good product as well as a good price. I called him telling him what I needed and without the usual stalling hustlers did, he told me to meet him on the westside. I agreed to do so but with this being my first time ever Dealing with him I had my body-guards load up their weapons and pray for the best but expect the worst. I tucked my Desert Eagle on my waist band and was ready to meet up with him, this was one hundred and fifty- thousand dollars worth of Work I was about to purchase so all precautions had to be made.

T-Dot had me pull up on one of the most nicest blocks on the westside. I assumed this was one of his spots judging by how many of his crew members were surrounding the entire house. T-Dot had at least twelve of his Crew members standing guard and when I pulled up they had me pull in backwards into the driveway. My bodyguards and I stepped out of the trucks when we seen T-Dot standing at the back door. "Yo Jay! Wassup Man! Come and follow me." He told me. Diago, OC and Myself followed him into the house and into the kitchen where the loud smell of strong Kush blessed our noses. There wasn't any household appliances inside the kitchen and where they would be sitting were all kinds of drugs tall as the ceiling. One corner had pounds of Kush. He was not bullshit-ting when he told me he has access to an unlimited supply of Work. Seeing all of this ruled out the question if he was a Fed or a Police officer too. There wasn't a government official who would have this much Work inside of a house.

One of the Workers he had was smoking a blunt of the Kush when T-Dot told him to give it up. T-Dot took three puffs and handed it to me. "Shid, that's how that shit taste Bro, you gone fuck up the streets with this shit." He told me handing me the blunt. I took the blunt hitting it a few time and indeed it was very strong and a very good quality of weed. I also tasted the Cocaine and licked the E-Pills to determine if they were strong and I was impressed by how good the quality was. "Yes this shit is straight.. i'll take it." I told him. T-Dot smiles, "Now that's what I like to hear.. that would be Seventy-Five thousand dollars". I nodded my head and turned back to OC who had the book bag telling him to hand it over. I then handed it over to T-Dot in the Louis Vutton bag when he turned it over to the Worker that was posted at the money counter.

After T-Dot's Worker put all the money into the counter and Diago and OC weight up the work that I was purchasing, both parties were satisfied and the business was finished. Diago and OC begin taking the bagged up work outside to the trucks as both T-Dot and I followed behind them. "So T-Dot, for future reference we have to find a better way to conduct our transactions. Having me meet you at the weight house ain't good for me or you. feel me? Who knows if either of us is being followed or anything like that. I'm to big to be meeting up at places such as these Dawg, for real." I told him. He nodded his head. "Yeah I feel you Homie, your right." T-Dot agreed knowing I was right. He reached his hand out for a play and told me next time he would pick a better location for us.

There was something about T-Dot that wouldn't allow me to trust him just yet. Just before I was about to hop in the truck T-Dot called my name stopping me. "Ummm, tonight i'm going down-town to go fuck wit' a club or two. You should come fuck wit me. Let's go pop a few bottles, pull a few bitches and relax a little, feel me? " he asked me. I stood there thinking if I wanted to hit the city up with him, I didn't know him for shit but I did want to know the type of Nigga I was dealing with better and the best way to find out what type of Nigga he was, was to be around him. I told him to just hit me up with locations and I would let him know then. How crazy my life has been I was paranoid in trusting new people. I had to do a background check on this Nigga and there was only one person that would be able to tell me the real about him. T-Dot told me he would hit me up a little later and let me know where it was he was going.......

Chapter Forty-Four
Close Call

(LATER THAT DAY)

I was in my white Chevrolet Camaro headed down to meet gutta and J.T and as usual I had my bodyguards in front of me as well as behind me. It wasn't only a nice fall day but today was the day I did my pickups all over the city. I even had to pick up my legit money from the Mainstrip locations. My pick ups were usually an easy process but now a days it was hard getting in contact with Gutta and J.T. I guess with them making more money now than they ever had, they were now feeling themselves more than they used to. For the last few pick ups they would have me meet up with their Workers to get the money, like they were too busy for the meet up. I swear everything they were doing I remember Rizzy, D-Money, and Myself doing but with it being my money on the other end I needed them to get back on their hustle shit that made us recruit them back in the day.....

The neighborhood that they were hustling out of was the same hood that MSN ran back in our coming up. We had put in a lot of time and hard hustling hours back in the day and one of the main spots that we hustled from was the gas station that the Arabs allowed us to hustle from. Reminiscing back and going down memory lane I decided to stop at the same gas station where we once hustled from. When we pulled inside the gas station there were at least six young Hustlers posted in front ready to serve the first customers they thought were ready to buy. They all watched my Bodyguards and I step out of the cars and head into the gas station. I couldn't help but to chuckle a bit as I remembered being just like them. I could tell that they badly wanted to ask me if I wanted to buy some weed but it wasn't hard to realize that I wasn't no regular Nigga By the MSN chain hanging from my neck.

One of the young Hustling niggas had that thirsty look and could care less who I was. "Yo, Big Homie! I got that strong kush for you, that fire!" He told me showing me a vial of it. I took a look at it and just by the orange hairs I could tell that it was my Product. It was clear that he had no idea who I was. "How much you want for that shit Young Dawg?" I asked him "Shid, I see you shining and shit and I know that you probably don't even need it so just give me a hot $25 for it" He told me. Not even knowing him I liked his determination to get his money. He was the only one to ask me if I wanted to buy and I admired his hustle. "How much more of this shit you got?" I asked him He got excited and reached in his pockets pulling out a sandwich bag full of vials. "I got nineteen more left." He answered I Looked back at Diago and OC then back at the young Hustler. "Give me all of them. All 19 of them. In fact, give me all the sacks that all of y'all got on y'all, fuck it!" I told all six young Hustlers standing in front of the gas station. Smiles had spread across all of their faces as they rushed to hand them over to me. Being that all of the sacks that the hustlers had on them was my product anyway, the money would come back to me anyway. All I was doing was putting a extra couple dollars into their pocket and getting them from in front of the hot ass gas station for a few hours. Soon as I bought all of their sacks the young hustlers began dispersing getting on their phones probably calling their Employer so they could Re-Up again.

My bodyguards and I stepped into the Gas station when I seen the Arab Hann and Ismail standing behind the glass. Their eyes widened as if they seen a ghost when they seen me. "Look what the cat done drugged in.... long time no see" Hann said to me. I grinned, "Yeah long time no see wassup Hann? wassup Ismail? y'all still alive huh?" I said to them. I never really liked them and I know they never really liked me, I remember all the times the police came up here fucking with us and I knew it was because they had called them. They hated that we use to hustle in front of their Gas Station back then but they just had to live with it.

Hann and Ismail looked at each other then back at me, "Are we still alive? we are surprised that you are still alive! We heard about one of your buddies that Darien that use to hang with you was dead and your Cousin was locked up, we just knew that you would've been killed by now also." Hann jokingly replied. Hearing the hate that they had towards me made me mad but taking a different road I decided to leave it alone and ignore his ignorance, both Hann and Ismail has to be at least 80 years old and a cough away from dying anyway. I walked to the back of the Gas Station and grabbed Myself a Everfresh juice and came back to the front counter asking them for a box of blunts. Before I walked out of the Gas Station Hann Said to me, "Have a nice day, stay out of jail and try not to get killed like your Buddies." Hann said as him and Ismail began laughing. I stopped in my steps badly wanting them to pay for what they just said, At the moment I told myself that I would have someone sitting outside for them waiting for them to get off work to beat the hell out of them.

When my bodyguards and I stepped outside there wasn't not one of the young hustlers who sacks I bought standing out there, I guess they had gone to re-up again. I walked over to my Camaro when I got a call from J.T, "Whatup doe? i'm bout to pull up on y'all in a few minutes. Huh? I'm at the B.P Gas Station right now. Aight I'll be there in a minute." I said before hanging up the phone. I hopped in my Camaro and Diago and OC hopped in their trucks ready to pull off. I sat in my drivers seat rolling up a blunt when I noticed a raggedy mini-van pulling into the Gas Station slowly. After being shot numerous times and being fucked over by people that I trusted, I was very cautious of my surrounding and refused to ever get caught slipping again. I Then reached for the Desert Eagle that was on my waist, and sat it on my lap as I kept a close eye on the Mini-Van.

The Mini-Van then stomped on the gas and pulled up on the side of my car with the sliding doors open and 4 mask shooters hopped out firing from their AK-47's. This was all Deja Vu all over again, dropping the weed I was rolling and picking up my pistol on my lap, my automatic reaction was to duck. It didn't take me long to remember that that I had all my cars bulletproofed so the bullets that they were shooting only bounced off my car. The Assassins didn't even realize that the bullets were to no affect and they continued firing non-stop. Up ahead at the bulletproof truck that OC was in, him and two more other bodyguards had made it out on the opposite side of the shooting and was ducked off behind the truck waiting on the right time to retaliate.

At this point I was tired of Niggas trying to kill me, I then hopped out and ducked on the opposite side waiting for the same opportunity to fire back. Before I knew it my whole Security team was all sitting ducking off on the opposite side of the cars and trucks just waiting for the assassins shooting to slow down just enough for us to react. I then yelled over to Diago on my left and OC on my right side giving them the head nod and they all knew what they meant, we all stood up and began firing our powerful firearms back at them non-stopped. My Desert Eagle was ripping through the mini-van doors and the M-16's the bodyguards had was damn near tipping the mini-van over. What we were firing was too strong for them, I was sure that they had already regretted coming to fuck with us. I heard them yell "RETREAT! LET'S GET THE FUCK OUTTA HERE!" The driver of the mini-van tried pulling off but my Crew and I chased them down on foot firing our weapons until the van was at a complete stop. Three of the Assassins has been killed before the van even pulled away.

I ran up on the Driver's side of the Mini-Van with Desert Eagle aimed to kill if I saw any movement and Diago and OC did the same thing on the passenger side. I snatched the drivers side door open with pistol still aimed when I saw that the driver had been shot multiple times in the back. I snatched the mask off his face only to see that the driver was a Baby. He couldn't have been no older than 17 years old. "Help.... Help me." The kid moaned, I chuckled at the nerve of the same nigga that tried to kill me. "Are you fucking serious?!? I tell you what.. tell me who you work for and i'll get you some medical help." I told him as the blood continued oozing from his mouth forcing him to knock on deaths door. "You... I work for you" He answered before nodding off into a painful death.

The sound of Ismail crying and calling out for help caught my bodyguards and I attention. I looked at the gas station and see that there was a lot of windows that had been shot out. Diago, OC and Myself went into the Gas Station asking if everyone was aight. When I seen Hann laid out on the ground covered in blood. "Please! Please, help him! help him please!" Ismail begged us, I kneeled down beside him. "Hann I will help you but I need the surveillance tapes first. I need them right now! Get me the tapes and we gon' get help!" I told him. without hesitation Ismail ran to the back where The surveillance systems tapes were kept. Hann looked me in the face with mouth filled with blood. "Help... me... Please Jay." He begged, I grinned "Damn... now look at you I knew you would die before me, fuck you Hann." I whispered to him. Ismail rushed back to us handing me the surveillance tapes, I stood up and told my bodyguards let's get out of here... "Wait, Wait. I thought y'all was going to get us some help!!??" Ismail stood up to his feet with concerned written all over his face. I turned back to him when at that very moment we all heard police and ambulance sirens echoing through the neighborhood. I chuckled, "Help is on the way right now, you don't hear that?" I asked him before heading to the cars to get out of there. I jumped in my Camaro and we all stabbed off heading to Gutta and J.T Spot.

We pulled up to Gutta and J.T's Trap House hopping out with weapons still in hand as we walked straight up to the door. Gutta opened the door eating an apple. "Jay?? Umm, wassup?" He asked. My bodyguards and I all entered the Trap-house with adrenaline still rushing from the shoot out we were just in. "Everybody except Gunna and J.T get the fuck out !" I yelled to all the little hood Rats and Spot Workers. J.T was sitting on the couch straight chilling and playing the game as I emptied their Spot.

"Niggas at the Gas Station just tried to kill me!" I said breathing heavy, Gutta's jaw dropped in shock "What?? who, what, who was it?!! This Just happened?" he asked. "Yeah it just happened! we killed them lil Niggas tho!" I said as I paced back and fourth on their trap house floor. J.T dropped the video game controller and was now tuned in. "You killed them all? All of them?" J.T asked. "All of them!!" I yelled back.

"Don't trip Jay, we gone find out who the fuck it was that tried to kill you, it was probably them Niggas we been beefing with lately from the Riverside!" Gutta said as if he was mad. I looked in J.T face and he looked like he had just seen a ghost. He was frozen stiff and completely silent. "J.T wassup? you aight?" I asked snapping him out of the zone that he was in. "Yea, Yea, Yea i'm good. We gotta find out who did this shit! I'll be right back!" J.T said rushing out the door. I didn't know what he was so jittery about when I was the one who almost got killed. Gutta looked at me and had kind of a worried face. "He's gonna find out what happened up there and we gon get on that shit for real!" Gutta said handing me the blunt that he just lit. I pulled from the blunt hard a couple times trying to relax Myself but I was still paranoid. I couldn't even sit down, I was so mad that I was just shot at. "A look, I gotta get the fuck outta here, it's right here but we ain't got it all right now." Gutta told me, I stopped pacing knowing that I had to had heard him wrong, they ain't never not had my money on time. "What you mean y'all ain't got it all? Where is it all then?! Shid, Y'all was suppose to have the cash for me last week!" I asked Gutta as I was getting even more mad.

Gutta walked over and grabbed a bag from behind the couch

handing it to me, "This is only a hundred thousand.. We gon' have the rest for you in a couple of days. Things just been a bit slow." Gutta explained. I took the bag of money and realized that I had to settle down. I was so mad at me just being shot at that I was ready to trip on Gutta and he's a great Hustler for the MSN. "Aight Dawg, I'll be back this weekend for the rest of it but tighten up Man. What y'all Trap do shouldn't determine when I get paid. I front y'all and give y'all a time to pay me back. Y'all been slacking up on y'all shit lately." I told him as me and my bodyguards headed out the door.

I had love for the young Hustlers but at the same time this was a business. If at any moment I felt like they were on some bullshit I wouldn't hesitate to kill them. . .

Chapter Forty-Five
Weekend Fun

(HOURS LATER. . .10P.M)

"COME TO THE ALL WHITE PARTY 2NITE DOG, WE BALLIN AND having fun!" The text message read from T-Dot. After a long and stressful day of being shot at and money shorted, all I wanted to do was chill out for the night and relax. Since the Boys were at Honey's Mother house I had the night to Myself. I stepped out on the balcony of my Mansion that ran me for a hot 2.5 million dollars and smoked on some of the loud Kush that I got from T-Dot. I stared up at the stars when my phone vibrated from a text message, "Hi Stranger?!" It read from Shanice. I haven't had the chance to call and kick it with her much after her Family Get-Together because I had been busy keeping my businesses running good. "Whasup my Baby? Good to hear from you, are you busy?" I texted back. I puffed my blunt asking Myself why haven't I been fucking with Shanice like that? Shanice was a very attractive woman and very independent like I liked my women but between having the boys and keeping all my business straight I never had time for any women.

"Not tonight, what's up?" Shanice answered back. "You should come and visit me and chill for a few." I replied back. I then headed over to my mini refrigerator grabbing myself a Red Bull. 'Sure, why not. Just send me the directions and I'm on my way." She answered. I smiled as I sent her the directions to my house. I quickly ran into the bathroom hopping in the shower and getting ready for the company that I was having.

(HOUR LATER)

I received a call from the security that was just outside of my gated mansion telling me that Shanice was here. I told them to let her in and I rushed down stairs eagerly anticipating her company. I opened the door for Shanice welcoming her inside my home. She looked all around my mansion in awe, "Wow Jay, your home is beautiful." She complimented taking her jacket off. "Thank you and your looking good Yourself I must say." I complimented her while admiring her body. She wore a skin tight jogging suit that was complimenting every curve her body had. Her ass was looking fatter since the last time I seen her and she looked so good that you couldn't even tell that she had a baby not to long ago. She turned facing me," Your looking pretty Handsome Yourself Jay. Oh, and look at you wearing a jogging suit like me, trynna' be my twin." Shanice said jokingly. "Nawl, nawl, nawl you was copying off of me but it's straight doe. You looking good doe and I missed you." I told her as I walked toward her with arms open for a hug. She couldn't help but to smile, "Awww, I missed you too but you couldn't have missed me that much, being that you haven't called me." She replied while we hugged each other tightly and longer than the average hug. I stepped back after our hug apologizing for not calling her and telling her that I had been very busy lately. Being the type of woman that she was, she totally understood.

I had Shanice follow me upstairs to my movie room, "So where are those cute lil' boys you have at?" She asked sitting down on the big long couch. "Ummm, they are over their Grandmother's house for the weekend. Where is your lil' one at?" I answered and returned the question. "My lil' Angel is at his Grandmother's house also but only for the night so. . .You have me to Yourself with no interruptions, No Cousins bothering us or anything like that." She answered with a smirk on her face. I liked where she was going with that statement and chuckled telling her that I must be a very lucky man then. The Chemistry between Shanice and I was certainly present and one thing that I liked about us was that neither one of us were rushing it. "Sooo. . .This is your movie room huh? Its nice, you probably bring all of your lil' girls up here and wine and dine them, don't you?" She asked with a grin but still wanting an answer. I shook my head, "Well for starters, I do not deal with girls, I deal with women. Secondly, I never bring any women up here because I never even invite women over to my home. You are the first woman that I ever invited over." I answered her as I stood at the Mini-Bar. She just smiled, "So you haven't never had a female over before? Im the first woman to ever visit your house?" Shanice asked for clarity. I pulled out a bottle of Greygoose pouring a glass, "I swear. . .I have real hard problem trusting people after all the stuff I been through and since its hard for me to trust people. I just decide not to deal with many and I invite no one to my Home." I answered raising the bottle up asking by gesture if she wanted some. "Yes please. . .Thats good that you don't invite random women to your home. Now I actually feel special." Shanice said smiling. I walked over to the couch with both of our glasses in hand and sitting right next to her. "You should feel special because I feel like your a special person." I told her. "Awww, that was so sweet Jay, Oh my God. You trying to make me cry or something?" She asked with a slight chuckle. I told her that I wasn't trying to make her cry but that was how I felt.

Shanice and I were drinking on our glasses of Greygoose making the night a straight chill night. The plan was to have a few drinks and watch a few movies but the conversations that we were having had the both of us tuned in on the other. The movie was playing but our attention was on each other rather than the movie.

We had so much to talk about and we were totally relaxed with each other. In fact, we were so relaxed around each other that we both found ourselves drunk and on the second bottle of Greygoose. We were both talking with a slur and very hands-on affectionate. Shanice and I both had came out of our Jordans and she let her hair down, the liquor had the both of us hot as hell and Shanice was looking so good right now that she was starting to look like Beyonce.

Shanice threw her feet over my lap and judging from how low and red her eyes were, I knew she was feeling horny just like I was. "Can I tell you something and you promise not to laugh?" I asked with one hand on her thick ass thighs and the other still holding my drink. "What? I promise I won't laugh." She said and instantly started laughing at the same time. "Nope! Nope! Nope, I ain't telling you nothing now. You already laughing!" I said no longer wanting to tell her anymore. She really started laughing when she seen my reaction, :Okay, okay, I promise I won't laugh!" She said pulling on my arm and trying to keep a straight face. I exhaled, "Okay but if you laugh we will really be beefing. . .Alright, I must start off with you are looking so good right now that you gotta' nigga's heart racing. Now I tell you that because when I lost my Ex and My Unborn child's mother it really messed me up and I haven't wanted any women since then. Right now I can't hold you up, I want you BAD!" I told her when she hit me with a look like what I just told her wasn't nothing. "Is that it? Thats what you made me promise not to laugh at?! That ain't nothing Bae, I know Im hot and truth be told I feel the same way about you. I been wanting you." Shanice replied. I shook my head, "Im glad that you feel the same way about me but that wasn't what I made you promise not to laugh at. What I made you promise not to laugh at is. . .its been offi- cially two whole years since I had sex." I told her putting my head down. Shanice lifted her legs from off my lap and sat up right beside placing her hand on my backhand rubbing it. "Don't feel bad Baby, you lost two people who were a very big part of your life so don't feel bad about your celibacy." She said to me in a comforting tone.

I drank more from my glass and taking in what Shanice had just said. Thats what I meant when I said that we were comfortable around each other because for me to even open up just with that information meant that I was developing feelings for her. Their was silence in the room between the two of us and the movie on the screen was continuing to play. Shanice than took the initiative and leaned over putting her arm over my shoulder and planting a kiss on my cheek. She began kissing me from my cheek around to my lips then down to my neck. It's been so long since I been kissed by a woman that I instantly got an Erection. I grabbed the remote to the projector and turned it off then turned on the sound system. R.Kelly's T-P2.COM "Strip for you" smoothly played through the surround sound speakers. With another remote I dimmed the lights in the room down which really had set the mood.

Kissing each other slowly and passionately felt so good and very much needed. After so long without sex I thought that when I finally did get some that I would be aggressive and like an animal but instead I was cool, calm and collected. Shanice climbed on top of me raising her jogging top over her head, Her breast was looking good inside the bra so I could only imagine how good they looked without the bra. We continued kissing each other when I reached behind her unsnapping her bra and releasing her big pretty breast. My dick was only getting harder and harder anxiously wanting too enjoy Shanice's body but patience was the key to a great sex session. Feeling the hard poke of my erected Rod through her jogging pants, Shanice raised off the top of me. "C'mon, lets go to the bedroom." She told me in a low and sexy tone.

We stepped into my Master Bedroom and since the music was connected through all of the speakers inside the house, all I had to do is hit the button and the music was now playing in the bedroom. I walked over to the King Sized bed where I removed all of my clothes except my basketball shorts, wife-beater and ankle socks.

Shanice then removed her jogging pants and was now standing in only her panties and jewelry. Shanice's body looked even more amazing than I had imagined. I took a sip from the bottle of Greygoose that I bought to the room with us when Shanice stepped in between my legs putting her Titties and breast in my face. I grabbed both of her Titties and sucked her nipples nice and softly when she placed her hands on the back of my head whispering for me to bite on her nipples softly. As she asked I nibbled on her titties and stuffed as much of her titty I could inside my mouth. I wrapped my hands around her waist and cuffed her ass tightly. "Ohhh Jay, I want you Baby. I swear I want you!" Shanice whispered. Hearing her tell me she wanted me did not need to be repeated, I picked her up and laid her flat on her back in my bed. Staring at her body on my bed made me even more anxious to do all of the freaky things I've been want to do to her. I climbed on top of her and kissed her from her lips, neck, titties and all the way down to her cleanly shaved pussy. I slid her panties down over her ankles and wasted no time pleasuring her.

I then cuffed my arms up and under her ass up to her waist and began eating on her pussy. I took slow passionate licks with my tongue on top of her clitoris causing her to moan and slide up toward my headboard. Eating her pussy was crazy because it actually smelled like strawberries and made me want to continue to eat on it nonstop. I began licking, sucking, and spitting all over her Pussy making it more wet than what it already was and she begged for more. "Oh shit! Oh shit! Right there! Right there Baby! Ohhh, yes. Yesss, Ohh Baby!" She began yelling out. The more she begged was the more I ate and I was going harder than ever. I stuck two fingers inside of her pussy and began finger-fucking her while licking on her clitoris. This was what was making her slide up toward the headboard in attempts to get away from the tongue. "Ohhhh My God Jay!!! Ohhh Shit! I'm Cumming! I'm Cumming!" She screamed. With my face in between her legs she then closed my head into a lock and shaking rapidly as she moaned. Shanice had Cum all over my face.

. . .

I then stood up over her when I wiped my mouth dry and smiled looking at her and her naked body lay in my bed satisfied, "Did you like that Baby? Was that good for you?" I asked already knowing the answer. She sat up with her hair all wild and out of place, "Oh my God Oh, I got something for you. You just set the tone!" She said as she got up and out of the bed.

Shanice then pushed me on the bed and pulled my basketball shorts all the way off of me, she lifted my wife-beater over my head where she began kissing me from the lips, neck, chest all the way down to my standing Tall and brick hard dick. With one hand she rubbed caressed on my Shaft and with the other hand massaged on my balls before putting the It inside of her mouth. Her mouth was so warm and with her saliva running down my dick and her licking the tip made me feel like I just entered heaven.

"THE GREATEST YOU, THE GREATEST ME, WE WILL FIND, THE GREATEST CHEMISTRY. THE GREATEST TOUCH, THE GREATEST KISS, THE BECAME TO BE, THE GREATEST WISH. . ." R.Kelly Echoed throughout the bedroom, surely he was the king of the lovemaking because how hard Shanice and I were going, you would've swore we were trying to have Ourselves a kid. Shanice had stuffed so much dick inside of her mouth that she was not only enjoying pleasuring me but she had a passion to suck dick like none other. Her head game was so good that I couldn't help but to sit back and close my eyes try not to cum so fast.

I then Had to stop her from sucking the dick to prevent myself from cumming so fast. I stood up and flipped her back onto the bed flat on her back. Enough was enough and now it was time for the grand finale. I badly wanted her pussy and was determined to make her Cum not only by my tongue but by this dick. I climbed on top of her in the missionary position where I slowly inserted the hard dick inside of her pussy. Her pussy was so tight that even with her pussy being soaking wet, it wouldn't allow me to just enter without a struggle. I knew how I had to handle the situation and patience with the key. I stuck just the tip inside of her then I started with slow and steady thrust, "Ohhh yea Baby, you feel so good inside of me. I feel you in my stomach." Shanice said as I was fucking her with a slow and patient bed-rock.

Her Pussy was feeling so good and she was looking so good that I couldn't help but to Lean down and begin kissing her. I wasn't only kissing her passionately but now we were at the point where we were just straight freaky and tongue kissing each other down. With the tongue kissing, me kissing all over her neck and then kissing her titties, her pussy was the wettest Pussy I ever had. The bed was rocking now and there wasn't any more slow pace fucking. We were both fucking the shit out of each other. I was throwing that long and big dick all the way inside of her and all the way out wanting her to feel all of me. She even was throwing her pussy at me which made me feel the urge of any upcoming eruption to take place.

"I'm Cumming Baby!! Ohhh, I'm Cumming Baby! Jay! Jay!" She moaned. I kept pounding my hard dick inside of her as I stared down at her big pretty titties bouncing and her pretty face looking up at me. Before I knew it her legs began rapidly shaking again and when I looked down at my dick only to see that I was covered in her creamy and wet Cum. Seeing that I made her Cum twice before me let me know that I had done a great job and now it was my turn to bust. I kept hitting her pussy hard, "I'm bout' to bust too Baby!" I told her. "Cum inside of me Jay! I want it all inside of me! Cum Inside of me!" She told me and I without a question I surely released all of my sperm inside of her. I flopped beside her naked body exhausted from the performance we just had. Just like R. Kelly said in the song, I think this was the best sex I ever had. We both threw the cover over our naked bodies and held each other until we fell asleep.

Chapter Forty-Six

THE BRIGHT LIGHTS FROM THE SUN RAYS BEAMED INTO MY BEDROOM waking me up. I looked at the clock it was already 9:45 AM. Laid up under the sheets with me was Shanice who was still asleep looking beautiful as ever. I remember E-Bo told me a long time ago that if a woman is still beautiful when she sleeps even without make up that she was Wifey and I was actually feeling that statement. It was crazy because it's been so long since I've been happy about a woman that it felt weird. I leaned over kissing her on the forehead and was the happiest I've been in a very long time.

"Awww man, I'm dealing with an early Bird." Shanice said with her eyes still closed. I smiled, "The early bird gets the worm." I told her. Opening her eyes and getting up, she leaned over toward me and kissed me. "Nothings wrong with being an early Bird. Speaking of, I have to go and pick up my son this morning so let me get ready to get up out of here." she said as she stepped out of the bed and headed to the bathroom still naked with one of the sexiest body I've ever seen. "I got toothbrushes and brand new towels in the cabinet in there too." I yelled to her from the bed. I picked up one of my cell phones when I seen I had missed calls from Gutta and T-Dot. I had no idea what neither one of them wanted but Gutta better been calling me to tell me that he had my money.

My phone vibrated from an unknown number and when I answered it, it said, "IF YOU WOULD LIKE TO ACCEPT A COLLECT CALL FROM A PRISONER AT THE CORREC-TIONAL FACILITY PLEASE PRESS 0" The recorded machine repeated. It was Rizzy calling from prison, "Whasup Cuzo', what's the deal wit you out there?" He asked with the same hyped up voice he always had when he called. I smiled hearing his voice in such good spirits, "Whasup Fam, what's the deal wit you in there? I ain't doing shit really. I'm just getting up and bout' to get ready to get up and start my day." I told him. "Oh okay, that's Whasup. I ain't doing shit in here but chilling and laughing at these broke niggas in here that be lying all day. You already know how this shit go." He replied. Shanice walked back into the bedroom, "Hey Babe, have you seen my cell phone?" She asked. I pointed over to the desk that it was sitting on and continued talking with my Cousin. "Yeah I already know how it go, Just make sho' you stay low-key in that Bitch and leave them sucka Niggas alone, feel me? When I get out on the streets Imma' go Moneygram you some money and shit." I told him."Aight fasho then but who was that in yo' background?" He asked me being nosy as hell. I grinned, "Aww Man that's just my lil' Friend." I answered him. Already knowing the deal he didn't ask anything else referring to her. "Fasho then, that's Whasup. Sound like your doing good out there. Tell me what was your latest purchase out there? I know you seen that new Bentley that came out?" He asked me. Rizzy like to hear me tell him of the things I purchased and how good I was doing, "I bought that new Infiniti Truck a couple of weeks ago but that was it. I went shopping for me and the boys and they so spoiled that they be asking for Gucci belts and shit now." I told him. He laughed tripping out on how much they had grown. I also told him that I been planning on building a Mainstrip Strip Club down in Miami. I told him if everything went right that I would even consider moving down to Miami for good.

He was silent for a slight second, "Umm, thats good Fam. Fuck the City. Well look, its almost count time in this Bitch so I gotta' go. I just called to check up on you and make sho' shit was straight out there. I'll call you in a couple of days Bro. I love you Dawg and be smooth out there." Rizzy told me. "Aight Fam, I love you too and you be smooth in that Bitch. Don't drop the soap." I told him jokingly before hangin up. I sat there thinking about how things would be different had I moved down to Miami. I would be leaving my Mainstrip Strip Clubs and my Street Hustles, now that I met Shanice I would be leaving her too and all of this had to be considered.

I looked around and noticed that Shanice had been in the bathroom for a nice minute. I walked over to the bathroom door and put my ear to it to listen, "YesI Im not doing this with you, I have to go!" Shanice said to whoever she was on the phone with. I knocked on the door, "Babe, you straight in there?" I asked. I could tell that she was a bit upset from her tone when she was on the phone so I opened the door, She stood right over the sink in front of the mirror. "You okay Baby, what's wrong?" I asked her. "My Child's father just called me making me mad but I would be alright." She answered as she washed her face. I stepped behind her body hugging her. "Don't let that Nigga make you mad, your too pretty to be trippin' off of that lame." I told her as I began kissing her down her neck and shoulders. I lowered my hand down to her pussy and hit that Clitoris causing her to moan and close her eyes, "Ohhh, Let me get outta' here before you start something and make me late picking my son up." Shanice said with a grin on her face trying to get away from me.

After getting Herself together, I walked Shanice out of the house and out to her car where we hugged and kissed each other, "You betta' make sure you call me." Shanice told me as she smiled and stared up at me with them big and pretty eyes. "You know I am, I'll hit you up a lil' bit later. Make sho' you answer then." I told her. She smiled before getting into her car, "You know I will." She said closing her door and then pulling off.

Chapter Forty-Seven

IT WAS A RAINY AFTERNOON WHEN I HOPPED IN MY RANGE ROVER TO go and pull up on Gutta and J.T. at their Trap-house. It was time for me to collect that money they shorted me from my last visit and this time I wasn't trying to hear any bullshit. I was now zero tolerance when it came to my business and even that included the two of them. Neither one of them still never called to tell me any information on the young Niggas that tried to kill me. Clearly they been getting so much money now that they were beginning to lose respect for the Big Homie so if they didn't have my money I was going to show them that I started them and could stop them as well, especially in my hood.

I pulled up to their Trap-house and only Gutta's car was parked in the driveway. My Bodyguards stood outside while Diago and Oc followed me inside their Trap, Gutta already had the front door open. Surprisingly the Trap was empty and only Gutta and two of his workers were inside. "Whasup Jay, I been waiting on you to come through. . .Here, that's another hundred thousand right there." He told me handing me a rubber band of money the long way. I took a look at it and it looked exactly what he said it was, "You only owed seventy-five thousand." I told him. He waved his hand, "Yea I know, I just put a extra something on it so that their wasn't any animosity between us for us being late. So. . .We straight?" Gutta asked sticking his hand out for a play. I looked at the money then looked at him knowing that I couldn't stay mad at the young Nigga for long, "Yea Man, y'all good." I answered giving him a play. I then walked around his Trap-house, "So where is everybody at? Where is the Hoes, the Niggas and where is that nigga J.T?" I asked. Gutta flopped down on the couch, "I kicked the hoes out cuz' all they wanna' do is smoke a Nigga shit up, The niggas just wanted to sit around and not put in any work and J.T. . .That nigga told me that he had to handle some business and he would be by later." Gutta answered firing up a blunt.

I started walking to the door telling him that I would be dropping off a package in the next couple of days, "Oh yea, did y'all ever find out who that was that tried to kill me at the Gas Station? I know word had spread by now." I asked him. Gutta kind of froze up when I asked him the question and began looking away which was a clear sign of a lie about to be told. "Umm, nawl we haven't heard any real info yet. You know how these Niggas gossip around here doe'. They can't keep their mouths closed so soon as I find out you already know that Im on it and telling you first thing." Gutta told me. I just nodded my head and headed to my truck not feeling to sure about his response. I knew how much this hood talked so for it to been me who was almost killed I knew word had got around and by now everybody and their mothers would've knew who it was that tried to kill me.

Its been so long since I really cruised the neighborhood that I grew up in and I decided to take a ride to check it out. The hood had changed a lot since Rizzy, D-Money and Myself had been younger. We use to be running up and down the streets chasing the hoes then when we got older we were chasing the money. Riding through the neighborhood was bringing so many old memories back and I couldn't help but to miss my Brothers. I hate what had to happen to D-Money and I hated that Rizzy was in Prison, no one could've told us that this would've been our future. All we wanted to do was be rich Niggas and with the wealth surly came the bullshit and problem after problem.

It was crazy riding pass the houses of old friends and females that we used to chase. A lot of the houses that we use to be at were burned down or became a Trap-house. I then turned down the block where Rizzy and I grew up at and chuckled thinking about the many fights we had, the Girls we ran trains on and all in the weed we smoked in the abandoned car in the backyard. As I passed the house I grew up in I passed Tiffany's house who everybody on the block wanted badly. The house looked vacant and I just assumed that Tiffany was doing so good somewhere that she moved her family up and out of the hood like the rest of us did that made it. I pulled up to the stop sign when I seen a female crossing the street not paying any attention to her surroundings. "Oh...My God.. It can't be!" I said to Myself. The female that was crossing the street was somebody who looked just like Tiffany but this couldn't have been her and I refused to believe it was. The person was a straight Dope-Fiend walking with a limp and totally in a different zone. I took a harder look to make sure I wasn't tripping and indeed I wasn't. It was the same Tiffany that lived across from us that everybody wanted. I rolled down my window looking at my childhood crush in the flesh. She had fallen to a ten to a flat out zero. I couldn't believe that it was her and if I told Rizzy about what I was seeing he would've swore I was lying.

I hit the blunt again rolling down the window, "Tiff?!.. Tiffany is that you??" I asked already knowing the answer. She turned to be with a ashy face and a swollen eye. What used to be a pretty face was now an abused face of a heroine attic. It's crazy because I remembered along time ago D-Money told Rizzy and that he paid her a fifty-pack of Dog-Food for the Pussy and neither of us believed him. We swore that he had gotten Tiffany confused with one of his other dope fiends. Tiffany smiled looking into my truck. "Jay?... Awww Hey Jay?! It's so good to see you. What you smoking on?" she asked as she approached the window. I was so in shock that I was speechless looking at a Dope Fiend Tiffany.

"Umm hop in real quick and take a ride for a few, get up out that cold." I told her even surprising Myself. Tiffany hopped in looking dusty as ever and had a loud odor sticking to her clothes and

body. There was even spots or dirt stuck to her skin like it was cloth-
ing. Tiffany was officially a straight Dope Fiend now. We pulled off
and even though it was cold outside I had to roll down all my
windows to keep the strong odor Tiffany carried from attacking my
nose and my seats. "So Jay, I see your still doing good. I always knew
that you would be successful and getting money every since you
hooked up with E-Bo. How is E-Bo by the way? I haven't seen him
in a long time" Tiffany asked scratching Herself like Dope Fiends
did. "Ummm, I don't know how he is doing but i'm sure that he's
not doing good. What I want to know is what happened to you?
How did you... How did you get so hooked?" I asked her. She
looked out the passenger window not even wanting to look at me,
she was embarrassed in what she become and and I didn't blame
her for it.

"I was in love with a Man, well I thought I was in love with a
Man who ended up lacing my weed. By the time I knew that I was
then fiending for it and it was to late. He then started passing me on
to his friends and before I knew it I was turned out. He then became
someone I worked for and now... I report to him just for a good fix.
I'm ashamed yes, but I plan to shake this bad habit sooner or later,
feel me?" Tiffany told me as a couple tears rolled down her face.
Tiffany was one of the baddest bitches in our neighborhood and
even though she never gave me the time of day, it still hurt me to
hear her story and how the drugs destroyed her life.

I hit another corner still not knowing what to say to her, "Well
enough about Me, how are you? I heard that Lil' Sammy and them
tried to rob and kill you the other day." she asked me. When she
asked me that I quickly turned my head toward her in shock to what
she just asked, " Lil' Sammy?????? Yea he tried to kill Me but I'm
good." I answered. I badly wanted more information but I had to
keep my cool if I wanted to get the details from her. "Who the fuck
is it that he work for doe? I'm trynna' find out who he is connected
to and willing to pay for any information. I asked her hoping that
she would take the bait that I was throwing out there. I hit another
corner and was deep in my thoughts wondering who this Lil'
Sammy Niggas was. Before the driver of that mini van died he told

me that he worked for me but I didn't understand what he meant. " What do you mean that I knew him? I don't know a Lil'Sammy" I told her. Tiffany shrugged her shoulders, "Well, he sold your Product, I figured that he worked for you. She answered.

I was now totally confused and knew that the truth was in the streets of who it was that tried killing me. "Why would somebody that worked for me try and kill me?" I asked Myself. "Ummm Jay, could I have a few dollars to buy Myself something to eat? I'm a little hungry." Tiffany asked me. I looked at her and could tell that she would go crazy if she had not got any drugs yet, I told her that if she told me more information on who tried to kill me that I would buy her some food and give her some money but she couldn't help me. I pulled up in a McDonald's Drive-Thru and bought her some food before dropping her off. I was going to find out who this Lil'Sammy was....

Chapter Forty-Eight
Shanice Part 2

(ONE MONTH LATER)

AFTER A GREAT SESSION OF MAKING LOVE WITH SHANICE, I HAD TO light up of fat blunt of that loud. Shanice and I been spending a lot of time together and in this last month we were inseparable. Every chance that we got we would spend it with each other and even been out in the public eye. The feelings that we had developed for each other had became more serious and neither one of us were ashamed to tell each other that we loved each other. We had even discussed building a future together and as bad as I wanted too, I was scared to get her involved with the lifestyle that I was living. This Past month had been crazier as ever and more stressful than anything I been through. Two of my strip clubs had been shot up to the point that I had to shut one of them down because one of the dancers were killed. Gutta and J.T told me that their trap house had been shot up so the business there were moving was slow now. I didn't know what was going on but one thing I did know that it wasn't just anybody just hating but it was somebody that was trying to kill me and slow my businesses down.......

. . .

Shanice turned the Television on in the bedroom as she laid under the sheets still naked, "Hey Babe, what do you think about Miami? Wanna pack the boys up and just go?" I asked her as I stood up putting my clothes on for the day. "Miami? I love Miami and I know the boys would love it. When are you talking about vacationing down there?" She answered and returned the question while flicking through the channels. I paused before answering. "Nawl, I'm not taking bout just for vacationing. I'm talking about moving down there for good. I been talking to some realtors down there and they have a few good locations where the Mainstrip would be good and.... I was just thinking, maybe we should move down there" I answered her Shanice turning the television off. "Your serious aren't you?" she asked me. I nodded my head fixing Myself up , "Yes Baby I am.. When I talked to the realtors about business properties I also asked about homes that I could purchase and they also had a few good ones that they were sure that we would love. I can't hold you up Babe, I'm from Detroit and I love it to death but i'm tired of it, I'm tired of all the hating ass Niggas, all the drama and stress that I deal with on a regular and I just want to start over. I want our boys to be able to live comfortably instead of with bodyguards every-where they go. I want us to be comfortable and to live happy instead of watching over our shoulders every time we go out. I got a lot of money and I know for sure that I could make a lot more but I want you.... No I need you to be with me. So what do you say Babe, are you riding with me?" I asked her sitting beside her in the bed.

Shanice sat Herself up and wasn't in a rush to answer, she exhaled " Wow Jay.. It sounds like you been doing a lot of thinking about this and have it all figured out. I'm from Detroit and I love my city Jay... But I love you more so if that's what you want to do then i'm riding with you" She answered, I was in total shock and how she started off had me scared of her answer. " So your with it? your moving down to Miami?!" I asked again. Shanice nodded her head with the biggest smile across her face, " Yes! Yes, I'll go!" She answered. I quickly leaned over toward her giving her the biggest hug and kiss in excitement. Right then I knew what we had was love and I was happy that I decided to love her. I jumped up, "Aight look, I gotta shoot a couple last minute moves and pick up the last couple dollars that I have in the streets so I'll see you a lil later okay Baby?! Start packing and when I come home I would help you!" I told her more excited than I been in a while. I leaned in kissing her again before I left the house to hit the streets.

I made it all the way outside to my car when I felt a bit empty and touched my waist noticing that I forgot my pistol in the house. I told Diego and OC that they could stay in the trucks while I ran inside for a quick second. When I made it back upstairs to the bedroom I heard the shower water running. "Hey Babe, that's you?" she yelled from the shower. " Yea, I forgot my gun" I yelled back "Oh Okay, Im taking a shower, I'll see you later. Love you!" she yelled "love you too Baby!" I told her as I walked to the side of the bed where I kept my Desert Eagle. I picked it up and put it into my holster. I then headed out the bedroom when I heard Shanice phone ringing. I never been the type to go through a woman's phone but being that the boys were all over her mothers house I decided to go over and make sure it wasn't her mother calling. By the time I made it over to the phone it had stopped ringing and when I picked her phone up I realized that it didn't ring but it was a text message. I seen that it was her cousin T-Dot who texted her, I looked at the bathroom door and still heard the shower water running. Curiosity was driving me crazy as to what he would want with her so I opened up the text message " IM GOING TO TEXT HIM TO PULL UP AND COP SOME WORK AND WE GON' KILL THEM TOGETHER SO DON'T SAY SHIT!" the text message read.

I was in total shock but it all had began to make sense. It was T-Dot who been trying to kill me all this time. He had been trying to kill me for at least this last month but what really broke my heart was that Shanice was apart of this. She was the one who introduced me to T-Dot in the first place so there was no telling how long they been plotting against me. I flopped down on my bed needing to have a seat and think but the fury that rushed through my body outweighed my thinking capability and I was all action. I had been shot at so many times and every time I regretted not being able to step ahead of the assassin and finally I was ahead with the plot of my death.

The bathroom door opened, "Oh, Hey Babe. I thought you were headed out to visit the city so we could start packing. Ummmm, why do you have my phone?" she asked with a confused smirk on her face and towel wrapped around her body. I stood up with so much rage rushing through my body that I felt that I was going to literally blow up. The tears filled my eyes and I quickly pulled out my gun aiming it at her. "Jay, Why the fuck are you doing?!" she asked with a face full of worry. I was hurt and couldn't believe what I just read in her phone. I really began to trust and love her and now she was plotting to kill me. "T-Dot texted you! Read it!" I yelled tossing the phone at her. "Awww nawl Jay, this is not what you......." She was saying but my Desert Eagle could no longer wait for an excuse before firing one shot to her chest. I stood there watching Shanice body hit the floor and my heart then began to feel worse. She had betrayed me and I couldn't allow her to finish her and her Cousin's Plot to kill me.

I walked down my mansion stairs when Diego and OC ran inside after hearing the gun shot, without explaining anything. " Follow Me, we got somebody else to kill!" I told them as we walked outside to the cars. I pushed my car full speed off of the property in a rush to get to T-Dot. If he thought he was going to set me up to kill me I was going to beat him to the punch. I should've known that it was him trying to kill me because he always tried to get me to come out and party with him but something told me to keep spinning him. Even though I had my bodyguards in my corner I still wanted more security since T-Dot kept a hundred niggas with him. Before visiting

T-Dot I was going down to my hood to recruit Gutta and J.T so they could join me. They were always talking about if I needed them to just call so this time I was going to pick them up, I was going to need all the help I could get.....

Chapter Forty-Nine
Betrayal

I PULLED UP TO GUTTA AND J.T'S TRAP-HOUSE WITH MY bodyguards behind me. On the way over I had already called to put both of them hip to what was going down. Of course they were for it and judging from the attitudes I could tell that they were ready to bust their guns. These were my young Dawgs who were trained to go, " COME HOLLA' AT ME BRO, I GOT BOES FOR THE LOW FOR YOU RIGHT NOW! 50 OF EM'" The text message from T-Dot finally came through. I grinned looking at the text message that I knew was coming , " Bet! look, this Nigga that we bout' to ride on just sent me a text message saying that he got 50 boes of the loud for the low for me. When we get here and kill this Nigga y'all can have that shit!" I told them. Both Gutta and J.T got excited "Hell Yea!" They shouted. At this point I didn't give a fuck about any work, all I wanted to do was kill this Nigga for plotting against me and trying to kill me all this time.

We finally made it to T-Dot's when Gutta, J.T , My bodyguards and I all stepped out of the cars and headed up to the front porch. T-Dot stepped out on the porch. "Bro? What........" He was about to say until his unwelcoming face dropped from seeing Gutta and J.T with me. Without hesitation I walked up to the first member of T-Dot's Crew pressing my Desert Eagle against his head letting off

one shot, sending the Workers body to the ground. When T-Dot
seen that he quickly ran into the house. Bullets began flying everywhere and my entire team was handling business killing everybody
that was part of T-Dots team. We barged into T-Dots where he laid
on the floor from catching a bullet to the leg. "Jay, Man! What the
fuck are you doing?! Why are you trynna' kill me? Are you fuckin'
crazy?" He yelled. I gave Gutta and J.T a head nod telling them to
search the house for the work. I stood over T-Dot's injured body,
"So you been tryna kill me huh?! I should've fuckin' knew but I had
to find out the hard way. I seen the text message you sent Shanice!"
I told him as I tossed her phone down on the floor to his. Gutta and
J.T came back into the front room excited. " We got it and a whole
lot more!" He said J.T stood beside me ready to watch and see what
I did with T-Dot.

T-Dot read the text message and looked at all of us, "Where is
my Cousin Jay?! Where is Shanice and why do you have her
phone?!" He asked. "You need to be asking Yourself what would be
your last word before I kill you!" I yelled back at him in fury. "Jay,
where is my Cousin?! Please tell me where she is?!" He asked
sounding more worried about her than he was about Hisself. I
grinned, "I killed her like Im going to kill you! Did y'all really think
y'all would try and kill me and get away with it?!" I yelled at him
with my gun pointed at his brain. T-Dot shook his head, "NO! NO!
NO! You are a fuckin' Dummy! Why would you kill her and she love
you?! You got it all wrong Jay. I sent her that text message because I
found out those two Niggas you got wit' you are the ones that been
trying to kill you! They were the ones that been trying to kill you for
all these months and I was telling Shanice that we, me and you were
going to kill them together! That young Nigga that you killed at the
Gas Station was his lil' brother Sammy!" T-Dot said with a lot of
blood coming from his leg. I stood there completely confused now
and I was even in denial. I lowered my gun and looked over at
Gutta and J.T. waiting for them to defend themselves but they
didn't.

.   .   .

Gutta lowered his gun down to T-Dot and sent three shots to his chest killing him. When I turned toward him trying to raise my pistol I was then shot in the leg causing me to fall to the floor. Shots started back ringing out and being that Gutta and J.T. had the ups on my Bodyguards, they shot all of them down leaving no one able to help me. J.T. stepped over me as I laid on the ground, "So um yea, he was right. Everything that he just told you was true. We were the ones trying to kill you for the past month. We been shooting up all of your Strip Clubs and yea. . .Thats what it is. If it makes you feel any better, it was hard as hell trying to catch you." J.T. said with a grin on his face. I couldn't believe what I was hearing, I trusted these Niggas and they were the ones trying to kill me the whole time? J.T. then circled around me, "Now I know that your wondering why we been trying to kill you but it wasn't our plan to kill you. It was our plan to just rob your tight ass until you killed my little brother Sammy. I mean, what did you think? Did you think that we were going to work for you forever and you keep dropping off work and think that you could Bird-Feed us?! I remembered I told you that if it wasn't for you and Rizzy that we wouldn't have shit. Well, that was a lie, if it wasn't for us then you wouldn't be shit!" J.T. yelled at me.

Gutta and J.T. were Rizzy and I Protege's and now they were becoming my Murderers. I bought them in this Game, showed them more money then they ever seen and this was how they were going to re-pay me? Gutta aimed his gun at me and fired off three more shots all to my Chest and shoulder. Again I felt Myself slowly starting to fade away but this time I was in more pain than the other times. Again my life had flashed before my eyes and the first person was Shanice. I felt terrible that I killed her all because I assumed instead f getting facts. Honey, Alicia, D-Money, Rizzy in Prison, My Boys Lil'K and Lil'Dez and all of the people that I killed in my lifetime. Before my eyes closed and took my last breath I heard more gun shots being fired but it wasn't at me. I watched both Gutta and J.T.'s bodies fall to the ground beside me. . . .

. . .

Somebody came to my rescue but the question was, who was it? I closed my eyes wondering who was my Angel that came to my rescue. . .

HUSTLE, LOVE AND BETRAYAL

TO BE CONTINUED. . . . .

Made in the USA
Monee, IL
10 November 2020